THE PUNISHMENT

From the bed came a silent command, and Jumel rose to his feet, sweating and shaking like one in the grip of malaria. The voice in his head was that of the Haitian sorcerer confronting him. Margal was ordering him to stand aside, against the wall on his right. He must wait there in silence.

Weak with terror, he stumbled to the wall and flattened himself against it.

On the bed Margal was equally motionless, gazing with crimson eyes at the doorway.

Presently Jumel heard an approaching sound of slow, mechanical footfalls. Into the room, like a zombie, trudged Brian Dawson.

Dawson took four steps and stopped dead, held rigid by the sorcerer's gaze. It was clear to him that the bocor on the bed was about to punish him.

Suddenly his mouth opened wide and he screamed.

Other *Leisure* books by Hugh B. Cave
THE DAWNING

HUGH B. CAVE

THE EVIL RETURNS

LEISURE BOOKS  NEW YORK CITY

For Peggy

A LEISURE BOOK®

July 2001

Published by

Dorchester Publishing Co., Inc.
276 Fifth Avenue
New York, NY 10001

ISBN 0-8439-4893-0

Printed in the United States of America.

THE EVIL RETURNS

Chapter One

Port-au-Prince, Haiti.
A midweek morning, 10 A.M.

The tree-lined streets of the elite Turgeau district are all but deserted.

Cooks and maids from the poorer parts of this Caribbean capital have already arrived at their employers' homes and begun the day's toil.

The flow of cars bearing businessmen and politicians to their downtown establishments has thinned to a trickle.

All but one of the morning's marchandes have finished their rounds and departed.

The sun is a blow torch, bubbling the asphalt and baking the cracked sidewalks. This is July. Haiti in July is hot.

At No. 84 Rue Printemps, a second-floor bedroom window has been opened wide to catch what little breeze there is. There, peering down at the street, sits a strange figure in a bright orange dressing gown that conceals his legs. He appears to be a dwarf.

Wasted away by some illness or accident that has scarred and shriveled him, he might be forty years old or sixty. His hair, touched with gray, is just beginning to grow back after being destroyed.

The room is small. This old wooden house is not one of the more elegant homes on Rue Printemps, though it might have been in years past. A frayed gray carpet covers part of the plank floor. There is an old bed made of taverneau, a handsome wood now rare and expensive. An ancient chest of drawers stands beside it. Two small mahogany tables flank the chair on which the dwarf-man sits.

This particular chair, old and big, is padded with remarkable pillows of sunrise red, passion-fruit yellow, the glowing purple of sea grapes. The dwarf-man has always reveled in bright colors and still seeks to immerse himself in them.

The chair itself is an iridescent blue green, the shade of shallow sea water along Haitian beaches from which, these days, peasant-made boats overloaded with the country's poor so often precariously set sail for that land of promise, America, six hundred miles or so to the west northwest.

For the past hour or so the man has been watching the passing parade of cars, maids, cooks, and peddler women, but except for a lone marchande on the opposite sidewalk, the show for today is now over.

In lilting Creole, as she strolls along with swinging buttocks, the peasant wench sings out that she is a seller of lovely brooms and is now about to leave.

"Mwen marchande bel balé! Mwen pr'allé kounyé a!"

The man is not interested in brooms. He has a housekeeper-companion who looks after such mundane matters. Certainly he himself is not able to use a broom.

He is, in fact, legless.

Actually, most of the inhabitants of this poor Caribbean country, including the president he tried to destroy, believe this man is dead, and are happy in that belief. If not happy, at least relieved. They believe he perished in a fire that destroyed a building from which he was not able to escape.

He did escape, however—able at the last minute to do so because his housekeeper, risking destruction, groped her way through the inferno to carry him out. But it was not she who healed him. While she helped by nursing him through the weeks when his life hung in the balance, he healed himself by calling upon the powers of his remarkable mind.

His name is Margal. Margal the Bocor. Margal the Sorcerer. By a miracle of his own making, he is alive.

With the disappearance of the broom peddler, Margal's eyelids drooped in boredom. But as the door of his room creaked open behind him, he indifferently turned his head.

The woman who entered was in her way almost as unique as the man she served. Six and a half feet tall, she weighed at least two hundred fifty pounds.

The dress she wore was striped with all the fiery colors of Margal's cushions. Her face was a full moon with sensuous lips and small, alert eyes.

Her name was Clarisse.

In one hand she carried a white enameled basin containing water and a sponge. Over one broad shoulder was draped a towel.

"So you finally got here," the legless man grumbled.

Without answering him, she placed the basin on a table beside his chair and stepped behind him. Her big hands were surprisingly gentle as they slipped his arms out of the sleeves of his orange dressing gown. Then, with her left arm lifting him, she removed the gown altogether, leaving him naked.

"How are you feeling?" she asked. Her voice was that of a friendly bear.

"I will recover."

"You already have." Lifting a bar of pink soap from a pocket of her multicolored dress, Clarisse reached into the basin for the sponge, then soaped the sponge and, as usual, began the morning ritual by washing the stumps of his legs. His legs had been amputated just above the knees two years before his joust with death in the fire.

"When are we going back to the mountains?" she asked while washing him.

"We're not."

Her hands hung suspended, dripping water onto him. "What are you saying? We can't stay here forever! Sooner or later they are bound to learn that the fire did not destroy you!"

"We will not be staying here."

"And not be returning to the mountains? Then where—"

"Be quiet, will you?" He slapped at her in anger. "For more than two months, woman, I have been sitting in this prison, thinking about our future. Thinking, if you must know, what a fool I have been. I, Margal, the greatest sorcerer this land of sorcerers has ever known, have wasted months of my life in the stupid pursuit of revenge."

"You had reason to seek revenge. They took your legs."

"The loss of my legs was my own fault, Clarisse."

Ceasing her ministrations again, Clarisse straightened, stepped back, and gazed at him, as though doubting his sanity. "Your fault?"

"When those politicians demanded my services, why did I refuse? It was an act of idiocy. I could have given them what they wanted and won their confidence. Then I could have gained control over them. But no, I had to defy them and be beaten half to death in my sleep by their thugs, losing my legs in the process. A fool, yes, that's what I was, Clarisse. A complete fool!"

Clarisse continued to gaze at him for a few seconds, then went on with her work, shrugging in a way that caused her vast bosom to brush his face as she leaned over him. Coiling his arms around her, Margal pressed his face between her breasts.

Normally she would have smiled when he did that. Not now. Now she said, still scowling, "If we are not to return to the mountains and not to stay here, what are we to do, please? If you don't mind enlightening me."

Burrowing more deeply, he merely grunted.

She repeated the question.

He leaned back, perhaps needing air at this point. From habit he glanced out the window beside him. On the far side of the street below, a white woman and a little white girl walked hand in hand along the cracked sidewalk, talking to each other. About thirty, the woman wore a sleeveless shift of pale blue that concealed her shape, but her movements left no doubt she was attractively slim and supple. The child wore a bright yellow sun dress.

"There they are again," the legless man said to his companion. "Have you called on your friend Edita yet?"

She shook her head. "I can't think of what to say to her."

Displeased, he slapped her hand away from his privates as she tried to sponge them. "Damn it, woman, I told you—"

"Not everything you want can be accomplished the moment you demand it," she protested. "Especially when you want a thing so hard to explain." Applying the sponge again, she peered suspiciously at his face. "What are you up to, anyway? I haven't liked the look in your eyes lately. To be truthful, I wish I had never told you about those two."

"But you did."

She had, yes—weeks ago, when he first saw the woman and child walking as they were now. Amused when he had leaned forward on his chair, almost falling off it to peer out the window at them, she had said, "Do you know who that woman is, Margal? She has just moved into a house on this street. Her husband works at the American Embassy, and the *ti-fi* is their daughter."

"What is their name?"

"Dawson."

"How do you know this?"

"Don't worry. I'm not clairvoyant like you. I met their cook in the market, that's all. We've become friends and look for each other each morning, so we can walk home together."

She referred, of course, to the huge Iron Market on Grand' Rue, where she went every day for fresh fruit, vegetables, and meat. A man of Margal's status could not be expected to rely on marchandes who trudged through the district with baskets on their heads. He craved cervelle, for instance, claiming the ingestion of an animal's brain was beneficial to a man whose own was the source of his power. Cervelle had to be fresh.

"What does M'sieu Dawson do at his Embassy?"

"My friend doesn't know, but thinks it must be something very important because his father is an assistant to the American president."

"His father is what?"

"An assistant to their president."

"You joke!"

"I do not. He even lives in their Palais National, which they call the White House."

"Interesting," Margal had murmured. "Indeed, yes."

On seeing the woman and child at other times, he had asked still more questions.

"What is the woman's *nom baptême?*"

"Sandra."

"And his, her husband's?"

"Brian."

"And the little one?"

"Hers is Marcia. They call her Merry."

"How old is she?"

"Six."

"She is an only child?"

"Yes, the only one."

Then one Sunday morning the father had accomapnied his wife and daughter on their stroll, and for the whole time they were in view Margal sat among his colored cushions like a spider in its web, watching them. She, Clarisse, could only stand there with a towel in her hands, waiting to dry him after his bath.

For a change, it had been a cool morning. He shivered because he was wet. But he would not allow her to interrupt his concentration by touching him.

"The man is young," he said in a low voice when the trio had passed from view. "I think about thirty."

She began to dry his legless, fire-scarred body.

"You agree? About thirty?"

"Yes. But why should you be interested in how old he is? You can't expect to meet him."

"There might be a way."

"Don't be foolish. If I were to ask him to come here to visit you, how do you know he would be discreet about it? You are supposed to be dead, in case you've forgotten. One careless word and the whole Garde d'Haiti would be at our door!"

He had seemed to ponder that for a time. Perhaps he was remembering his two weeks of hiding with a cousin of hers in the miserable slums of La Saline after she rescued him from the blazing house where he had been left to die. It had taken her that long to find a house she could rent. This one. This house they were hiding in now.

Finally he had shrugged. "Very well. You are probably right."

But now, as she finished the morning ritual again and turned to leave the room, he was saying something different. With his gaze fixed on the sidewalk where Madame Dawson and her small daughter had disappeared from sight, he was saying, "Wait. I want you to call on your friend this afternoon."

She paused on her way to the door. "It is not a good day for me to do that."

"Why isn't it?"

"M'sieu is leaving for Miami tomorrow, to be gone for two weeks or more, she told me in the market this morning. She has to prepare a special dinner this evening. There will be guests coming to bid him good-bye."

Margal's eyes always mirrored the machinations of his mind. Now a telltale glitter flashed in them. "He is going to Miami?"

"Yes."

"For two or more weeks?"

"That's how long he usually stays, according to Clarisse."

As Margal leaned toward her, his hands were the talons of a hawk about to seize a rabbit. "Now you *must* see your friend this afternoon!" he hissed. "There is something I want from that house!"

"What are you talking about? *What* do you want?"

He told her.

She gazed at him as though he had asked for a piece of the sun. "Are you out of your mind? How in the world am I supposed to—"

"And in the morning you will go by camion to Léogane with a letter. Do you hear?"

"I hear," she said, frightened now. "But I don't understand."

"It is not necessary for you to understand! Just do as I tell you!"

She knew that tone. When he used it, he would tolerate no argument, even from her. She knew, too, what he could do to those who offended him. Wondering why he so determinedly wanted something that belonged to the Dawsons' little girl, she turned and hurried from the room.

Chapter Two

Later that day, in another bedroom on Rue Printemps, Sandra Dawson packed a suitcase for her husband.

This room had two beds. The suitcase lay on Brian's. His face a mask of boredom, Brian himself sat on a window seat and watched his wife. Thirty years old and six feet tall, he was considered by most women outrageously handsome.

This afternoon he had just returned from a mile of jogging in the capital's cruel heat and still wore running shoes.

"How many shirts will you need?" his wife asked. At the time of their marriage seven years before, her face had possessed a rare natural beauty. Now, though still attractive, she could have been mistaken for a zombie merely going through certain civilized motions.

"How many what?"

"Shirts."

"Lord, I don't know."

"I'll put in four. You can ask someone at the hotel to wash them out if you have to." Or your girlfriend, she thought.

Tomorrow her husband would fly to Miami for talks with Immigration people. The latter were in trouble because so many Haitians were arriving in Florida illegally, most of them in makeshift sailing craft. The Haitian government could hardly be expected to do much about it. In political turmoil since the overthrow of the long-lived Duvalier regime, why should they weep because some of their desperate poor fled to affluent America?

So all right. Brian again had a legitimate excuse for going to Miami, and it would be a relief to have him out of the way for a time. I should have married Ken, God help me, when I had the chance, she thought. Why was I so stupid?

"Where's Merry?" her husband suddenly asked.

"Out in the backyard, with Edita."

"Doing what?"

"The laundress didn't show up today, so I asked Edita to wash out a few things. Merry's helping."

"For God's sake," he said, rising from the window seat.

"What's the matter?"

"Helping with the laundry?"

"Little girls enjoy doing things like that. When you

were her age, didn't you ever help mow the lawn or rake leaves?"

The look he directed at her was an optic sneer. "I'm going downstairs for a drink. You want one?"

"No, but run along. I can finish this."

For some reason she felt instantly free of stress when he walked out of the room.

Entering the yard just then, Clarisse wondered how she was going to persuade her friend Edita to give her what Margal wanted. All the way from her employer's house she had frowned over the problem.

She found Edita at a backyard standpipe with little Merry Dawson, washing out some clothes.

"Bon soir, ti-fi," she said to the child. Then, "Hello, Edita. You doing a washing?"

"Hello yourself, Clarisse. As I told you this morning, m'sieu leaves for Miami tomorrow. Madame wanted some of his things washed, and the laundress is sick, so I said I would do them."

"And you have no machine?"

"It's broken. Being fixed."

This was a piece of good fortune, Clarisse told herself. Yes, it was. Especially as she could see that not all the laundry being done was for the man of the house. In the basket were some items that certainly belonged to her friend's little helper.

Edita and Merry sat on stools beside a big wash pan, and there was a yard chair nearby. Clarisse dragged it over and sat. "So this is the little girl you told me about." She smiled at the Dawson's six-year-old, but, of course, spoke in Creole. Though she had often seen the child walking with Madame Dawson, she had never before been face-to-face with her. What a lovely child Merry was, with her silky, golden hair and chocolate eyes!

Edita placed an affectionate hand on the child's shoulder. "Yes, and isn't she a darling?" She herself was not yet twenty-five but already had four children of her own. Her mother looked after them while she was at work. Their father had fled to America months ago, and she had not heard from him. Perhaps he had never reached there. In those ramshackle boats it was always a gamble.

"What's wrong with your laundress?" Clarisse asked. In a difficult situation such as this, you had to be friendly, take your time, and hope for sudden inspiration. "The *fiév* is going around, I hear."

"It's not the fever. It's what her boyfriend gave her."

"Oh?"

"He picked it up from some slut, and now she has it."

The moon face did not smile, but Clarisse did so inwardly. All you had to do was be patient and there it was: the answer. She turned her head to gaze at the little girl.

Merry was trying to imitate Edita, rubbing a tiny panty between her hands. Clarisse glanced at the basket of dirty clothes.

"Your answer could be right there, Edita."

"Eh?"

"In the child's panties."

"I don't follow you."

"It's a known fact. If you have the sickness and wear something belonging to a virgin, it will go away. The very best thing is a child's panty."

"Anna is too big to wear such a trifle!"

"She wouldn't have to wear it. She can just place it inside her own garment next to where the trouble is." Clarisse leaned so far forward, she was in danger of falling into the wash pan. "Where does this Anna live?"

"Just off the Pétionville Road, in Lalue."

"Would you like me to take her one?"

"Would you?"

"A friend of yours is a friend of mine. Just tell me how to find her. And you'd better give me two of those. Two you haven't washed yet. It's better if they haven't been washed since the virgin wore them. And the person with the sickness mustn't wash them either, so she ought to have more than one."

Edita gazed at the child, whose small white face now wore a pout. Though she had been taught a few words of Creole by the servants, Merry of course could comprehend nothing of the conversation in progress and obviously felt left out.

"Look, honey," Edita said in halting English. "Go bring the towel by the kitchen sink, will you? We should wash it."

Happy to be included again, the youngster sped toward the house.

Edita's hand darted to the basket and plucked out two panties. "Quick! Hide them!" she told her friend.

The woman from Margal's home stuffed the garments down the front of her dress. They were safely out of sight when the child returned.

"Now tell me where this Anna lives exactly," Clarisse said.

"You know Rue Carmeleau?"

"Yes."

"On the right side, just before you reach the Pétionville Road, there is a gray house with a veranda. You'll see a little lane beside it. Go down that lane, and in back of the big house you'll find a small one with a door painted blue." Edita leaned from her stool to clasp the other's hand. "Clarisse, may *le bon Dieu* bless you for your kindness!"

"It's nothing," Clarisse murmured as she turned away.

She would, of course, deliver one of the panties to the house with the blue door. She would have to do that, because Anna ought to be cured. But not both. No, indeed. And Margal would be pleased with her, even though he had not bothered to tell her why he wanted something worn by the little girl.

At the gate she waved farewell. Edita waved back. The child sang out "Good-bye!" in a voice as pure as the flute song of the mountain musician-bird.

Now that's odd, the Dawson's cook thought as their caller disappeared from view. Yes, that's really a little strange. Clarisse never did say why she came here this afternoon, did she?

Returning to the bedroom with a drink in his hand, Brian Dawson said to his wife, "I'll be staying at the

Greenway, in case you need to reach me. You have the phone number."

She had finished packing for him and now stood by the bed with her back to him. How much would he drink, she wondered, before their guests arrived for dinner? In giving him the afternoon off, had the Embassy really thought he would use it to prepare notes for the people in Miami?

"Yes, I know it," she said. "By heart."

"What's that supposed to mean?"

"Don't you always go to the Greenway?"

"Is there some reason I shouldn't?"

"Of course not."

"All right, then. If you have to get in touch with me, that's where I'll be. And if you call and I'm not there, just leave a message."

If you're not there, Sandra Dawson thought. Which, of course, you won't be—will you?

Chapter Three

While Sandra Dawson was driving her husband to the airport the following morning, Margal's Clarisse walked down through the city to the waterfront. From there, amid perpetual bedlam, gaudy open buses with fanciful names embarked on long, dusty journeys to all part of Haiti.

All Clarisse knew about Léogane was that it was a coastal town, said to be a hotbed of voodoo, twenty-odd miles out on the Southern Peninsula. Perhaps the voodoo had something to do with her being sent there? Though Margal was not a houngan but a bocor—there was a distinct difference—he sometimes dealt with important voodoo practitioners.

Actually, Margal had told her nothing about her mission except how to find the man whose name was on the envelope she carried.

A dozen or so buses were lined up at the place of departure this morning. Some were empty, some half full, some seemingly ready to be on their way. One that could take her to Léogane was already crowded, she saw with dismay. Even its roof was piled high with assorted goods belonging to its passengers. Someone was taking two live chickens, tied by their legs to the roof rail. Others were transporting baskets of fruit, sacks of flour, stems of green bananas.

There were better ways of getting to Léogane, she had complained to Margal. By the smaller, more comfortable *tap-taps,* for instance. But no, he had insisted she ride a *camion.* On a tap-tap, the wrong kind of person might recognize and question her.

She paused by the front of the vehicle and spoke in Creole to the driver, who had not yet climbed onto his seat. "I am going to Léogane. When are you leaving, please?"

"Right now."

"The seat beside you—is it taken?"

"It will cost you extra."

"Why?"

Looking her over, he grinned. "Well, you're not an ordinary passenger. You'll be crowding me more than most." The grin excised the insult from his remark. "Shall we say an extra ten *gourdes?"*

She paid without argument, and he helped her onto the seat. A moment later the vehicle lumbered out of line to begin its journey.

While negotiating city traffic the driver remained

voiceless. Only when the outskirts village of Carrefour was behind them did he relax and begin humming a little tune. At the market town of Gressier, fourteen miles from the capital, some of his passengers got off and he climbed onto the roof to hand down their belongings.

As the *camion* rolled on again, swaying less frighteningly on the curves now because it was less top-heavy, he glanced at Clarisse with interest. "Where are you going in Léogane, m'selle? I live there, as it happens. If you don't know the town, perhaps I can help you."

"No, I don't know the town, and I'm concerned. I have to find someone."

"Who, may I ask? Perhaps I know the person."

She opened her sisal handbag and took out the letter. "Paul Polivien. He lives near the marketplace."

"And owns a fishing boat?"

"I wasn't told that."

"He is the one, though. Unless there are two Paul Poliviens in Léogane, which I doubt." Removing a hand from the wheel, he patted her thigh. "Don't worry. You have no problem. When we stop at the market I will point out where you must go."

A fishing boat, Clarisse thought, unaware that she was frowning. Now what could Margal want with a man who owned a fishing boat?

Had she been able to see what her Margal was doing just then, she might have been even more puzzled.

Though he usually did not move about without her, preferring to call her and be carried, he could do so if he had to. It involved employing his powerful arms to lower himself from bed or chair to the floor, then using them as crutches. His pride found this distasteful, but despite the damage done to his body by the fire that had so nearly destroyed him, he was far from helpless.

Clarisse had left him seated by the window, as usual, but now he was in motion. Crossing the room to the chest of drawers beside his bed, he pulled open the bottom drawer and rummaged amid certain paraphernalia of his trade for a piece of white chalk and a candle. The candle was black.

Black candles could be bought in certain shops in the city, of course. People had need of them for voodoo rites. Margal made his own, however, and more went into the making of them than a mere knowledge of how to dip a string in melted wax.

His candles contained a blend of ingredients known only to himself, and the dipping was accompanied by incantations of his own invention.

With the selected candle in his shirt pocket—for he needed both hands to move himself about the room—he went now to an uncarpeted part of the floor where he used the chalk to draw a circle five feet in diameter. Inside that circle he drew another, and inside that one, a third. Seating himself within the innermost circle, he lit the black candle and set it upright in front of him in a puddle of its own wax.

The smoke it gave off contained an unpleasantly sweet odor, like that to be encountered in, say, a closed room in which a dead rat was rotting.

From inside his shirt the legless man now extracted the soft white garment delivered to him the afternoon before by Clarisse. Through the night it had been stored for safekeeping under his pillow, where it had kept him awake half the night with anticipation. Holding the panty up in front of him now, he fixed his gaze on it.

His eyes glittered. Remarkable eyes anyway, as any enemy of his could testify if still alive, they acquired a redness now that made them resemble smoldering coals. An observer might have expected the fragile bit of cloth dangling in front of them to burst into flames. But it did not.

After a moment of this, a sound began to vibrate in the room, reaching into the corners and crannies, as did the smoke and dead-rat odor of the black candle. The sound emanated from Margal's mouth, though his lips scarcely moved. It consisted of words sometimes heard in voodoo services, but not in the usual order. In a church it might have been a prayer spoken backward.

As it droned on, his upthrust hands brought the stolen garment slowly toward his face, until it pressed against his lips and he was breathing the incantation through it.

The chant continued. The panty grew warm against his skin. The candle burned with a greenish-yellow flame in front of him. Time passed.

* * *

In the living room of the Dawsons' house, farther down the street, six-year-old Marcia Dawson, called Merry, knelt on the floor with a box of crayons and a coloring book.

With her protruding pink tongue seemingly alert to lick up any mistakes, she concentrated on adding color to a picture of children skating on a frozen lake. Her father had bought the book for her on one of his trips to Miami.

Suddenly, in spite of her concentration, the child stopped what she was doing and stood up, her head atilt, as though she had heard her name called.

"What, Edita?"

From the kitchen came the young woman who had been doing the washing the afternoon before. "You want me, *ti-fi?*"

"I thought you called me."

"Uh-uh. *M' pa té rélé ou.*"

Merry struck a hands-on-hips pose and pretended to be indignant. "Now what does that mean?"

"It means 'I did not call you.' Say it now. *M' pa té relé ou.*"

Merry solemnly tried to repeat it, was as solemnly corrected, and tried again. The two of them played this game often. "You can learn Creole quicker than I can learn your English," Edita had insisted. "You're smarter than I am."

"But I heard someone calling me! I know I did!"

"Nobody is here but you and me, honey. Your mother will be home soon, though, so don't worry."

* * *

Sandra Dawson at that moment was returning alone from the airport. The plane had been late taking off, and she had stayed with Brian until he boarded. Neither of them had said much. All through the long wait she had thought mostly about the fact that she would be alone now for two weeks.

As she drove along Grand' Rue, past the Iron Market, she caught herself wishing she had the courage to phone Ken Forrest at his north-coast sisal plantation and ask if by any chance he would be coming to the capital in the next few days.

She wouldn't, of course. But even thinking about it caused her pulse to quicken.

At that moment, in Léogane, Clarisse was in the presence of the man whose name was on the envelope she had been told to deliver.

The driver of the *camion*, true to his promise, had shown her where to find Paul Polivien, who lived only a little distance from the town's big marketplace. Fortunately she had found him at home.

Now she sat with him in his quite respectable parlor, where he had finished reading the letter and was frowning at her across a cup of coffee brought to her at his command by a woman he had introduced as his wife. About fifty years old, he was a short, wiry fellow with such prominent ears, she felt she ought to put her hands on them and press them against his head.

"It will be best if I go back with you, I think," he was saying.

Having no idea what was in the letter, Clarisse could only look at him and say, "Oh?"

"I believe so. To give you a message for him would not be enough. I should know his response to it. Unless I talk to him face-to-face, you could be coming and going more times than you care to."

"I do what he tells me to," said Clarisse.

"As will I, of course. Who would not, when dealing with such a man? But certain plans have already been made and—well, as I say, I will go back with you. I know a man with a car who can be persuaded to take us, I think." He stood up. "Make yourself at home, please. I'll return soon."

She drank her coffee. The wife came and asked whether she would like more, and on being told "No, thank you," gave her a curiously searching look and took the cup and saucer away.

In twenty minutes a car stopped outside the house, and Polivien reappeared.

"You are ready, madame?"

She rose.

Turning toward the kitchen doorway, he called out, "Yolande! I am going to the city."

His wife showed herself and said, "When will you be back, if I may ask?"

"I don't know."

"If some of those people come looking for you, what am I to tell them?"

"You needn't worry. They will not arrive until tomorrow."

She shrugged. Polivien motioned to Clarisse and strode to the door.

The car waiting there, with a bearded man at the wheel, was a big one but old and battered, as were so many of the machines in the country towns. The driver leaned back to open a rear door for Clarisse. Polivien sat in front.

When they had put a few miles behind them in silence, Polivien turned around and said, "Are you comfortable, madame?"

"Thank you, yes."

"You must tell me where our friend is to be found. The letter did not say."

There was a reason, of course, for his not using the name *Margal* in the presence of the driver, Clarisse told herself. It was a name well known, and its owner was believed to be dead. "In Turgeau," she said. "Rue Printemps."

"Ah, yes." He turned to the driver. "You know where that is, Albert?"

"I think so."

"I will direct him when the times comes," Clarisse offered. Then, having Polivien's attention, she added almost casually, "I hear you own a boat, M'sieu Polivien."

"That is so."

"A fishing boat?"

"Yes, though at times I find other uses for it."

She frowned at him. "Not to take our people to Florida, I hope."

"My boat has never been close to Florida, madame. Or any other part of the United States." He put an end to the questioning by turning around and lighting a cigarette. No one spoke again until the driver took a wrong turn near their destination and Clarisse had to correct him.

Margal was seated on the sea-green chair by his bedroom window when the car stopped at the curb below. The black candle had been returned to its drawer, the circles erased from the floor with a wet rag he always insisted Clarisse leave with him. Nothing remained to indicate what he had done there during his housekeeper's absence.

Assuming she had hired a taxi in Léogane to bring her home, he watched her struggle out of the machine and was pleased with her for returning so promptly. Then, when he saw her followed by the small man with the protruding ears, he leaned closer to the glass, not pleased at all. He had expected only a message from that one, not a visit.

In a moment, hearing footsteps on the stairs, he turned his head to direct his scowl at the door of the room. Someone knocked—it was Clarisse, of course. At his growled "Come in!" she opened the door for Polivien to enter and then, following him, said with a shrug, "M'sieu Polivien insisted on speaking with you, Margal. Shall I bring some refreshment?"

"No. Just leave us." He motioned the other to a chair.

Polivien sat and said nervously, "You did not instruct me to come, but I felt I ought to." His gaze traveled slowly from the bocor's face to his arms and hands, taking in the disfigurations left by the fire. "*Mon dieu!*" he whispered. "We heard the fire consumed you. How did you escape?"

"With the help of Clarisse. But you are to say nothing to anyone about it. Do you understand?"

"Of course."

"Why are you here?"

"Because in your letter you said 'a week or so' and I already have a firm commitment to make a trip the day after tomorrow. After that I must do some work on the boat and will not be able to go again for perhaps a month."

The corners of Margal's mouth turned down. "The day after tomorrow? Can't you delay for a day or two?"

"Not safely. I have twelve passengers arriving tomorrow, some from so far away they have left home already. My neighbors will be suspicious if that many people stay long at my house."

"Why should that be a threat? Everyone knows what is going on."

"Not everyone knows who is doing it. If they did, many might demand to be taken themselves—free of charge for not reporting me."

"This is awkward." Margal let his breath out in a soft growl. "You give me too little time to make ready!"

"Please—you can do it. For the great Margal, nothing is impossible. Or even difficult."

The compliment had its effect. In the seconds of silence that followed, Margal's look of annoyance faded. "Well, all right, yes. I can make adjustments. The day after tomorrow, you say?"

"Yes."

"And you will be taking your passengers aboard

before daybreak, of course, to avoid attracting attention? And sailing with the first light?"

"As usual. Yes."

"You will come here to pick us up, of course."

The boat owner looked distressed. "M'sieu, I expect—"

"By midnight. There will be three of us, by the way."

"Three?" Polivien was startled. It was known, of course, that this legless man never went anywhere without his Clarisse. But a third passenger? "May I ask—"

"You will see when you get here," Margal said. "Now go home. And remember—I have ways of dealing with people who fail me."

Chapter Four

When Clarisse brought his evening meal just before eight o'clock, the legless man in the green chair by the window ordered her to remain in the room. Timing, he knew, could mean the difference between success and failure.

"But my own food is in the kitchen," she protested vigorously.

"Bring it here, then. I want you with me."

Indignant, she made more than the usual noise while thumping down the old wooden staircase. But she returned with her meal of rice and black mushrooms on a tray, and sat with him to eat it.

When she would have taken the dishes down to wash them, Margal growled an impatient, "No!"

"What are you up to?" she demanded.

"Polivien is coming for us at midnight. We have much to do before then."

"Coming with his friend, you mean? In the car?"

"Yes."

"To take us where? If I may ask."

"You will learn that in due time."

"How long are we to be gone?"

He shrugged. "Several weeks, perhaps."

"Several weeks! Then, God in heaven, we will need some clothes! Both of us."

Margal had more important things on his mind this evening. But she was right, he supposed. Frowning at her from his chair, he said, "Well, yes, we may need a few things. But only a few, hear? One suitcase for the two of us."

"Only one? You must be out of your—"

"One! And don't argue! You'll have trouble enough transporting me from place to place without encumbering yourself with luggage." He aimed his scowl at the watch on his wrist. "Before you go to pack, put me on the floor. Over there." He pointed to the patch of bare floor where he had sat before in the center of the three rings, with the black candle and the child's white garment.

She lifted him easily from his chair and placed him where he wished to be.

"Bring me my chalk and one of my candles."

She did so, peering at him suspiciously as she handed them to him.

"Now you may go, but don't be long."

This time she went quietly.

While she was absent, Margal drew the three circles again, with himself in the center, and set the black candle up as before. After plucking the stolen panty from inside his shirt and laying it on the floor between his stumps, he looked at his watch a second time.

Nine o'clock. Outside, Rue Printemps was dark and quiet. In a residential neighborhood such as this, nothing much happened after the dinner hour. A dog barked in a nearby yard. Others answered. The silence returned.

Lifting the panty from the floor, Margal held it for a moment in both hands and unblinkingly gazed at it. Then he closed his eyes and pressed the garment against them as though it were a blindfold. He was in this position when Clarisse returned.

She looked at him and frowned. "What are you doing, if I may ask?"

"I am watching the Dawson child."

"Watching her?"

"Yes."

"What is she doing?"

"At the moment she is walking up a flight of stairs. Now she has turned at the top and is going along a hall. Now she is in a bedroom."

"You see this clearly?"

"As if I were there."

"The fire has not diminished your powers, then. For that I am thankful, master."

It was only on occasions such as this that she called him "master" and showed him total respect. As for his statement that he could see what the Dawson child was doing in her home down the street, it was, of course, not to be questioned. Give him some object that had been close to a person—an article of clothing, a ring, a bracelet, even something as ordinary as a coin from a person's pocket—and he could sometimes even see with its owner's eyes and think with its owner's mind. She knew this to be true. Time and again he had done it.

"The child is going to bed," he said.

Clarisse nodded. "Yes, this would be about her bedtime."

"There is but one bed in the room where she is undressing. The mother sleeps in another room."

"With her husband, no doubt. Though he is not there tonight."

He was silent a moment. "She has put on pajamas, white ones, and is kneeling beside the bed. Asking *le bon Dieu* to protect her while she sleeps, I suppose. I must concentrate now, so be quiet. She must fall asleep with my command in her thoughts, so that when I wake her, she will obey me."

"Yes, master."

"One question: Have you any idea what time her mother retires?"

"No, Margal. But with the husband away she will do so early, I think. They had guests last evening, too. She will be tired."

The room filled with silence. Again a dog barked somewhere and others answered. Margal sat in the lotus position with the child's garment now hiding his whole face. But Clarisse knew what was going on behind it.

He was using his mind. When dealing with someone in his presence, he used his eyes as well, but his incredible mind alone was sufficient when he was properly prepared. With a slight shiver of fear she watched him.

What did he want with the Dawsons' little daughter, anyway? What kind of journey were they about to embark upon with Paul Polivien of Léogane, who owned a boat?

For half an hour the silence persisted, and Margal remained unmoving. The smoke and the smell of the black candle permeated the room. Then with a noisy sigh the bocor removed the panty from his face and said, "Put me to bed now, but don't undress me. With Polivien coming at midnight, I must rest a little."

Obeying, she said with a frown, "Why did I have to be here for what you have just done? You had no need of me."

He reached up to pat her face as she leaned over him. "You give me strength, woman."

"Well, if that's true, I'm glad. But I don't see—"

"You too must rest now. Come back at eleven." His eyes flickered shut. "Set your alarm clock," he murmured as he drifted into sleep. "We must not be late."

In the house down the street, Sandra Dawson had kissed her six-year-old good night and watched the little girl go upstairs. Now she sat in the living room with a book. The servants had gone home.

Her thoughts wandered. For a time they focused

loosely on how peaceful the house seemed without her husband. Then, with her eyes half closed, she drifted back in time to the days before her impulsive marriage.

She had been a senior at Brookline, Massachusetts, High School when a drunk driver killed her father in the prime of his life. An insurance executive, he had left her mother and herself well enough off. She could still go to Miami University as planned. But the sense of loss haunted her, while Mother sought a solution in too quickly marrying a near stranger.

Was that the reason Brian had been able to convince her to marry him? Because he offered security, while Ken Forrest preferred flying a plane to hitting the books?

I should have married Ken, God help me. Why was I so stupid?

She had expected to marry Ken. By their senior year at Miami they had been spending nearly all their time together. But Brian had turned up as a transfer student from Georgetown and decided she was for him.

She turned her head to look at the telephone. In this country, phones did not always function, but if she were to try calling the north-coast sisal plantation where Ken now worked, she would probably get through to him in time.

To say what? "Ken, my marriage is washed up. Can you come?"

He could come if he wanted to. Quickly, too. When the plantation people had business in town, he was the one who flew them in. And, in a way, she was responsible for his having the job.

The plantation had asked the Embassy to recommend an American who knew tropical agriculture and could fly a small plane. Brian had tossed the request to her for suggestions.

"Well, I know a pilot who at least studied tropical ag."

Knowing nothing of her past with Ken, Brian had passed the name along. Ken was hired.

He had been in Haiti two years now, but she had kept her distance for fear of being found out. For fear of having her husband say, "What a bitch you are, persuading me to find work for an old flame so you could have an affair with him!"

And now? What if she called Ken after two years and he said he wasn't interested? Could she live with that?

She tried to read again, but not for long. Putting the book down, she went to close the shutters at the living room windows. The servants would have secured the others before leaving.

That done, she bolted the veranda door, then repeated the routine at the kitchen door. Port-au-Prince had more than its quota of nighttime thieves.

At the top of the stairs she peered into Merry's room, where a nightlight glowed. Her daughter was peacefully sleeping. My daughter who loves me, she thought as she went along the hall to her own room. Even if her father doesn't.

She was tired. Perhaps from thinking too much about her problems. Soon after getting into bed, she too was fast asleep.

* * *

"Margal!" Clarisse leaned over him and gently shook his shoulder. "Margal, wake up! It is eleven o'clock."

The man without legs opened his eyes and used his powerful arms to push himself to a sitting position. "Light the candle."

Going to that part of the room, she stepped with care over the three chalked circles and held a match to the candle wick, then returned to the bed. Margal did not have to tell her to carry him to the candle. She knew what was expected.

He had slept with the child's garment inside his shirt, and now closed his eyes and held it against them as before. The room was again full of stillness. Outside, a car coming up Rue Printemps rattled over a ridge of dirt where the road had been poorly put back over a repaired water pipe. There was no other sound. Even the dogs were quiet.

Margal's lips moved, but he spoke so softly that Clarisse had to listen intently to hear what he said. What he said was, "The little one sleeps."

"Is that what you want?"

"Partly. I put a thought into her mind before she slept. She has had it all this time. Now she will do what I tell her to."

Clarisse did not argue. If he said the world would end in a moment, it would end.

But for what purpose did he wish to capture the mind of a child?

Chapter Five

"Wake up, little one!"

Merry Dawson stirred in her sleep, then opened her eyes. Had she really heard someone tell her to wake up? It seemed so. But there was no one in the room. Moonlight streaming through the east window revealed nothing unfamiliar.

"Don't be afraid, little one. No one will harm you."

Yes, there was a voice. A man's voice, speaking English like the Haitians who sometimes came to the house to see Daddy.

But where was it coming from?

It was inside her head, she decided.

"Listen to me now, little one, because I am going to tell you what to do and you must not be afraid to do it. No harm will come to you. Are you listening?"

She sat up in bed. "Yes, I'm listening."

"I want you to get up very quietly, little one, and dress yourself to go outdoors. Don't make any noise. We don't want to wake your mother. Get up now."

She got off the bed the way she always did, dropping onto her tummy and sliding feet first off the edge. What should she wear? The dress she had taken off before going to bed was in the wicker clothes hamper beside her bureau, where she put her taken-off clothes every night before getting into pajamas. This was a really hot country in summer. You had to put on clean clothes every morning.

Peering into her closet, she decided on a yellow dress. Yellow was her favorite color. But first, of course, underwear and socks. You had to wear socks because there were things like Spanish needles and sandburs in the grass. And because if you lost a shoe and didn't have socks on, you could get a bad thing called hookworm.

Dressed, she went back and stood by the bed, waiting for the voice to tell her what to do next.

"Are you ready, little one?"

"Uh-huh."

"Listen, then. I want you to go along the hall past your mother's room without waking her. Don't go in to talk to her. Don't even stop. Keep right on going to the stairs, and go down the stairs and through the kitchen to the back door. Do you understand?"

"Yes."

"Unlock the back door, go out into the yard, and close the door behind you very quietly. When you have done that, I will tell you what to do next. Go now."

For the last time she looked around, with a strange feeling she might not see her room again for a long time. Being careful to do exactly what the voice had told her to—not out of fear, but to win the speaker's approval—she merely glanced into her mothers room as she went along the hall. The door was open because Daddy was not home, and in the moonlight from the windows she could see Mommy sleeping.

Downstairs she went, and through the kitchen to the back door as instructed. There she had a little trouble, because the door had bolts at top and bottom, and to slide the top one down she had to pull on a chain that was almost too high for her. But by straining on tiptoe she finally reached it, and a moment later she was in the yard.

Shining with moonlight, the yard was really pretty tonight. All the trees cast shadows. Standing by the door, she wished she could stay a while just to look at it, but the voice was in her head again.

"Go out to the gate now, Merry. The small gate, not the wide one for cars. Be sure not to make a noise when you close it behind you."

Through the shimmer of moonlight she obeyed, and again the voice spoke.

"Now come to me, little one! Turn up the hill and just keep walking until you reach me. My name is Margal and I am your friend. Come!"

Unafraid, she turned and went up the sidewalk. Never before had she been out alone at this hour. Never, in fact, had she been alone on a Port-au-

Prince street at any hour. But it was what Margal wanted, so it must be all right.

And there he was, seated on the sidewalk in front of one of the older houses near the top of the street!

A car was at the curb. It, too, was old. Beside it stood a big, fat lady and a man with large ears. But they didn't count. It was the seated man who had called her from her bed and told her to come here to him, and she saw now why he was not standing like the others.

He hadn't any legs.

He was holding his arms out toward her now, so she ran the last few steps with her own arms outstretched. He caught hold of her hands.

"Hello, little one." It was the same voice. "Hello, Merry Dawson."

"Hi, Mr. Margal!"

"You're a good girl. Because you're so good, I'm going to take you on a very special trip." He let go her hands and beckoned the lady to come forward. "This is Clarisse, Merry. She'll be your friend too."

The lady nodded.

"And this is Mr. Polivien," Margal said. "Now we can all get into the car, eh?"

Mr. Polivien frowned as he opened the car's rear door for Merry. He did not look happy. But the lady smiled her approval as Merry climbed onto the seat.

"Move over, child," she instructed, "so Margal can sit with you." Proud of her English, she beamed at the child.

Long before going to live in the mountains and encountering the man she now served, Clarisse had attended school in the capital, where English had been her favorite subject. As for Margal, he too had studied English in school, his incredible mind finding it as easy to master as everything else he sought to learn.

Returning to the man who had no legs, Clarisse now picked him up as though he were a doll and carried him to the car. She put him on the rear seat beside Merry. She and Mr. Polivien got in front beside a silent, scowling driver, and Mr. Polivien, turning his head, spoke to Margal in Creole.

Margal answered him by saying, *"Bon. Nou kapab allé, koun yé a."*

From the Creole lessons Edita had given her, Merry knew what that meant. Or almost, anyway. It meant something like, "Good. We can go now."

What fun this was!

It was certainly a fun journey. First the car rattled through the city streets, and those were not like when she rode with Daddy or Mommy in the daytime. They were so quiet they were spooky. The only moving things were sad, hungry-looking dogs that slunk out of the way when the car's lights hit them, making their eyes shine.

Then the city fell behind and there was just the one road running wide and straight through the moonlight.

Margal put his arm around her. "You are not afraid, little one?"

"Oh, no!"

"I knew you would not be."

Not often had she been outside the city. Once

Daddy had driven them to a beach where the water was so clear you could see even the smallest shells on the bottom. Another time he had to go through the mountains to a place called Jacmel. But you didn't do those things at night.

"Why not shut your eyes and sleep, little one?" Margal said.

"Will it be all right?" She really was kind of drowsy.

"Of course. You are very young to be up so late."

"Thank you."

When she awoke, she was not in the car any more. The moon had disappeared, and the fat lady was carrying her along a path. The night smelled like the seashore. There was a sound of small waves breaking. Then a light came on ahead—a lantern, not an electric light—and she saw a boat in front of her. On its deck next to the lantern stood Mr. Polivien.

He reached down, and the fat lady handed Merry up to him, and there was some talk in Creole that Merry did not understand. Then Mr. Polivien reached down again to help Clarisse onto the boat.

Merry was not sleepy any more. She had never been on a boat before and was curious. This one had a kind of a house in the middle. In front of that was a big pole with ropes hanging from it. Everything looked old and dirty, though.

"Come, little one." Taking her by the hand, the fat lady led her into the boat's house, where another lantern provided light, and walked her across a dirty floor to a kind of bed. She was supposed to use the bed, she guessed, so she sat on it. There were two others like it. Margal sat on one, and Clarisse, with a sigh of weariness, went and sank onto the other.

"Are you all right, little one?" Margal said.

"Oh, yes."

"Then you should try to sleep again. Before daylight, people at Polivien's house will be coming aboard. I have warned him to keep them quiet, but he won't be able to."

"Yes, go to sleep," Clarisse urged. "And may *le bon Dieu* protect you, *ti-fi!*"

"Who?"

"The one you call God."

Margal turned quickly to look at her and said something angrily in Creole that Merry did not understand. After staring back at him for a few seconds, the fat lady shrugged. Then she lay down with her back to both of them and did not speak again.

Chapter Six

Rising at seven, Sandra Dawson donned a robe over her pajamas and went downstairs to the kitchen. On mornings when they needed fresh fruit and vegetables from the Iron Market, she always prepared breakfast herself, so that the cook, Edita, could stop at the market on her way to work.

After setting the table for two, she went to unlock the back door and found its bolts already drawn.

Had she neglected to lock the door last night?

What about the front door and the living room shutters?

She went to look, and found that part of the house properly secured. Strange.

The situation was ironic, too. With Brian away she felt so much less tense but had to face the fact that she and Merry were alone in a big house, in a city where a door left unlocked at night could be an invitation to terror.

She must be more careful tonight.

At the bottom of the stairs she called Merry's name. No answer. Ah, to be six and able to sleep so soundly! Again she called. Again no reply.

"If you're just looking for a morning giggle session, young lady, I'll paddle your tush for making me climb these stairs!"

Up she went, half amused. At the top she paced along the hall with her hands on her hips, past her own open door to the one at the end.

Merry liked to burrow under the sheet and pretend she wasn't there, then giggle when "discovered." There was no bulge under the sheet this morning.

A new game? The child did have a lively imagination. And a wicked sense of humor.

"All right, I'll find you. They don't call me Sherlock Sandy for nothing, young lady."

Dropping to one knee, she peered under the bed. No one there. With a dramatic lunge at the closet, she swept apart the clothes hanging there. No one was hiding behind them to grab her around the legs with a game-ending squeal of delight.

Puzzled now, she turned to the bed again and saw the white pajamas lying on it.

"Merry, where are you? Stop this, now!"

The silence was frightening.

"Merry! I'm not in the mood this morning. Where are you?"

Not here in the room, obviously. The child must

be somewhere else in the house. But naked? Or had she put on some clothes after shedding the pajamas?

This was a big house. Much larger than the one in Canapé Vert that they had occupied while waiting for something Brian felt was more appropriate to his position at the Embassy. She went along the upstairs hall to a bedroom Merry used as a playroom.

The child's red tricycle was neatly parked in a corner. Dolls of assorted sizes sat on the bed where she played at teaching school.

"Merry, are you hiding in here?"

No answer. A quick search proved Merry was not.

Sandra sped down the stairs, shouting the child's name. It could no longer be a game her daughter was playing. The games never lasted this long!

Downstairs was just as empty. Then she remembered the unlocked back door.

Could her daughter have unlocked it? Was she tall enough now to reach the chain that controlled the top bolt? *I secured that door when I went to bed last night. I know I did! Even thinking about Ken, I wouldn't have neglected to do that, with two break-ins on this street in the past week.*

The door clattered against the wall as she jerked it open. Shouting Merry's name, she ran into the yard. The part of it where the child always played was empty. Still calling, she sped around to the front, where the swimming pool was. Merry never had come here alone after being told she mustn't, but if she were caught up in some frenzy of independence this morning . . .

The front was deserted, too. Her shouts went unanswered. There was no one in the pool. Numb with fear, she ran around to the back again.

Was it possible the child could have opened the gate and left the yard for some reason? To chase a ball, say? Or talk to some passerby who might have called out to her? The marchandes did that sometimes.

Sandra hurried to the gate and opened it. This was the time of day when servants were on their way to work. Seeing her there in her dressing gown and slippers, two such women peered at her in passing. One offered a hesitant, "*Bon jour*, madame."

She did not answer. There was no sign of her daughter. Dear God, what should she do?

Don't panic. She's a sensible child, not one to do something really foolish. She isn't in the house and she isn't in the yard, so for some reason that seemed to make sense to her, she must have gone somewhere.

Remember the time in Canapé Vert when she found the Dantaves' kitten in our yard and walked half a mile to take it back to them?

Get dressed now. Get organized. Then go look for her!

It was all very well to preach calmness to herself, but she was back at the gate, dressed, in less than three minutes, and again faced the need to make a decision. If she left the house and the child returned while she was gone—what then? It would be Merry's turn to panic.

I can't help it. I can't just stay here and wait! And if

she returns and is frightened, it may teach her not to do this again.

Leaving the gate open behind her, she looked up the street, then down. Which way? Dear God, there were so many decisions to make! She turned left, down the hill.

For half an hour she knocked on locked gates, causing watchdogs to howl and bark, or opened unlocked gates and rang doorbells. And asked people she did not even know if they had seen her daughter.

No one had.

Call the police, she told herself. The child could be far from here by now. Perhaps someone coaxed her into a car.

Into her mind came memories of lurid tales she had read about this land of superstition and black magic. Tales of secret voodoo rites in which children were said to be used.

She ran most of the way home. Bursting into the house, she frantically called Merry's name again until convinced the child had not returned. Then she forced her hands to stop shaking while she pawed through the telephone directory.

Police Department? It wasn't listed. But they didn't call it that here, did they? Dear God, what did they call it? Her mind would not function. Department of Police? No. Ministry? No, no. Bureau—that was it. Bureau de la Police. She found the number and dialed it. The answer came in French, of course.

She could speak a little French. Even a little Creole. Not enough for this. Did someone there speak

English? Please? This was an emergency!

"I speak English, madame. What is the problem?"

He listened without interrupting, then questioned her. She got the impression it was not to him an earth-shaking problem, but for the sake of good public relations he would be cooperative. "Your husband is at the United States Embassy, is he not, Mrs. Dawson?"

"Yes, yes. But not now. He's in Miami."

"I see. Well, please be assured we shall do our best. And, of course, if the child returns, you will call us?"

"Yes, of course."

"Don't be alarmed, Mrs. Dawson. No harm will come to your daughter. We will soon find her."

His mention of the Embassy had put a thought in her head. One she should have had before, she told herself. The only homes Merry was likely to think of visiting were those of Brian's colleagues. She had been taken to most of them at one time or another. Some were in this area.

If the child knew how to reach them on foot . . .

One after another she phoned them and talked to Embassy wives. No, they had not seen Merry but would alert their servants. She mustn't worry.

"That daughter of yours is a bit of a pixie, you know, Sandy."

"She'll be back when she's had her little fling, dear."

"The police are really efficient here, Sandra. They'll find her."

"I'll send Luc"—her yard boy—"out on his motorbike to search the neighborhood. He knows her, and he's very intelligent."

Should she call Brian in Miami? No, no—at least, not yet. He would be furious. He would say she should have been more careful. And the Embassy women were right, of course. Merry hadn't been kidnapped. She had just wandered off somewhere.

If only she could believe that!

At this point Edita arrived from the market and, on being told what had happened, went out again at once, wide-eyed, to make inquiries of her own.

Chapter Seven

The Greenway was not one of the Miami area's better-known hotels. A few blocks south of Flagler in Coral Gables, it catered to visitors who appreciated quiet more than chrome. Its lobby was small, its roof only six floors above the street.

Brian Dawson took a taxi from the airport to a foreign-car establishment run by a college buddy. From machines available in its used-car section he leased one suited to his temperament.

It was a silver Jaguar with a hood ornament depicting a cat of that species leaping into space. The car itself resembled a sleek feline ready to pounce. Arriving at the Greenway in it, Brian nevertheless carried his suitcase himself rather than wait for assistance.

He offered his hand to the middle-aged manager

at the desk. "How are you, Norman. You got my telegram?"

"We did indeed, Mr. Dawson. Would you like your usual room?"

"Fine."

Norman tapped a bell. A man about his own age but wearing a dark brown uniform came to carry Brian's bag. He, too, greeted Brian by name. On the way up to the fourth floor he said, "Will you be with us long this time, sir?"

"I wish I knew, Henry."

"I took the liberty of putting some bourbon in your room. Doubted you'd be carrying anything so breakable, the way they handle one's luggage these days."

"Bless you."

Unlocking the door of 402, Henry stood aside to let Brian enter, then followed and placed the bag on a luggage stand. Brian tipped him, watched him depart, then opened the bottle on the writing desk and poured two inches into a glass. Having downed this with an "Ah!" of appreciation, he poured a second two inches and reached for the phone.

When given an outside line, he dialed a number he did not have to look up. He was more than familiar, too, with the sultry voice that answered.

"Hello, love," he said. "Have you been sitting by the phone waiting for it to ring?" He had, of course, called her from the Embassy in Port-au-Prince to say he was coming.

"Where are you?"

"At the hotel."

"And didn't call me from the airport? Shame on you."

"Career before pleasure, darling. You know that." His mock-solemn tone implied she knew precisely the opposite. "Look, I ought to shower before coming over, but, damn it, I don't want to take the time. I'll have one there while we talk."

"I'll have the water running," she said. "I might even be under it, waiting."

"I'm on my way."

Downstairs he stopped at the desk for a necessary word with the manager. "As usual, I don't expect to be spending much time here, Norman. But you needn't tell that to anyone who might call. Just give them this number."

But when he produced a card from his billfold, Norman stopped him. "We have it on file, Mr. Dawson."

"Now that's what I call efficiency."

"Unless you have a different one this time."

"No. It's still the same."

"And if you'll just let us know when you are using your room, there'll be no problem."

"Of course."

Strange, the man at the desk thought, watching his handsome guest stride out to the Jaguar at the curb. He comes here with a suitcase, then goes to stay somewhere else without taking it with him. Wherever he disappears to for days at a time, he must keep a supply of clothes there.

* * *

Brian drove to Le Jeune Road and south on that main artery to Poinciana Avenue. Heading east there, he arrived after other familiar turns at a Coconut Grove apartment building as unpretentious as the hotel he had left. Here again he was able to park without difficulty.

In the building's small foyer he pressed a button and waited to be asked who was calling.

He wasn't asked. The door release buzzed. Letting himself in, he took the stairs two at a time to the second floor, where the door of apartment 203 opened as he reached it.

He had known, of course, that she would not be waiting for him naked in the shower. She lived alone, and someone had to push the button to release the downstairs door. She was almost ready for the shower, though, he saw with a sudden surge of excitement as he pulled her into his arms and hungrily sought her mouth. All she had on was a dressing gown.

While kissing her, he kicked the door shut. His hands were never still as they renewed their acquaintance with her body.

This was the woman he should have married, not Sandra. He knew it now. He so easily could have done so, too, for she had slept with him when they were both students. It was only because of her name that he had chosen Sandra instead. A name like Carmen Alvaranga had seemed so synonymous with promiscuity.

With his mouth still on hers, he succeeded at last in removing the dressing gown, and God, what a gorgeous creature she was! That raven hair, that creamy skin, that seductive body, and that sensual mouth with its hungry tongue. But then she managed to escape from his arms, shaking her head at him despite her provocative smile.

"Let's shower," she said. "With me like this and you still dressed, we're going to get nowhere."

That was another thing. She had that way of making him feel she fiercely wanted him. Sandra, for God's sake, always made him feel she didn't.

"Should we have a drink first?" There were times when he had trouble coping without one.

"Well—"

"Just one?"

With a little frown she went into the kitchen.

In the bedroom, Brian removed his clothes. From the chest of drawers that held his things he tossed clean underwear and socks onto a chair. Shirts and slacks of his, even suits, hung at the back of the bedroom closet, and he had shoes on the closet floor.

His wife would be slightly shocked, he thought with satisfaction.

Stripped, he returned to the living room and found two drinks on a small table there. Bourbon for him, vodka for Carmen. She stood nude by the table, facing him.

Downing his drink quickly, he reached for her. But she stepped back.

"After we shower."

Reluctantly, he let his hands drop. "For God's sake, let's get at it, then. It's been three months!"

"Closer to four this time. And I should know better than you. I've been alone."

"Damn it, Carmen, I don't get anything from Sandy. You know that."

"Don't you?" she said. "Really?"

He looked at her and was suddenly angry. So often now it came to this. He would arrive full of his need for her, and somehow they would blunder into a stupid argument before anything good happened. As though he were being punished for having married the wrong woman.

"Please," he begged. "Drink your drink."

Slowly she did. Slowly to taunt him, he was certain. And if he said anything, she would remind him that it was he who had wanted the drink, not she. But at last her glass was empty, and when he reached for her hand to walk her to the bathroom, she did not resist.

In the shower they soaped each other exploringly, and when the soap was rinsed off he kissed her all over, kneeling for the part of the ritual he enjoyed most. It never failed to arouse her too, and from bathroom to bed was only a matter of minutes.

Half an hour later, when they were still naked on the bed but no longer playing with each other's bodies, she said with a frown, "How long are you here for this time?"

"Two weeks. Maybe three."

"Really? How did you manage to get away?"

With his hands clasped behind his head he grinned at the ceiling. "Immigration asked the Embassy to send someone over to talk about the Haitian boat people. I got myself the job."

"For two or three weeks?"

"It won't take more than a few days. But I can say it took longer."

"What about your wife?"

"I told her not to expect me back until she saw me. She won't be trying to get in touch."

"M'm." She pressed her lips to his. "Sounds good."

"If you can get away, we might drive up to North Carolina for a while, out of this heat. Can you?" He knew she could. She owned and ran an art gallery in the Grove, and the young fellow who was her assistant could easily take over.

"You know"—she reached out to use her fingertips on him in a provocative caress—"sometimes I really am fond of you. North Carolina sounds like heaven."

"Do that again."

"Do what?"

"What you just did."

Everything was going to be all right after all, he told himself when she complied.

Chapter Eight

They were bound for an island in the Bahamas, Clarisse now knew.

"Since you are not familiar with the many specks of land scattered through those waters, there is no point in telling you more," Polivien had added.

Why they were going to an island in the Bahamas she could not imagine, but she was heartily sick of the voyage. They had left Haiti at dawn on Saturday. It was now Tuesday, unless she had lost track of time. So for four days and three nights their world had consisted of this ugly fishing boat, not more than thirty feet long, with its stinking beast of an engine that was never silent.

"Can't we go faster and get there sooner?" she had asked Polivien's younger brother, Louis, who appeared to be second in command.

"Madame, we are making a commendable eight knots."

"I am not a sailor. How fast is that?"

"Slightly more than nine miles an hour."

"And how long a journey are we embarked upon?"

He shrugged. "Who knows, exactly? We should be there before midnight tonight."

"I'm delighted to hear it," she had replied sarcastically, though in truth she did not dislike Louis or even Polivien himself. Since leaving her homeland she had learned something about them from the twelve other passengers who, with their possessions, occupied the boat's crowded deck.

Formerly poor but respected fishermen, the brothers earned a somewhat better living now by netting fees from unhappy countrymen who sought transportation to the States. But they did not overload the boat or set forth with insufficient food and water, as some of the greedier ones did. They could even produce letters of gratitude from some of their former passengers.

Yes, the Poliviens were good men and probably capable, though on this voyage—thank *le bon Dieu!*—they had not been tested. The sea had remained reasonably calm, the weather had not once threatened, and no watchdog vessel of the United States had put in an appearance.

That was a worry, of course. Fear had been a ghostly passenger on this humble craft ever since its departure from Léogane. U.S. ships were known to be constantly on patrol, and no one could be certain when one might suddenly materialize.

But if all continued to go well, the voyage would end before midnight tonight. Good. It was nearly that now, and the sky glittered with stars.

But wasn't that a cluster of earthly lights just becoming visible off to the right, up ahead?

She must inform Margal.

He would be relieved, no doubt, though until today he had been content to sleep the time away or talk to the little girl. Even more amazing had been the behavior of the child. One would have expected little Merry Dawson to be frightened at being cooped up for so long. But when not with Margal, answering his endless questions about her parents and home life, she had made friends with the people on deck, watching the men at their card games and dominoes, helping the women prepare food over charcoal fires in cut-down oil drums.

To Merry this dreary voyage was obviously an exciting adventure. Did Margal control her mind?

Margal himself had seemed somewhat restless today, though. He had not talked much or taken his usual naps. For the past hour he had been sitting stiffly erect on his bunk, with his back against the cabin wall, like one who at any moment might spring into furious action. As though he were expecting something unusual to happen at any moment.

Did he already know what she was about to tell him? It would not surprise her.

Approaching his bunk, she waited for him to look

at her. Then she said, "We are coming to something."

"I know."

"There are lights in the distance."

"Are they on land?"

"I think so. They don't move."

He looked at the bed where the child lay. "The *ti-fi* sleeps?"

She nodded.

"And you believe we are nearly there?"

"Louis said we would arrive before midnight." She glanced at the watch on her wrist. "It is now twenty minutes to."

"Get our things together, then. Tell Polivien we must be the first to leave the boat."

She carried out his instructions, then stood beside the boat's owner, at the wheel, for the last few moments of the voyage. The lights she had first seen were behind them now. The man with the protruding ears pointed to others ahead. "You see Bootle Bay Village there? The spit of land we are approaching is part of Grand Bahama Island, less than a hundred miles from the east coast of Florida."

"And that is supposed to mean something to me?"

"Only that we are where we should be, and on time."

Apparently where they were supposed to be was a long stretch of beach, and except for a single boat lying at anchor in shallow water, it appeared to be deserted. The boat was a sailing craft. At least, it had two short masts that stood dark against the stars.

To her surprise, Polivien turned his craft in that direction.

"Are you mad?" she protested. "If any people are there, they will see us!"

"They are waiting for us."

"But—"

"Not now, please. I have things to do."

In the next half hour he indeed had things to do, and as he did them she recalled his telling her in Léogane that his boat had never been close to Florida.

Not his boat, perhaps. No. But there was a Creole peasant proverb that applied here, without a doubt: *Pa blié grand chemin pou chemin travès.* Don't let the crossroads make you forget the main road. Indeed.

She watched him with interest. First he brought his boat close to the sailboat so his brother could throw a line to two men on the other's deck. Then he talked with the pair for a moment while his passengers strained to hear what was said, which was impossible because all three voices were kept low.

Ignoring a barrage of questions from his passengers, Polivien then instructed Clarisse to go for Margal. And when she returned from the cabin with the legless one in her arms, she found Polivien standing shoulder deep in the sea, between the two boats, waiting for her.

He raised his arms. "Hand him down to me, madame."

She looked at Margal. He nodded. Having received him with the greatest of care, Polivien passed him up to the two men on the sailboat.

"Now the child."

Merry Dawson went aboard the other craft the same way, and was followed by their suitcase. Then the little man with bat-wing ears frowned up at Clarisse and shook his head. "Not you, madame," he said.

As though struck by lightning, she stood rigid for a moment, gazing down at him, then exploded. "What do you mean, not me? I go where my master goes!"

"No, no—you misunderstand. I simply mean I cannot be of help. You weigh too much."

"Oh." She was instantly mollified. "Well, then, I shall have to get wet, I suppose. But not these clothes. Oh, no."

Calmly lifting her dress over her head and removing it, then stepping out of her shoes and underwear, she handed her things down to him and waited, huge and naked in front of them all, for him to pass them up to the men on the sailboat and position himself. When he had done that, she went over the side backward, with Polivien's hands on her buttocks to steady her, and joined him in the water.

Then she raised her arms to be helped aboard the sailing vessel by the two startled men standing on its deck.

When Polivien's other passengers had transferred themselves and their possessions, he came aboard the sailboat to introduce the two strangers now in charge of their destiny. M'sieu Sassine and M'sieu Treveau, he informed them, were Haitians living in the Bahamas. Sassine, Clarisse decided, had the face of a sick donkey.

"Good luck to all of you," Polivien said in dismissal. But before leaving, he escorted Donkey-face and Treveau to Margal, who sat between Clarisse's legs on the deck—she had put her clothes back on—and explained to them that the man with no legs was a last-minute addition to the passenger list, along with his woman and the white child, but was to be given special treatment.

"You have been out of Haiti for several years," Polivien told them in Creole, "and perhaps have not heard of M'sieu Margal. Be assured he is a man of great repute, the most revered bocor our country has ever known, and you would be wise to help him in any way you can."

Impressed, the two solemnly shook Margal's hand, and the small donkey-faced man said fervently, "Whatever you wish on our brief voyage, m'sieu, you have only to ask for it."

Margal merely nodded.

Then Polivien returned to his boat, and the other craft, under rags of sail, crept away from the beach.

Chapter Nine

It was a pathetic wreck, this boat. Filled with apprehension, Clarisse approached the donkey-faced Sassine at the wheel to seek reassurance.

"We are going to Florida, I presume."

"We are, madame."

"I do not understand. Why have we changed to this boat when Polivien could have taken us the whole way?"

"Because, madame, were Polivien caught trying to land you from his excellent craft, you would be sent back to Haiti without question."

"But—"

"Whereas if we are caught in this miserable craft, and tell the Americans we have come all the way in it, risking our very lives in a desperate attempt to attain freedom, our chances will be somewhat better.

That, at least, is the situation at present. It changes from time to time." He shrugged. "I shall explain all this to the others presently, so that all will know what to say if we are apprehended."

The boat lumbered along through the darkness with its timbers incessantly groaning and the sea gurgling past its ancient sides. Clarisse returned to Margal, who lay near the bow with his head on their suitcase because now there was no cabin to shelter him. The child slept at his side.

When she repeated the boatman's words, Margal only nodded. She lay down next to him on the side away from the child and closed her eyes. After a while he reached out to grasp her shoulder.

"Do something for me."

She sat up, waiting to be told what.

"Tell Sassine or the other one I wish to talk."

"All right." Both men were at the wheel now. By the light of the stars she felt her way through the other passengers on deck, most of whom slept. She and Margal and the child had been blessed, she realized. What an ordeal the journey from Léogane must have been for those forced to spend the entire time exposed to blazing sun and cold night air!

It was the tall man, Treveau, who returned with her. Gazing up at him, Margal said, "Madame has already asked a number of questions, I know. But I have a few more."

"Certainly, m'sieu." Treveau squatted to bring his face closer.

"First, how long does your part of this journey usually take?"

"About twenty hours, m'sieu. We should arrive at dusk, which is good. The time and tide must be right."

"You land at a place called Sebastian, Polivien said."

"Yes. That is to say, we sail through Sebastian Inlet to the Intracoastal Waterway, which is wide there and called the Indian River. Then we go south a little way to an abandoned pier in Wabasso."

"Your passengers have friends there?"

"No, m'sieu. They are going to Little Haiti in Miami. But it is perilous to land near Miami."

"How will they get there?"

"Cars will be waiting where we land."

"I see."

A sudden gust struck the boat's ragged sails, and the squatting man had to put a hand on the deck to steady himself. When the moment passed, he said with a frown, "Where will you be going, m'sieu, if I may ask?"

"Polivien told me of a cousin of his who lives in a place called Gifford."

"Gifford?"

"A country town or village not far from where you will be putting us ashore, he said."

Plucking a worn and dirty map from his pocket, the tall man unfolded it with care lest it fall apart. For a moment he studied it by starlight. "Ah, yes, here it is—just north of Vero Beach. How will you get there, m'sieu?"

"I'll find a way."

"I must warn you not to depend on the cars I mentioned. They will be overcrowded even without you. A taxi is out of the question also. No one must know we—"

"I will find a way," Margal calmly repeated.

Treveau looked at the three of them. "I know of no way to help you, m'sieu, and I am sorry. Had we been told you three would be with this group . . . But Polivien had no time."

"It will not be a problem."

Shaking his head, the tall man returned to his donkey-faced partner at the wheel.

The boat lurched on through the night, and in time the sun rose flaming from the sea behind it. During the hours of daylight that followed, no other craft came suspiciously close. Still, the faces of the passengers showed relief when the same sun sank upon the land of their destination, now visible as a low dark streak on the horizon.

But as darkness fell and the craft neared the end of its journey, signs of tension appeared.

"We must all be very quiet now," Treveau warned. "No talking, please. No noise at all."

He was obeyed. The only sounds to be heard were the creaking of the craft itself, the occasional flapping of its sails, and the slither of the sea along its hull.

All at once an engine sputtered to life somewhere in the boat's bowels.

Startled, Clarisse reached out to halt Sassine as he appeared from below and would have hurried past.

"What is this? You warn us to make no sound, and now—"

"You see that light ahead, madame?"

"Well, yes."

"It marks the entrance to Sebastian Inlet, where the current will be swift and treacherous even though the tide is with us. To rely on our sails there would be dangerous. We could be swept onto the rocks. But I assure you, the moment we are through the inlet—"

"You said we had to be a sailing craft in case the Americans intercepted us!"

"True."

"But if we have an engine—"

"Madame, it is a very old engine." The look of innocence on Sassine's donkey face was comical. "Had the Americans apprehended us before, they would have thought, ah, those stupid Haitians, when it comes to machinery they know absolutely nothing, not even that a part is missing. And one moment after we are safely through the inlet, that part will be missing again."

"I see."

"Now, madame, I must shorten sail. Excuse me, please."

The engine continued its rumbling, and Clarisse now noted a difference in the way the craft moved through the water. The change was reassuring, like discovering that a drunken man leading her along some dark and dangerous road had suddenly become sober.

Presently there was the sound of swift water sucking and gurgling through a narrow passage, and, peering ahead, she saw a pair of white lights marking rocky shores. Another two, closer in, were like red eyes on what appeared to be pillars of a bridge.

The man at the wheel was intent upon steering the boat between the red ones, it seemed.

Suddenly, overhead, the bridge flew past like a huge, low-flying bird, and she knew why this particular boat had short masts. Taller ones could not have cleared such a structure.

Bridge and lights disappeared behind them, and now Donkey-face, who had been at the bow calling out instructions to his partner at the wheel, scurried past again on his way below. The sound of the engine ceased. Slithering on like a ghost ship, once more under sail, the deceptively ancient craft entered what appeared to be a broad lagoon pocked with small, dark islands, with the man at the wheel occasionally—and no doubt reluctantly—switching on a spotlight to catch the red and green glint of reflectors marking the channel. Then a blinking light indicated a place where the channel turned, and presently assorted other lights became visible on the right, some apparently on piers, others in houses.

The boat glided on past these until Donkey-face trimmed the sails and hurried below again. The engine recommenced its sullen growl beneath the deck. But not for long. Only long enough for them to slide up alongside a dock that appeared to be as unsound as the boat itself.

The two men made the craft fast. Clarisse, feeling

safe for the first time in hours, exhaled a moan of relief.

Sassine was at her side, she realized, speaking to Margal. "M'sieu, I will ask you three to depart first. Proceed along the pier, and you will come to a small road." He turned to one of the other passengers. "Alcide, go with them and carry their suitcase, please. You must walk to the road in any case to reach the cars. Make as little noise as possible."

A big fellow, the man spoken to responded with a shrug and picked up the suitcase as though it contained feathers. Clarisse knew what it weighed, and was grateful. She had been forced to cope with it since their departure from the house in Rue Printemps.

She lifted the legless Margal in her arms. With a quiet "Come, *ti-fi*," to the child, she stepped gingerly from deck to pier and trailed the big man along thirty yards of warped planks to solid ground, with dark water making soft gurgling sounds under her feet.

It was quite dark now. Were there houses here? If so, there were no lights turned on in them. With the little girl clinging to her hand she continued to follow the man with the luggage until he unexpectedly halted and she bumped into him.

"Here is the road," he said. "I leave you here."

"Wait," Margal told him.

"I can't wait. Don't you see the cars over there? They'll be crowded, and I want a good seat." He pointed, and Clarisse saw two hulking automobile-shapes standing without lights at the road's edge some twenty feet away. Putting the suitcase down, Alcide started toward them.

"Wait, I said." It was the tone Margal used when he would permit no discussion.

The man halted.

"Which car will you be riding in?"

"How should I know? We are supposed to be taken to Miami in two of them, that's all I know!"

"Go to the first one, then. Put the suitcase in it. Instruct the driver to come here."

"What are you talking about? There won't be room for extra passengers!"

"Look at me."

The man did so, and Clarisse knew what was happening. Her master's eyes would be live coals glowing red in the dark, and gazing into them would be nearly as painful as having hot coals pressed against one's own eyeballs. Yet it would not be possible to look away.

"Go," Margal said.

"But if he will not talk to you—"

"He will talk to me. Go." And to Clarisse, "Put me down."

She placed him on the ground and stood behind him, again knowing what would happen. And because he was using his eyes on the car now, it did.

She saw a light wink on as the driver opened his door and stepped from the machine. It went out as the door clicked shut. The man walked toward them like a zombie.

Halting before them, he simply stood there motionless with his arms dangling. He was a thin man with bony wrists and limp, long-fingered hands.

"What is your name?" Margal asked him.

"Zepherin, m'sieu."

"I am hiring you to drive the three of us to Gifford."

"Where is that, m'sieu?"

"A few miles south of here."

"I am supposed to drive people to Miami."

"They can wait."

"Of course."

"You may carry me to the car," Margal said. "My lady is tired."

The driver picked him up as though he had been taking such orders for years. It was usually so, Clarisse reflected as she followed them, holding Merry Dawson's hand. Behind them now came others from the boat.

At the car, the driver waited for her to open the rear door, then deposited Margal on the seat. She and the child got in to share it with him. The suitcase was already on the floor, and the man who had carried it stood a few paces distant, silently staring.

Clarisse closed the door. The driver had just turned the ignition key and switched on the headlights when the people from the boat appeared out of the darkness. Seeing the three already in the car, some surged forward with cries of protest.

Margal looked at them, and they halted.

"Tell them you will return for them," he instructed the driver.

Zepherin did so, as though the words had no meaning to him.

"Now drive on."

The car moved forward while the boat people stood in silence, watching it leave them stranded.

It was a large car, air conditioned, and once it reached a concrete highway it ate up the miles swiftly. Clarisse made herself comfortable, welcoming the change from the sea voyage. But by the taste of the air, she knew the ocean was still close by.

The child gazed out the window. Margal sat with his eyes closed and a look of concentration on his scarred face. Nothing was said for ten minutes or so.

Then the headlights picked out a sign bearing the name of the town that was their destination, and the driver said, "We seem to be here, m'sieu. Where in Gifford am I to take you?"

"Turn right just ahead."

"As you say, m'sieu."

Clarisse almost spoke but decided not to. Never before had Margal been here, she was certain. Or anywhere else in the United States. How, then, could he know?

But, of course, he did.

They turned from the four-lane highway onto a narrow strip of blacktop. "Go slow here," Margal said. "There will soon be a road on the left."

There was, and he ordered Zepherin to take it: another narrow, black road with nothing on either side for the headlights to reveal except sand and scrub, with now and then a stunted pine or cabbage palm. To Clarisse it was desolation, even in the dark. What, dear God, could have persuaded the master to come to such a place?

"Turn to the right, ahead."

This road was unpaved and rutted.

"Now watch for a house on the left, with a light burning on its veranda."

"They are expecting you, m'sieu?"

"No, but the light is burning, as I say. By the driveway is a mailbox with the name 'Jumel' on it. Stop beside it."

And there it all was, just around the next bend. The house, the light, the driveway, the mailbox, the name. Zepherin stopped the car.

Margal said, "Go to the door for me, please, Clarisse. Ask if M'sieu Jumel is at home. If he is, come back and carry me to him, so that I may talk to him face-to-face."

And make him know, she thought as she opened the car door, that he, too, is now part of this mysterious game we are playing, whether he wishes to be or not.

Chapter Ten

In her daughter's deserted playroom, Sandy Dawson gazed through a haze of despair at the red tricycle. Today was Thursday. Merry had disappeared last Friday night.

Six days. Six centuries.

She had driven every street in Port-au-Prince that could be driven, she was certain. She had walked many of them. She had spent hours begging the police to do more than they were doing.

"Perhaps the child has been stolen for ransom, madame."

"But no one has made any demands!"

Stolen. His word. It was growing in her mind now like a malignant tumor. Not just because of what she had read in sensational books. She didn't believe most of that. Though there was such a thing as voodoo here, of course—affecting the life of this country as surely as an underground stream affected plant life in the earth above it.

But there could be other reasons for stealing a little girl as attractive as Merry. Sexual reasons. Or to fill a void in a childless family. And if Merry had been taken for one of those reasons, there would be no demand for ransom, only an endless silence. The child would be kept hidden until everyone but her parents had forgotten about her.

Going down the stairs, Sandy clung to the railing. In the living room she sat and gazed blankly at the telephone.

Six days.

She had tried to phone Brian in Miami. Had called his hotel time and again, only to be told that he was not there and given another number to call. But calls to the other number had also gone unanswered, no matter what the time. Once she had phoned at three in the morning.

The Embassy, too, had tried without success. But while she was frantic, they were merely furious. On one of her visits she had overheard something not meant for her ears: that Brian Dawson was able to do "these stinking things" only because his father was close to the President. "I'd like to see the bastard get his comeuppance just once, damn him."

Walk the streets. Hound the police. Hammer at the Embassy. She had even tried to enlist the help of an army officer she knew slightly, and a Catholic priest who taught at the College St. Martial. Anyone. While Edita, who really loved the child, had doggedly sought information in places a white woman would be neither understood nor welcome.

All in vain.

What else could she do?

One more thing. She looked at her watch. Quarter to ten. How Ken Forrest could possibly help she did not know. But he might know someone to whom she could turn.

She never had called the plantation where Ken worked, though its number was in the phone book. As she waited for the connection, her fingers whitened around the phone.

She heard sputters and clicks, and then a ringing.

"Plantation Margot. *Bon jour.*"

"Ken Forrest, please. This is Mrs. Brian Dawson."

"Mrs. Dawson in Port-au-Prince?"

"Yes. It's urgent that I—"

"I'm sorry, Mrs. Dawson. Ken isn't here."

"Oh."

Her voice must have told him something. He came back quickly with, "You might be able to contact him this evening, though, right there in Port at the Pension Etoile. Do you know where that is?"

"Yes." It was a small hotel on the Champ-de-Mars, generally ignored by tourists. The kind of place Ken would stay.

"He's on his way to the city now. Flying in. He has to be in Miami tomorrow."

She discovered her mind was still working, after all. "What time is he due here? Can I catch him at the airport?"

"You might. In fact, I think yes." The voice was

cheerful now. "He got a new camera from the States yesterday and said he'd be trying for some aerial shots of the Citadelle on his way in this morning. That should stretch his flight time a bit."

"Thank you!" Sandy shouted. "I'm on my way!"

Ken Forrest had indeed gone out of his way to take new pictures of the incredible mountaintop fortress built years before by King Christophe. One of the special rewards of working in Haiti was the freedom his job provided to explore and photograph—sometimes by plane but more often by Jeep or on muleback—this mysterious country that for most outsiders ended at the outskirts of the capital.

Coming in for a landing at Port-au-Prince now, he set the company's light plane down with a touch of a flourish, just to prove a point to the cowboys who flew for the Haitian Air Force. Some were nightclub buddies of his when he spent an evening in the city. Being sons of the elite, they delighted in telling him that he looked more like a farmer than a pilot.

"Well, hell, I am a farmer. I was born on a farm."

He had been born, he liked to tell them, in Aroostook County, Maine, where his father was still one of that state's top potato growers. "But there are only two seasons in that part of the U.S—July and winter—so I opted for college in Miami and ended up here at the plantation."

None of his pals appeared to be present this morning, however. Mildly disappointed, he picked up his suitcase and headed for the terminal to catch a taxi. While loping past the bar, he heard his name called.

He stopped. The voice had been female, with an unmistakable note of invitation. Wheeling, he saw waving to him the wife of a man who worked at the U.S. Embassy. At a recent Embassy get-together, she had not seemed to mind that he looked like a farmer. If, indeed, he did.

A striking blonde, Veronica Holly was married to a man who believed an employee of State should always wear, even in the tropics, dark trousers, white shirt, a jacket, and a tie. She would have liked to know better this man who stood six-two, flew a plane, had the rugged features of one who spent most of his time outdoors, and, so far as she knew, never dressed up unless he had to.

"Well, hi," she said as he approached the bar. "What brought you to town?"

Ken put down his bag and accepted her hand. "Have to go to Miami tomorrow. Business."

And what, she quickly asked herself, might he be doing until then? Today was Thursday. Her husband, Hal, was in Jérémie and would be there until Sunday. "You've time for a drink, then." Her smile made it more than a casual invitation.

Ken ordered a Barbancourt-and-soda from the hovering bartender. "And what are you doing here at the airport?"

"I came to see a friend off."

"Oh."

He was not a man for small talk, she recalled. At least, at the Embassy party he hadn't been. Not that it mattered. Small talk was something she received from her husband seven days a week. And nights. It was not what she wanted now.

Still, you couldn't just stand and stare at a man, could you?

To fill the gap, she said, "Have you heard about the kidnapping?"

"Kidnapping? I've been in the bush all week."

"Sandy Dawson's little girl."

She saw his fingers tighten on his glass and was surprised it didn't break. "Merry? What happened? When?"

She had made a mistake, she realized. He knew the Dawsons. And she didn't want to . . . But it was too late now. Damn.

"Well, no one seems to know wht did happen, exactly." How could she keep the telling brief? "Brian left for Miami Friday. Next morning, when Sandy got up, their child was gone. The whole city's been looking for her."

"My God." His face was actually pale. "What do they think happened?"

She shrugged, then wished she hadn't. She mustn't seem indifferent. Nobody ought to be indifferent to the disappearance of a little girl, even when the child's father was a bastard. "Well, you know the stories that circulate here when something like this happens. The crazy voodoo tales."

"But Sandy must be frantic! And Brian. Has he come back?"

"She can't locate him. Even the Embassy can't." She reached for his arm. "Look. Drink up and let's go to my place for a refill. It's a long story."

But he was not hearing her.

He was not hearing because he was looking past her at something. And when she turned to see what had caught his attention, she could have kicked herself for having asked him to have a drink here. *What you should have done, stupid, was offer him a lift to town.* Because the person coming toward them at a run was the woman they were talking about. And the look on the face of Ken Forrest was the one she herself had been hoping to arouse.

Well, perhaps not really hoping. But when you were wed to a man who wore embroidered purple pajamas to bed in Haiti's summer heat, you had to at least try.

With a sigh of surrender, the wife of Hal Holly stepped back against the bar to avoid being caught in the middle as the two came together.

"Sandy!" Ken Forrest said. "I've just heard—"

"Thank God you're still here. I got caught in traffic."

"—about Merry."

"That's why I'm here. Oh, Ken, I need help! Do you have time to help me?"

"Of course." Still holding her hands, he turned to Veronica. "Excuse me, will you, Mrs. Holly?"

Her "Run along" was merely a vocal shrug.

Ken put money on the bar and let Sandy lead him out to her car. "Better let me drive," he advised. "You look a bit rocky."

"I am."

He opened the door for her. "Where to? Your house?"

"Do you mind?"

As he drove, she told him what had happened, and he managed to steal a few close looks at her despite the traffic. How long was it since he had been this close to her?

A long time. Much too long a time.

On coming to work in Haiti he had not looked her up. He knew, of course, that Brian was the Embassy man who had given the plantation his name, and that could only mean Sandy had suggested it. But it didn't have to mean she wanted to see him.

If she did, she knew where to find him and how to use a phone.

They had met twice at events in the capital, but only as impersonal parts of a crowd. Two totally unsatisfactory meetings in nearly two years.

She hadn't changed much, had she?—except she now looked as though she hadn't slept for days. But then, maybe he didn't look any different, either. Maybe the ache didn't show.

By the time they reached Rue Printemps she had finished briefing him. Following her into the house, he sank onto a chair in the living room.

"Where do you suppose Brian is?"

"With some woman somewhere."

"You can't mean that."

"In all the time we've been in Haiti, he's taken me to Miami only twice. Why does he go alone?"

"You think he checks in at the Greenway and then moves in with a girlfriend?"

She shrugged.

"You've called the hotel, you say."

"So has the Embassy. Time and again. He told the hotel people he'd be gone for a few days. They haven't seen him since."

Ken's scowl lowered bushy brows over his intense brown eyes. "If he planned on being away for a few days, he'd have given them a number to call."

"He did. No one answers."

"Have you tried to locate him through his father?"

"By calling the White House? I'm not that close to dear Daddy. I haven't seen him since the day of our wedding, when he turned up late and stayed less than an hour."

"All right. When I get to Miami tomorrow, I'll see what I can do. Meanwhile, let me make some local calls."

Sandy said helplessly, "Who to? I've called everyone."

"I know some police and army guys. It won't hurt to tell them I'm your friend."

She came to him and stood with a hand on his shoulder. It was not an answer to the question in his mind, but it was something. If Brian was cheating, the marriage couldn't be all that great anyway.

Why, for God's sake, hadn't he taken the trouble to find out?

He made four calls. The last, to a Captain Roger Labrousse at a police post in the area, was the only one that produced results. The man was an older brother of one of his Haitian pilot pals.

"Come see me. We have just uncovered something that may be important."

"Should I bring Mrs. Dawson?"

"I think not. Come alone."

Chapter Eleven

They sat across a long, bare table in a back room at the police station.

"Have you ever heard of a man named Margal?"

Ken hesitated. "I don't think so. But many Haitian names still sound pretty much alike to me."

"You would remember this man. He has no legs."

"He what?"

"The man is a sorcerer. Some years ago, by order of—we think—a certain politician whom he refused to serve with his magic, he was so badly beaten up that his legs had to be amputated."

"A sorcerer? A voodoo houngan, you mean?"

Labrousse shrugged. With his height and supple grace, he should have been a basketball player. "Not a houngan. Voodoo people are not necessarily evil; in fact, usually they are not. Margal is a witch doctor, a bocor. Probably the most feared one in all Haiti."

"And?"

"Some time ago he masterminded a plot against our president. It failed at the last minute, and we thought he had perished in a fire." The captain paused to shake his head, as though he still found it difficult to believe what he was about to say. "Now we know we were mistaken. Margal did not die. He has been hiding in a house in Rue Printemps."

"Sandy's street."

"Pardon?"

"Mrs. Dawson's street."

"Where the child disappeared. Yes."

Ken stared.

Labrousse's eyebrows went up a little. "You are not impressed?"

"Well, I—"

"Of course. You have not been in Haiti that long, have you? Until now you had not even heard of our infamous Margal."

"I've been here nearly two years, Roger."

"But, like most outsiders, you still inwardly smile when witchcraft is mentioned, eh? So, then, I will simply state the facts as we have learned them."

"Roger, don't think for a minute I'm una—"

The tall captain waved Ken to silence. "Only the facts. Then form your own conclusions. In questioning people who lived or worked near the Dawsons' home we were, of course, merely hoping for a report of something unusual or suspicious. A lead, you might say."

"And?"

"We came up with a live-in maid who said she worked next door to a house in which lived a man with no legs. She had seen him but twice. On each occasion he had been carried into the yard by a very large woman and deposited on a chair there for several hours. She thought it remarkable that she had seen him outdoors only twice in the heat of the summer, when the interior of an old house such as his, without air conditioning, must have been all but unendurable."

Ken could only nod.

"We investigated and found the house empty," the captain went on. "But ah, the things in that house! We found a man's clothing cut down to be comfortable to a wearer with no legs. We found other clothing to fit the very large woman described by the maid next door. And"—the dramatic pause was typically Haitian—"we found all sorts of paraphernalia used by sorcerers, including black candles of a kind not to be found in any shop. Without a shadow of doubt, *mon ami,* the man was our thought-to-be-dead Margal."

"But what does it prove, except that a man thought to be dead is not dead?"

"He left that house the night the child disappeared."

"You know this, Roger? How can you, if no one except this maid ever saw him, and she saw him only a couple of times all summer?"

"We know it." Smiling, Labrousse became the basketball player who had personally scored the winning point in a game of great importance. "You are looking at the man responsible. Across the street from this house we have been talking about is one occupied by a lawyer named Claude Etienne, whom I know well. He and his wife are in Europe this summer. The day I went to the house occupied by our sorcerer, the Etiennes' yard boy was trimming their hedge, and I talked to him. He knew nothing of the Dawson child's disappearance, he said. He worked at the Etiennes' only an hour each day. But I felt he was concealing something, so I questioned him more—ah—thoroughly and learned that he also slept on their veranda every night without their permission. They have a sofa that swings—you know the type?—which he adored. And on the night the little girl disappeared, he was there and saw something."

"What did he see, Roger?"

"Voices across the street awoke him, and he saw a car in front of that house, and people talking. One was a man with no legs, seated on the sidewalk. A large, fat woman was leading a small child to the car. The woman went back to the man with no legs and picked him up and put him in the car. Then she herself got in, and the car was driven off."

The captain's penchant for histrionics was no longer amusing. Leaning across the table, Ken said in a low voice, "For God's sake, Roger, that was a kidnapping! Where did they take her?"

"That we do not know. Not yet."

"Did he get the car's number, this boy?"

"Unfortunately, no. But we know for certain that

Margal is alive, that he lived for months in that house undetected, that he disappeared when the child did, and—if we are to believe our frightened yard boy—it was Margal who took her."

"Why haven't you told Mrs. Dawson this?"

Labrousse shrugged. "We are not keen to have a hysterical woman on our hands in addition to our other problems, *mon ami.* Can you imagine the consequences if we tell her that her child is in the hands of Haiti's most feared bocor?"

"But this Margal—what will he do?"

"Who knows? The file we have on him is not one I enjoy looking at. The last time he was involved with a child, he turned her into a zombie."

"The living dead? You believe that?"

Labrousse chose not to reply.

"All right, you believe it. What are you doing to find the man?"

"Everything humanly possible." The Haitian aimed a scowl at Ken's pleading face. "And what about you? Are you a special friend of the Dawsons? Until you phoned, I wasn't aware you even knew them."

"I almost married Sandy Dawson, Roger."

"Really? You do keep things to yourself."

"I'm supposed to go to Miami tomorrow on company business. But if there's any way I can help her, I'll postpone it."

"Your company would permit that?"

"They'll understand. On the other hand, Sandy's husband is in Miami, or is supposed to be, and she hasn't been able to reach him. He should be here, damn him!"

"Acting like an indignant Embassy shit-ass?"

"Or just sharing the burden with his wife. Their daughter is missing, Roger."

"Go to Miami," Labrousse advised. "We are doing everything that can be done here."

"You're sure?"

"I give you my word. When will you return?"

"A day or two."

"Come see me then. I may have something more to tell you." The captain rose and offered his hand. "So you nearly married her, did you? Interesting. I have met her husband a few times; that's why I used the term 'Embassy shit-ass.' Women do have their stupid moments, don't they, *mon ami?*"

How much should he tell Sandy? Ken wondered as he drove her car back to the house. Not everything. Not what Labrousse had told him about Margal's background. Yet any attempt to tell only part of the truth might trap him in a bog of lies, with Sandy demanding to know what he was hiding.

"I've learned something," he said when she opened the door. He could not have lied to her anyway. "Can we sit down?"

She led him to the dining room, where the table was set for two. He was expected to stay for lunch, then. They sat, and he told her the story much as Roger Labrousse had told it to him.

While he did so, the cook put sandwiches and an avocado salad before them, but he saw no need to interrupt the story on her account. A bright-eyed young woman whom Sandy addressed as Edita, she appeared to be a peasant who spoke only a few words of English.

When he finished, Sandy was more in control of herself. "What, exactly, is a bocor, Ken? I know I've been in this country longer than you, but you're closer to the real Haiti. Does he have something to do with voodoo?"

"I asked Roger, and he said no."

"It would be for money, then, that Margal took Merry?"

"He must know Brian works at the Embassy and assumes you're wealthy."

"I wonder how he got her out of the house." Sandy seemed to be forcing herself to think about it calmly. "I mean, someone must have come here for her. She didn't just walk up the street to where they were waiting."

How was he to answer that? Unless the concept of sorcery here were merely superstition, a bocor had real powers. But what powers?

She did not wait for a reply. "What will you do now?" she asked.

"Well, Labrousse said to have faith in him."

"I don't mean that. What will *you* do?"

"I?"

"For the rest of today. Tonight. You don't leave for Miami till tomorrow."

"Oh. I usually go to the Etoile."

"Stay here, why don't you?"

He hesitated. It was not the kind of invitation it might seem to be, of course.

"Well . . . all right. I'd like that, Sandy. We can talk."

Chapter Twelve

At six o'clock the Dawsons' cook, Edita, stepped into the living room, where her mistress and M'sieu Forrest were talking.

"Madame *est servi,*" she announced.

Six o'clock was an early hour for dinner in this part of Port-au-Prince, but madame would not object, she was fairly certain. Not in front of a handsome guest like the pilot from Plantation Margot.

Edita had something special to do this evening and wished to depart early.

Leaving the house soon after seven, she walked home by way of Avenue José Marti and went into the Eglise Sacré Coeur. There were but two others in the church at this hour: a young couple seated near the front with their heads together. Entering a pew near the back, Edita sank to her knees and closed her eyes in prayer.

What she had done was a terrible thing, she knew now, though of course she had not been aware of that while doing it. The fat woman from up the street had deceived her. The child's panty had not been for the laundress at all, but for that awful man with no legs, the sorcerer Margal.

And everyone in Haiti who knew anything about him had thought him dead!

So Margal was not dead. He had somehow survived the fire that was said to have destroyed him. And now for reasons of his own—wholly evil ones, no doubt—he had found a way to kidnap Madame Dawson's lovely little daughter.

As she thought about it and mentally reviewed the part she had innocently played in it, Edita wept. She truly loved the child. Not for anything in the world would she knowingly have done a thing that might cause Merry harm.

What, oh God, was she to do now? Confess and lose her job, when jobs were so hard to find and she had children of her own to feed?

For half an hour she knelt in the church, weeping and praying. The young couple from the front pew looked at her with curiosity as they walked out.

When she herself departed, she stood for a time on the sidewalk, undecided. Should she obey her conscience and return to the house in Rue Printemps to confess what she had done? Or should she follow her instinct for self-preservation and go home with her lips sealed?

In the end she went home.

"If you're to catch a plane in the morning, I suppose we ought to stop talking," Sandy said much later to Ken Forrest. Ken never flew the company's small plane to Florida. He took commercial flights.

He glanced at his watch. "After midnight. We *have* talked, haven't we?"

Mostly about themselves, he realized. After, of course, discussing the disappearance of her daughter until they were only repeating themselves.

At first Sandy had seemed reluctant to discuss her marriage. Had, in fact, tried to ward off questions by asking about himself and his work. But with that subject exhausted, she had come around to being honest.

So now he knew. This woman he had loved in college was about ready to throw in the towel. Would probably, in fact, have done so already but for their child. Brian Dawson was a womanizer. A snob. A boor.

"He loves Merry, though," she insisted. "He really does."

She had not meant to say all these things, he guessed. Mostly she had just wanted to stop being afraid for a while.

And what had he told her about himself? The truth, for what it was worth. He liked his plantation job. He was grateful to her for recommending him for it. He thought Haiti exciting. He hadn't found another woman to take her place.

So much for that.

"Just let me lock up and I'll show you your room," she said.

He followed her about while she checked the shutters and doors. "Most people around here have a live-in housekeeper or house boy," she said. "I told Brian I didn't want one. Maybe if I'd listened to him, this wouldn't have happened."

"Stop blaming yourself."

"Is that what I'm doing?"

He took her hand. "I think you are, for a lot of things. And you're wrong."

At the foot of the stairs she turned to face him. "I'm to blame for one thing, at least. You didn't leave me."

No, he thought, I didn't.

As they climbed the stairs together, he found himself remembering what might have happened. He had known she was seeing a lot of Dawson. She hadn't kept that from him. But the cutoff had been a real thunderbolt all the same—just a phone call to say she wouldn't be seeing him again because she was going to marry Brian. It was the one night of his life he'd got blind drunk.

At the top of the stairs she halted. "That's your room at the end of the hall."

"Okay."

"I'm glad you could stay. I haven't said all I wanted to, I guess you know."

"Both of us."

She turned to face him. Touched his hand. "Maybe it's best, no? Good night, Ken."

He was aware of the stillness. It was a big house, they were the only ones in it, and except for the hall light it was now dark. It seemed to be holding its breath, waiting to find out what they would do.

He drew her close and touched his lips to her forehead. With her six-year-old daughter in the hands of a kidnapper, how could he do more?

" 'Night, pal. Try to sleep."

She nodded. He waited for her to go into her room and close the door, then went down the hall and switched on the light in the room he was to occupy. Edita had brought up his bag earlier.

The room had its own bathroom. Undressed, he decided he could use a shower and took one, then put out the light and got into bed.

He was not too surprised when Sandy came to him a few minutes later in her pajamas. What really startled him was that, after touching her lips to his, she stepped back, said, "Thank you—oh, thank you!" in a whisper, and then fled from the room like a frightened ghost.

Chapter Thirteen

Elie Jumel was not a man Clarisse felt inclined to trust. About forty, with beady eyes and a dark-roast coffee complexion, he made her think of a small, hungry mouse.

He worked, he had told them, for a company that looked after the maintenance of certain citrus groves in the area. Mostly he drove trucks and tractors. For a modest rent the company allowed him to use this house he lived in. But they, M'sieu Margal and M'selle Clarisse, must not judge all Florida citrus by the sad-looking orange trees surrounding it. These had grown old and been abandoned. One day they would be removed and new ones planted.

"I have lived here six years," the mouse told them, "and you can see how I have fixed this old place up. In Haiti I was an electrician and a mason, and I came to this country legally and am a citizen now. Which is not to say you are not welcome as Haitians," he quickly added with a glance at Margal. "I am totally at your service!"

His shrillness indicated that he was also more than a little apprehensive. Sizing him up, Clarisse wondered what was in the letter from his cousin Polivien, handed to him by Margal when they arrived.

But, yes, the house was not bad. The unpainted cypress of which it was constructed was the color of silver and not unattractive. Jumel also had two large, ugly, coal-black dogs to guard it, but after getting it through their heads that the intruders were present with their master's approval, they suspended their growling and merely prowled about like sooty ghosts.

Margal and she, with the child, shared a large bedroom. Jumel had a smaller one, separated from theirs by a bathroom. The kitchen would be adequate after she had given it a thorough cleaning. The mouse did not have a wife to attend to such things.

And—a point that pleased Margal immensely—the house was equipped with a telephone. "The company had it installed because I am sometimes needed quickly," Jumel explained. "For instance, when the weather becomes suddenly cold in winter and there is danger of the citrus freezing, I am wanted in a hurry to help with the heaters in the groves."

So then, good. They had arrived in this country without being detected. They had a roof over their heads. Their host dared not be other than eager to accommodate them.

Still, something appeared to have gone wrong.

They had arrived yesterday evening. On awakening this morning, Margal had ordered her to place him on the floor and had sent her and the child out of their bedroom, saying he wished to be alone. It was now seven in the evening and he was still there with the door shut, refusing to allow her to enter even to feed him.

It was time, she decided, to put an end to such dangerous nonsense.

Bearing a tray with his supper on it, the third lot of food she had prepared since morning, she hesitated before his door, then dared to turn the knob and shoulder the door open.

"Why are you behaving this way?" she demanded. "Don't you know you must eat?"

"Go away. I am not hungry."

"You must be hungry. You haven't touched food all day!"

He turned his head to scowl at her. From the look of him, he had been sitting there in the center of his three circles since daybreak. The black candle burning before him was not the same one, of course. Many must have contributed to the mound of wax in which this one stood. "I am not able to reach him," he said in sullen anger. "We are too far from where he is."

She placed the tray of food beside him. "Reach whom?"

"The child's father, of course. Who else?"

"Don't growl at me as if I'm stupid. You haven't yet told me why we are here, you know. It's as if I'm not worth talking to."

He sat there quizzically gazing at her, the way he sometimes did when she worked up the courage to remind him that she was a human being. Not that he ever remembered it for long. This evening she had on a dress he liked—a red one she had worn often in their mountain village before he lost his legs. Perhaps that mellowed him a little.

"I must reach the child's father." Beckoning her to come closer, he reached up and took hold of her hand. "I foresaw a problem when that fellow on the boat said we would be so far from Miami. To reach Dawson at that distance I must have something he has worn or had in his possession. Something that is a part of him."

She took her hand back and buried her fists in the fat above her hips. "And you have nothing that is a part of him?"

"No. When I told you to get something that belonged to the child, I should have—"

"Margal, where is your mind today? You have the child herself!"

"What?"

"Is she not a part of him? Where did she come from, if not from his seed?"

He looked at her long and hard. "You know, Clarisse, I underestimate you sometimes. Yes. Bring the child here!"

Merry was in the front room, looking at pictures in old magazines with which Jumel had enlarged his

English. Or so he claimed. She did not protest when told that Margal wished to see her. She was a classic example, Clarisse reflected, of the way he was able to control a mind. Just as he controls mine, she thought.

When they entered the bedroom together, Margal held out his arms and Merry went to him. "Sit here, *ti-fi*," he said, patting the floor.

Guided by his hands, she sat with her back to him.

"Put the candle in front of her, Clarisse."

Clarisse did so, dripping some wax to secure it.

"Now," he said to Merry, leaning forward to touch his face to hers, "you may sleep if you wish. Watch the candle burning. It will help you."

"Do I have to sleep?"

"No, but watch the candle flame for me, eh? And if you do sleep, it will be all right." Coiling his arms around her, he put his hands on her infant breasts and pressed her against him. "Are you comfortable?"

"Oh, yes."

"I'm not hurting you?"

"Uh-uh."

He glanced at Clarisse, who was watching intently. "So now we begin in earnest."

Though Clarisse had anticipated the performance, the intensity of it startled her. Ridges formed on Margal's forehead. A glistening film of sweat coated his face. His body trembled or vibrated, as though all the nerves in it were being stretched to the breaking point.

She stepped back in alarm, but he paid no attention to her now. His fingers on Merry's body were a hawk's talons clutching a helpless chicken. The astonishing thing was that the child did not cry out. Narrowed to slits, Margal's eyes stared without wavering at the candle flame.

For a while there was no change. Then the child began to whimper.

Margal sighed in surrender and let himself go limp. "It will take time. This land is not my home. I am a stranger here."

Clarisse stepped forward to frown down at him. "May I offer a suggestion?"

He shrugged.

"The purpose of all this is to make contact with the child's father, is it not?" She spoke in Creole.

"Of course."

"But you have no idea where he is. Why not ask her if she knows where he might be staying? If she can even tell you the name of a hotel—"

"Ti-fi." He stroked the child's shoulder. "Look at me."

Merry did so.

"Do you know the name of the hotel in Miami where your father is?"

"He always goes to a place called the Greenway."

"Thank you."

"Is something wrong?"

"Only that I am trying to talk to him, to tell him that you are here, and I could not reach him."

"That happens sometimes when my mother tries to call him on the telephone."

"Well, let me try again. Just look at the candle,

please, and think about him for me. Think hard about him." He gazed at the candle himself, and again Clarisse saw his body tremble.

What now?

She retreated to a chair and watched him. Sweat ran down his face like rain on a windowpane. Every little while he trembled violently for a few seconds.

The child went to sleep.

"I see something," Margal said at last.

"You see what?"

"Not the hotel. A building with a lighted sign beside the walkway to its door. 'Burl'—'Burling'—never mind. The second word is 'Apartments.' A man and a woman are approaching the door. The man is Dawson. The woman is not his wife."

Clarisse would have spoken, but he silenced her with a wave of his hand and said, "Wait!" Then he said, "They are inside now, climbing a flight of stairs. They have stopped before a door with the number 203 on it, and the woman is looking in her handbag, no doubt for a key. Yes, a key. She is opening the door. Now they have walked into the apartment and shut the door and are embracing. He has hungry hands, that man—yet, as I told you, the woman is not his wife. But at last I have found him!"

Triumph sharpened his voice. "Yes, I have found him at last! Take the child away. I have work to do!"

Chapter Fourteen

"One of these days, damn it, you're going to have to do some cooking." Stretched out on the sofa in Carmen Alvaranga's apartment, Brian Dawson said this to the woman locked in his embrace.

"So we can eat without leaving here, you mean?"

"Right. I'll buy you some cookbooks."

"Do that, darling." *And be sure I'll never open one, even if every restaurant in reach is closed and you're starving.* There were some things she just would not do for this man, and cooking was high on the list. She wouldn't look after his laundry, either; he could damn well lug it to the laundry room himself.

Things might be different if he showed any inclination to divorce his wife and marry her. But when she brought that up, he never failed to back off.

It was a stupid situation. Within a week after his

transfer from Georgetown to Miami U., all those years ago, she had been sleeping with him. Even before she knew his father was big in Washington. He was good-looking, sexy, and a spender.

When she found out who he was—or, rather, who his father was—she had felt even better about being his bedmate. Then, damn it, he had dropped her for Sandra.

Since the clandestine renewal of their old relationship, he had tried more than once to tell her the why of that. "I was dumb, baby, that's all. College-kid dumb. A gorgeous doll like you, going to bed with me on our second date—I figured you were sleeping around."

"You could have asked me."

"If you'd said no, I wouldn't have believed you. Forget it. When the time is right, I'll get rid of Sandra and make it up to you."

Would he? It was possible, she supposed. And if she could maneuver him into marriage, she certainly would. You could build quite a future on being the daughter-in-law of Rutherford Dawson, confidant of the President. There sure as hell was no such future in running a minor art gallery, even with a young and virile male helper who adored you.

At the moment, the only son of Rutherford Dawson was doing his best to undress her. As he had every few hours at the North Carolina resort from which they had just returned. And at the Savannah motel last night on their way home. Even in the restaurant this evening, all through dinner, he'd kept finding ways to touch her.

"Damn it, don't!" she said now on the sofa. "You'll tear my dress."

"To hell with your dress."

"To hell with you! I bought this to go to Carolina in, and it wasn't cheap." She slapped his hand away. *"I'll* take it off, if you don't mind. If you want to undress somebody, go undress yourself." Eluding his hands, she got up and stalked into the bedroom.

When he came in a moment later he was undressed, and she was on the bed ready for him. He sat beside her and kissed her, working his way up from between her legs to her mouth. By the time he reached her mouth he was frantic.

As usual, she was, too.

When she finished guiding him into her, to save what could be a brutal assault were he left on his own, she put her arms around his neck and prepared to enjoy herself.

Then a strange thing happened. The expression on his face suddenly changed from hunger to bewilderment, and he went limp inside her.

"What's the matter, for God's sake?"

"I don't know." He swung himself off the bed and stood there, staring. Not at her, but apparently at some invisible thing dangling in space just over the bed. "Five six two what?" he whispered. His face had become as white as the sheets.

Frightened, she cried out, "Brian! What's wrong?"

"A number I have to call. Right now. Right this minute." He was talking to himself rather than answering her, though perhaps there was some of both in it. "All right, all right!" he shouted. "I understand!"

Wheeling, he stumbled from the room.

Her phone was on a small table in the living room. She heard him dialing. When she got off the bed and went to the door to watch, he had begun to talk. "Yes, yes," she heard him say. "This is Brian Dawson. What?"

Listening, he turned his face toward her, and she saw such a look of panic on it, she felt sorry for him. "My daughter?" His cry nearly caused her hair to stand on end. "Here? In Florida? Where?"

Listening again, he sank limply onto a chair and fixed his gaze on her but was not really aware of her, she was certain. He looked—what was the word? Mesmerized. Hypnotized. Spellbound. Mechanically pulling a pad and pencil toward him, he wrote something, tore off the page, and stared at it, then looked at her again.

In a way it was totally ridiculous: a grown man sitting naked at a telephone, clutching a bit of paper while he stared unseeing at a naked woman in the doorway of the bedroom from which, for no apparent reason, he had just wildly fled.

"All right," she heard him mutter then. "All right. I'll be there." He let the phone fall back onto its cradle and still sat there, gazing at her without seeing her. Then, as she again cried out, "Brian, what is it?" he rose and turned to the couch where his clothes lay, and began to dress himself.

Filled with compassion now, she went to him. "What is it about your daughter, Brian? Please!" He loved the child; she knew that. He might not love Merry's mother, but he worshipped the ground his daughter walked on.

Brian only shook his head at her while pushing the bit of paper into a pocket of his slacks.

"Who were you talking to?"

"No one I know. A Haitian." Like a man three times his age, he sank trembling onto the couch to put his shoes on, thereby completing the task of dressing himself. Then he struggled to his feet and lurched to the door.

"Brian!" she heard herself screaming. "Where are you going?"

"To him," he said over his shoulder. "He said I must, if I want her back."

"But where?"

Ignoring the question, he walked out of the apartment, leaving the door open behind him.

She ran to the threshold and tried once more as he started down the stairs. "Brian, for God's sake—" Naked, she could not follow him. Again ignored, she could only stand there, wondering whether he was ill or had gone mad.

A man is making ardent love and suddenly goes limp? He mumbles part of a phone number, then stumbles to the phone and calls someone he doesn't know? He is told something about his daughter, who should be miles away in a foreign country, and that he must go to the person he is talking to if he "wants her back"?

It was crazy.

Except, she thought as she closed the door and

went to a window from which she watched him get into the silver Jaguar at the curb . . . except that the country his daughter should be in was not just any foreign land. It was a land of voodoo and sorcery.

What was the number he had cried out in the bedroom? Five six two? It could be important. She ought to write it down before she forgot it.

In a daze she walked to the table and reached for the pad and pencil there.

Chapter Fifteen

Suitcase in hand, Ken Forrest strode out of Miami's airport to a line of waiting taxis. The hour was near noon, the day hot. Even in a short-sleeved sport shirt, with his jacket slung over a shoulder, he could feel sweat trickling down his back and chest.

"The Greenway."

Traffic was heavy. He had plenty of time to wonder what he would do if the man he sought were not at the hotel. For days Sandy had been trying to reach her husband by phone. So had the Embassy. For days the manager of the Greenway, one Norman Sack, had been almost frantically claiming he could not locate Brian Dawson.

What kind of hotel was the Greenway, anyway?

It turned out to be a small one on a quiet Coral Gables street. The lobby was empty except for a gray-haired man at the desk—Norman Sack, himself. When Ken had explained the reason for his visit, Sack nervously leaned forward.

"Mr. Forrest, I don't know how to help you." His heavy sigh gave off an odor of sour stomach. "I have been calling and calling the number Mr. Dawson left with us. I must have tried twenty times. No one answers."

"You don't know whose number it is?"

"No, sir. In fact, I—ah—I'm afraid I have behaved badly about this. Mr. Dawson is an old friend of ours and specifically said we were not to give the number to any third party. 'If anyone wants me,' he always said, 'get their name and number and call me, and I will call them back.' "

"You don't know where he goes?"

"No, sir. It would hardly be proper for us to—"

"You haven't seen him since he checked in here?"

"No, we haven't."

"Is that normal? He usually just signs in and disappears?"

The manager hesitated. "Well, I . . . He does that sometimes. Yes."

"Do you mind giving me the number, Mr. Sack? Perhaps the phone company will tell me whose it is."

"Will they, do you think?"

"I'm not up on such things. But, as I told you, Mr. Dawson's daughter has been kidnapped. When I tell them that, maybe they'll cooperate."

"Of course!" Obviously the Greenway was not a hostelry that liked having its guests' children kidnapped. The man with the bad breath hastily flipped open a phone index and copied a number onto a sheet of paper.

Peering at it, Ken said, "Before I check with the company, why don't we give it one more try?" Reaching for the phone on the desk, he dialed the number.

A woman's voice said guardedly, "Yes?"

Ken flashed a glance of triumph at the manager. "Mr. Dawson, please. This is a friend of his, Ken Forrest."

"Who?"

"Ken Forrest. An old friend from Haiti."

"Oh. I'm sorry. He is not here."

Ken took in a breath. "Please," he said carefully. "It's very important that I speak with him. I'm just in from Port-au-Prince and—"

"He isn't here!"

"Tell me where I can reach him, then. His daughter has been kidnapped."

He heard a hiss of indrawn breath. Then, "What?"

"His little girl, Merry, has been abducted. His wife is frantic. I must talk to him."

"Oh, my God." Suddenly her voice was scarcely audible. "I don't know where he is. Believe me, I don't. He just walked out. But he said something about Merry, and I have part of a—" She paused to catch her breath. "Look. Can you come over here?"

"Of course."

Her tongue seemed to tremble as she gave him her address. Then she said, "Where are you? I'll tell you how to get here."

"The Greenway."

"All right. It's easy."

Ken listened to her directions and was told her name and apartment number, so he would know which bell to ring. He hung up and looked at the man across the desk. "Can you give me a room here, Mr. Sack?"

"Certainly, sir."

"Have my bag put in it, will you? And I need a cab. Right now."

"That will take but a minute." With a sigh of relief this time, the manager reached for the phone. "You could even go outside and wait, Mr. Forrest. He only has to come from around the corner."

Carmen Alvaranga, Ken thought. Brian had played around with a girl of that name at the university before his marriage to Sandy. It had to be the same one. There wouldn't be two women with that name in a man's life, even in a city where Latin names filled the phone book.

He had met her, he recalled. A beauty. Was she again Brian's girlfriend?

A cab swung to the curb to pick him up, and presently he was at the door of the woman's apartment.

"I've seen you before," Alvaranga said, motioning him to enter. "You went to college here."

"Yes."

"And knew Brian?"

He nodded.

"I was a student then, too." She waved him to a chair. "Tell me about his daughter."

Briefly, impatiently, he told her of the child's disappearance and Sandy's anguish. How Sandy and the Embassy had been calling the Hotel Greenway and her number for days, trying to reach Merry's father.

"We—" She quickly corrected herself. "He was away on some kind of business. He got back only yesterday."

And you were with him or you would have answered your phone, Ken thought. "And now?"

"I don't know where he is." She leaned toward him. Her skirt was bright red and her blouse a Guatamalan Indian thing, brilliantly embroidered, that let him look down between exquisitely shaped breasts.

"Brian and I were—sitting here," she said. "Just sitting here, talking. All of a sudden a faraway look came into his eyes and he stood up, as if he were listening not to me but to someone else. He mumbled a number and said he had to make a phone call. 'All right!' he yelled. 'I understand!' Then he rushed to the phone."

'And called the number? What was it? You remember?"

"I wrote it down after he left." She went to the phone table and returned with a pad, On it was written 562.

"This is only part of a number. Did you hear what he said on the phone?"

"It was about his daughter. I didn't know she'd been kidnapped then, of course. He said something like, 'My daughter, here in Florida?' and sounded as if someone had clubbed him."

"Did you ask who he was talking to?"

"He didn't answer me."

"And then?"

"He left. He just got dressed—I mean, he grabbed his tie and jacket—and went out the door as if I didn't exist. As if I—" She took in a breath. "Wait a minute. I should have known the child had been kidnapped. When he went out the door and I asked him again where he was going—almost screamed it at him, I was so upset—he said something like, 'To him. I have to if I want her back.' "

"So Merry is here in Florida." Ken looked at the number again and saw something he hadn't noticed the first time. Under it were indentations of a scribble that must have been written on a page torn off. They were too faint to be readable. But below them was a single word on which the writer must have borne down hard in anger or fear.

Margal.

He looked at Alvaranga. "Did Brian use this pad while he was phoning?"

"He wrote on it and took the page with him."

Margal. Here in Florida with Sandy's little girl? Striding across the room, Ken reached for a directory on the phone table. What he wanted was a list of Southeast Calling Zone Prefix Codes.

Five-six-two was Vero Beach.

Chapter Sixteen

He had telephoned Sandy to come to Miami on the next flight out of Port-au-Prince. He had rented a car. Now the car was parked in front of a shabby two-story apartment building in the section of Miami known as Little Haiti.

In one of its second-floor apartments Ken faced a man he had known on the plantation: a small, wiry Haitian who, unlike many others here, had come to Florida legally. Raoul Monestimé, a carpenter, had been in the city a year or so.

Ken leaned from his chair to peer into the man's lined face. "Raoul, the number Mr. Dawson called is in the Vero Beach area. Do you know any Haitians there?"

Monestimé frowned in thought, then shook his

head. "No, M'sieu Ken. In fact, I am not sure I even know where Vero Beach is."

Ken produced a map of Florida. "It's north of here about a hundred fifty miles, on the coast. Other towns in the area are Gifford, Wabasso, Sebastian, Grant—"

"Wabasso? You said Wabasso?" The little man stood up. "Let me call in some friends of mine. There's a young fellow staying with them who came in at Wabasso only yesterday." He went to the door. "I'll be back in a minute," he called over his shoulder as he stepped onto the wooden walkway outside.

Ken looked around. The apartment seemed to consist of this room, an even smaller kitchen, and a grubby little bedroom. There were four rickety chairs, a cot, a table for dining.

More space could be found—certainly more fresh air!—in many of the poorest peasant *cailles* in Haiti, at least in those out in the country, where most of the people had a bit of land to cultivate as well. So why in God's name did so many Haitians sell everything they owned to buy their way here, sometimes risking their lives on homemade boats held together with bailing wire?

He had no answer. He himself had found Haiti fascinating, and had liked nothing better than to explore its mountains and mysteries. But he wasn't a peasant with no hope of ever improving his lot, was he? Or a peasant citizen of a country whose leaders cared only for themselves and to hell with the barefoot masses under them.

There were footsteps outside. Into the room came Monestimé, followed by two middle-aged men and a younger one. Of the older pair, one was stout and grinning, the other reed-thin with shifty eyes. The young fellow, in shirt and pants of sweat-stained denim, was no doubt the new arrival.

At Monestimé's bidding they sat, while their host perched on the edge of the cot. "M'sieu Ken," the carpenter said, "allow me to introduce to you Fortune Boiset"—the smiling, fat one—"and Marcel Odiol"—the one whose eyes would not be still. "They live here in the building."

The fat man beamed. Shifty eyes nodded.

"And this young man, m'sieu, is the one who just arrived."

"You came yesterday?" Ken asked the youth.

"He speaks only Creole, m'sieu."

"Ou té vini ici hier, compère?"

The youth looked frightened enough to leap to his feet and race out the door if anyone made a move toward him. "*Oui,* m-m-m'sieu," he stammered.

"Ask him," Ken said to the man on the cot, "if there was a little white girl on the boat that brought him. My Creole comes hard."

Monestimé and the youth chattered back and forth in the Haitian peasant tongue while the others listened.

"He says yes. There was a little white girl. Her companions were a very big black woman called Clarisse, and a black man with no legs."

"Ask him the name of the legless man, Raoul."

Again an exchange of Creole. "He doesn't know.

The man stayed in the cabin throughout the voyage. Only the woman came on deck, with the little girl. They didn't talk much."

"Ask him if he has ever heard of a legless Haitian bocor named Margal."

Monestimé put the question. "He says yes, but Margal is dead."

Tired of the three-way dialogue, Ken tried his own Creole again. "*Compère,* are you saying this man on the boat could not have been Margal?"

"Well, I don't know," the youth replied. "I mean, I have never seen the terrible Margal. But everyone in Haiti knows he died in a fire in Port-au-Prince many months ago."

"All right. Tell me what happened when you landed. In Wabasso, was it?"

"Yes, in Wabasso. And that man with no legs did a wicked thing. The passengers had paid for two cars to meet them and bring them here to Miami. He commandeered one and kept six people waiting there, in danger of being caught, until it returned."

"How could he do that? Was he armed?"

The youth wagged his head.

"How, then?"

"I don't—well, I don't know. He just did. The driver seemed afraid of him."

"Let me be sure I understand this." The outrush of Creole had left Ken groping a little. He had a genuine flair for languages, but that strange mixture of corrupted old French, African, and Spanish was far from being one of the easiest to master. Besides, even in Haiti it differed in different regions.

"You are saying that this man without legs, traveling with the white child and the fat woman, commandeered a car that others were depending on for transportation to Miami?"

"Yes, m'sieu."

"But the car did bring them here eventually?"

"It did. Yes."

"Is the driver here now?"

"No, no, m'sieu. He was hired there, not here."

"Very well, how long did you have to wait at the dock for the car to return after it went off with those three?"

The youth frowned in thought. "About forty minutes."

"You're sure?"

"I am sure, m'sieu."

So they didn't go far, Ken thought. They've got to be holed up somewhere within twenty minutes of where the boat docked. "Tell me—why did the boat land at Wabasso? Why not closer to Miami?" It was probably a stupid question. Wabasso must be a place where illegal aliens could be brought ashore at less risk.

The youth surprised him. "Polivien has a cousin near there."

"Polivien? Who's he?"

"The owner of the fishing boat that brought us to the Bahamas."

"And your contact at Wabasso was this cousin?"

"I understand everything was arranged through him."

"Do you suppose the three who took the car went to him?"

"Well, perhaps. Who can say?"

"Where does he live?"

"In a place called Gifford, where many black people live."

Ken's pulse was pounding. "Do you know his name, friend?"

The youth looked at his companions. Fortune Boiset still smiled happily, as though proud to be part of such a dramatic performance. Marcel Odiol of the shifty eyes stared at Ken as though trying to memorize his face. Finally the boy looked at Monestimé, and the carpenter gave him a nod.

"His name is Elie Jumel, m'sieu."

And I'll bet I have part of his phone number, Ken thought, barely suppressing a shout of elation. *Sandy, darling, I think I've found your daughter!*

Rising, he thanked Monestimé and the others for their help, then turned to leave. But the shifty-eyed man, Odiol, stepped in front of him.

"M'sieu, do you have a cigarette?"

"I don't smoke. Sorry."

"The means of buying some, then?"

"Well, yes." From his billfold Ken extracted a five-dollar bill.

It was a small price to pay for what he had learned here, he thought as he departed.

Chapter Seventeen

It wasn't a very nice house, Merry decided.

She was especially afraid of Mr. Jumel's big black dogs, who never seemed to stop prowling. She had a feeling they were watching her all the time with their ugly, red-flecked eyes and might decide all of a sudden to leap at her.

The truth was that she wouldn't want to stay in this house another single minute if Clarisse were not here.

On the voyage from Haiti, Margal had been the one who talked to her a lot. Clarisse had only done what he told her to. But now that Daddy was here, Margal was too busy.

Even Daddy was too busy. Ever since his arrival yesterday, he and Margal had been shut up in the big bedroom with the door closed. Even last night they had stayed in there together, making it necessary for Clarisse and herself to sleep on an old mattress that "the mouse," as they secretly called Mr. Jumel, put on the living room floor for them.

All through the night Merry had kept waking up because the mattress was so hard. And every time she did, she heard the two men talking. They must have talked the whole night through.

She couldn't hear what they were saying. The bedroom door muffled it. But first Margal would say something, and then Daddy would seem to repeat it. Mumble, mumble, mumble from Margal, then mumble, mumble, mumble from Daddy, just like an echo. On and on and on, as if Margal was a teacher and Daddy was someone being taught.

She was tired now. It was like Mommy said sometimes: a little girl who didn't get enough sleep would be dopey next day. Seated on the mattress with a magazine, she looked at Clarisse.

There was a picture in the magazine of a whale on a beach, and that was what Clarisse looked like, lying there on the mattress. She hadn't slept much last night, either, and was making up for it now by taking an afternoon nap. But her eyes were open. "Hello, *ti-fi,*" she said with a smile.

"How are you feeling?" Merry asked her.

"Better, but still full of aches. I hope we get our beds back tonight."

"Me, too."

"Has your daddy talked to you yet?"

Merry wagged her head. "Not even once."

"I'm sure he will when the two of them finish." If,

Clarisse thought, Margal decides to let him.

Recalling what had happened when the child's father arrived, she frowned in disapproval. First the dogs had begun to bark—a thing they didn't do often, thank heaven, for when they did they bared their fangs and the sound was enough to curdle one's blood. Then the ugly brutes had run to the front door, still barking, and she looked out a window and saw a car stopping by the mailbox.

Brian Dawson jumped out of it, stumbling in the soft sand in his haste to reach the house. And knowing he was expected, she had shouted at Margal to do something lest the brutes attack him when she opened the door to him.

"All right," Margal called from the bedroom, where he was busy doing something she was not permitted to watch. And suddenly, like whipped curs, the two brutes put their bellies to the floor and slunk into Jumel's room. So she was able to open the door, and Daddy saw his daughter in the kitchen and ran to her, calling her name and moaning something like, "Oh, thank God, thank God!"

The little girl had been drinking some milk. When she put the glass down on the counter and ran to him, he fell to his knees and put his arms around her. She kept crying "Daddy!" and he kept sobbing her name while they hugged each other.

Then Margal called from the bedroom, "Bring him straight here to me, Clarisse! At once!"

When the legless one spoke in that tone, you didn't disobey him even if you thought him heartless. She had gone to Merry's father, who also had heard the shouted command, of course, and said to him, "It would not be wise to keep him waiting." So he had let her lead him into the bedroom, and there he had been ever since.

She had gone into that room several times herself, of course, to perform her various duties. After all, Margal had to be taken to the bathroom, he had to be bathed, he had to be fed. Both men ought to have been fed, but the legless one ordered food only for himself, letting the white man go hungry.

Each time, on entering the room, she had found M'sieu Dawson seated on a chair beside the bed, unmoving, staring at her master as though hypnotized. Or, more accurately, like someone dead who was propped up to participate in his own funeral, as was sometimes done by certain people in the mountains of Haiti.

No one else had been allowed in that room, however. Not Merry. Not Jumel. Not even the dogs. During the daytime, of course, the mouse worked at his job. He couldn't stop working just because a bocor from his homeland had descended upon him and taken over his home. But on returning from work yesterday he had not even tried to talk to Margal. Hearing the teacher-pupil voices from behind that closed door, he was careful to keep his distance.

Only once, in fact, had Jumel even allowed himself to display any curiosity about what was happening. "Whose fancy car is that out front?" he asked while eating supper in the kitchen.

"The child's father came in it."

"Oh," he replied, and then talked about the food—

how it was good, thank you, but he missed the *pois-et-di-ri,* the *jonjon,* the *mirlitons* of Haiti. "Of course, one can buy *mirlitons* here," he said, perhaps to demonstrate how indifferent he was to what Margal and the child's father were doing. "They're called chayotes. But somehow they don't taste the same as those I used to buy from our *marchandes."*

Then after supper he had retired to his small bedroom and shut the door, as if to say, "Whatever is going on here, I don't want to know about it."

"What are you looking at, *ti-fi?"* Clarisse asked now. Not that she cared. But she had slept awhile, leaving the child with no one to talk to, and felt she ought to make up for it.

Merry put her magazine back with the others. "Nothing special. Just some pictures of things to eat."

"Are you hungry?"

"A little."

"Let's see what we can find in the kitchen, shall we?"

"I don't want to bother you."

"You're not. I have to think about what to fix for supper anyway." Clarisse glanced at the door of Jumel's bedroom. "Is the mouse back from work yet?"

"He came while you were sleeping. He's in his room."

Purchasing the food was Jumel's responsibility. Margal paid for it. She cooked it. In the kitchen she spread peanut butter and jelly on some bread for Merry, then opened the refrigerator to see what the mouse had brought. She found a piece of pork that had not been there before.

As she began to prepare a Haitian meal of fried pork and rice, she wondered whether Margal was paying the mouse for allowing them to use his home. He could, of course; he was wealthy. But then again, he might feel that whatever he needed or wanted was his by some kind of divine right.

Her Margal at that moment sat fully clothed on his bed, propped against a pillow which, at his command, the terrified father of Merry Dawson had arranged for him without protest. Brian Dawson no longer sat beside the bed but stood rigid with his back to a wall, as far from his tutor as the dimensions of the room would permit.

The two stared at each other, the sorcerer's eyes glowing and pulsing like red-hot coals, the other's as empty as frozen spheres of water.

"What am I commanding you to do?" Margal asked in a voice barely audible.

"To kneel."

"Why are you not doing it, then?"

Still returning the bocor's gaze, Dawson sank to his knees.

"Now what am I commanding you to do?"

"To come to you on my knees."

"Well?"

As though his whole body had become lead-heavy, Dawson inched himself forward on his knees without letting his hands touch the floor. On reaching the bed he became a kneeling statue, his face oily with sweat.

Margal leaned forward to look down at him. "You have learned well how to obey. That is good. Those who learn quickly are most often able to teach others. Command me."

"I don't understand."

"Command me to do something. Use your eyes as I do. Use your mind, and the power within yourself that I have made you aware of." He watched the other's eyes and waited. But after a moment he shattered the stillness by saying sharply, "No! You are using your lips!"

"But I said nothing."

"Nevertheless, your lips moved. You are projecting words instead of thoughts. Use your mind!"

The learner tried again, and again was harshly reprimanded. For nearly an hour this part of the lesson continued, while the agony of remaining on his knees caused Dawson's once handsome face to age.

Then came a moment when the man on the bed smiled with satisfaction.

"You instructed me to lie back and go to sleep, did you not?"

Dawson seemed startled, then afraid. "Well—yes."

"Excellent. Of course, had I obeyed you, you would have rushed from this room and fled with your daughter to the car outside. Is that not so?"

"I—I—"

"Never mind. It seems I have taught you well. Be grateful, even though we are both tired now."

"Tired!" The word was a groan. "For God's sake, can we sleep now?" the kneeling man begged. "We've been at this all night, all day—"

"One more little test, if you please."

"Oh, God," Dawson moaned.

Margal peered down at him. "What am I telling you to do?"

"To—to go into the kitchen where the others are eating their supper and give Jumel a command to see if he will obey me."

"Good."

"But—what shall I tell him to do?"

"Whatever you wish." A shrug. "Tell him to fondle my Clarisse if that appeals to you. Her reaction might be amusing, and we've earned a little recreation, no?"

"I—I will think of something."

"Go, then. If he obeys you, I'll let you sleep for a few hours."

Dawson rose from his knees and turned his back to the bed. Like a somnambulist he walked to the door and opened it. Leaving it open behind him, he paced through the living room into the kitchen, where his daughter sat with Clarisse and Jumel at a plastic-topped table.

With a happy cry of "Daddy!" the child scrambled from her chair and ran to him.

He knelt and put his arms around her, but not for long. Whispering into her ear, "Stay with me! Hold on to my hand!" he lurched to his feet. The other two watched from the table.

Ignoring Clarisse, Dawson focused his gaze on Jumel, concentrating fiercely on the little man's eyes. His own took on a tinge of red as he did so. Not the unearthly glow achieved by Margal at such times, but at least a hint of it.

The mouse gazed back at him like a mesmerized bird responding to the death stare of a snake. Merry looked up at her father in bewilderment.

A moment passed. No one had spoken—not even Clarisse, who was not involved in what was happening. Then Jumel murmured, "Yes, yes, I understand," and slid from his chair.

Crossing the kitchen, he drew open a drawer beside the sink and took out a knife with a six-inch blade. The blade caught the light and glistened as he turned with it. As he glided through the living room to the door of Margal's bedroom, he held the weapon behind his back.

Clarisse at this point sucked in a noisy breath and staggered to her feet, struggling to cry out. But Brian Dawson had by then focused his gaze on her, and the cry died on her lips.

He had the power to command, she realized, and was commanding her to be silent. Even the two black dogs were silently cringing. They, of course, belonged to Jumel and perhaps would not have tried to intercept the mouse anyway, but they appeared to be helpless.

As he neared the bedroom door, Jumel slowed his pace. He had been commanded to approach that door with great stealth, then rush to the bed and plunge his knife into Margal's heart. The command had burned its way into his brain, leaving him no power to think of anything else.

Kill Margal. Rush to the bed and stab him. Stab him again and again until he is dead!

He had reached the doorway. On the other side of the room, on the bed, Margal sat facing him with head erect, arms folded, eyes bright as stars.

Whipping the knife into view from behind his back, Jumel raced forward. And stopped as though he had hurled himself against an invisible stone wall.

Moaning, he sank to the floor. As the knife slid from his quivering fingers, he put his hands to his face and sobbed into them, whimpering for mercy.

"He made me do it, master! I didn't want to! You must believe me! You must forgive me!"

From the bed came a silent command, and he rose to his feet, sweating and shaking like one in the grip of malaria. The voice in his head was no longer that of the white man in the kitchen. It was that of the Haitian sorcerer confronting him. Margal was ordering him to stand aside, against the wall on his right. He must wait there in silence.

Weak with terror, he stumbled to the wall and flattened himself against it.

On the bed Margal was equally motionless, gazing with crimson eyes at the doorway.

Presently Jumel heard an approaching sound of slow, mechanical footfalls. Into the room, like a zombie, trudged Brian Dawson.

Dawson took four steps and stopped dead, held rigid by the sorcerer's gaze. It was clear to him that the bocor on the bed was about to punish him.

Suddenly his mouth opened wide and he screamed.

Never before in his life had he felt such pain as blazed at that moment inside his head. It was as though a lightning bolt had pierced his skull and set his brain on fire.

His eyeballs were twice their normal size and bulging from their sockets, he was absolutely certain. They were melting and would in a moment be no more than streaks of slime crawling down his face.

There was a noise in his ears so loud, so shrill, so unbearably high that it was cutting away his eardrums as surely as though a surgeon were slicing them out with a scalpel.

His head was no longer a head at all—just a container for agony.

No longer screaming, no long able to, he sank to the floor and lay there writhing like a stepped-on snake. Arms, legs, head, torso—every inch of him twitched and trembled in torment.

Then, suddenly, the pain left him.

"Stand up," the man on the bed commanded.

Dawson was certain he could not obey, but he did.

"Undress yourself."

Again Dawson obeyed, dropping back onto the floor to remove his shoes and socks but, at some silent command, able to stand erect again when he was naked.

"Now the knife," Margal said. "Jumel, hand him the knife."

The mouse picked up the blade he had dropped

and passed it to Dawson. Then he returned to the wall and watched, drenched with sweat but shivering. Would he be next?

The man on the bed said coldly, "Place the point of the knife against your belly, M'sieu Dawson."

Violently shaking but unable to utter a sound in protest, Dawson did so.

"Now shall I command you to drive it home? You may answer me."

"No," Dawson whimpered. "Please . . . no!"

"Do you still imagine the pupil can become the master?"

"No, no, master! Never!"

A moment of nothingness passed. The man on the bed seemed to be weighing what he should do next. At that moment, in the living room, the telephone rang.

Clarisse answered it. "Margal," she called, "it is for you. A man named Marcel Odiol, in Miami. The place called Little Haiti. He says he served you once."

"I know him," Margal called back. "Come and carry me to the phone."

While waiting for her, he looked at the others. "You, Jumel, may return to the kitchen. As for you, M'sieu Dawson, you would have destroyed me with the powers I gave you. So now you may kneel here naked and think about it, until I decide whether or not to have pity on you. If I do so decide, we will begin your training anew."

The mouse scurried from the room. Brian Dawson shut his eyes and sank to his knees, moaning. The fat woman came into the room and, lifting Margal from the bed, carried him to the telephone. Handing him the instrument, she continued to hold him while he talked into it.

"Marcel?"

"Yes, master. I have something important to tell you, or I would not have dreamed of daring to call."

"What is it?"

"There is a man here in Miami, master, a white man named Forrest, who works in Haiti and is trying to find the little girl you brought from there. He knows you are at Elie Jumel's house, and where that is. I felt I should warn you."

"A warning is not enough. Do you have something of his? You know what I refer to."

"The best I could do was some money from his pocket, master. A five-dollar bill he thought he was giving me for cigarettes."

"Bring it to me."

"Yes, yes."

"At once, before he gets too close."

"I will leave this minute, master. And—"

"Yes, Marcel?"

"You will remember this, in case I ever happen to displease you?"

"Of course." Margal's mind was already at work on this unseen new problem, and his reply was mechanical. "Do I ever forget those who serve me well?"

Chapter Eighteen

Ken Forrest was waiting in the hotel lobby when the cab from the airport pulled up outside and Sandra Dawson got out of it. He hurried to her with his arms outstretched, and without a word she stepped into his embrace. Suddenly it was how it had been in the old days, before her marriage.

He held her for a few seconds, then stepped back and looked at her. She seemed tired. The flight from Port-a-Prince was not all that long, but for days now she had faced the terrible realization that her daughter was in danger.

Reaching for her single piece of luggage on the sidewalk, Ken said, "You'll want to freshen up before we start? It will be a fairly long ride." He had told her on the phone where he thought Merry was being held.

"I need a bathroom."

He took her arm and led her into the hotel, where the man at the desk eyed them without comment as they crossed the lobby to the stairs. The room the manager had given him was on the second floor. He walked her up to it to save waiting for what was probably the slowest elevator in the city.

Inside the room, with the door shut, Sandy turned to face him again. "Have you called the police, Ken?"

"No."

"But why not? If you know where Merry is—"

"I'll explain in the car," he said quietly. "Then if you want to call the police, we can."

"Oh, my God," she whispered. "I want my baby back!"

"In the car. You said you need the bathroom, Sandy."

While she was gone he stood there beside her suitcase and looked at his watch. He had phoned her after his visit to Little Haiti. The time now was four-fifty. She had been lucky to get out of Port-au-Prince so fast. Perhaps the Embassy had helped her. But now what?

The town of Gifford, where Merry was almost certainly being held, was how far from here? Say about three and a half to four hours over Interstate 95 and the Florida Turnpike. He had bought a good road map earlier and studied it. He had also located a Vero Beach directory at a phone company office and found in it the name supplied by the youth in Little Haiti. Elie Jumel lived at 21 Petrea Road.

So they should arrive in Gifford about nine o'clock this evening. But he had no idea how large the town was, or where Petrea Road might be, or what their next step ought to be when they got there.

Coming from the bathroom, Sandy said, "I'm ready, Ken." She touched his arm. "And I do thank you for what you're doing. Don't think I—"

"Quiet, lady."

"All right."

"I have a rented car parked down the street." He picked up her suitcase. "And we'd better take this. We may be gone awhile."

"What about you?"

"I have a bag in the car."

She had little to say until they were out of Coral Gables traffic and bound north on I-95. Then, "How did you find out where she is, Ken? On the phone it only confused me."

He told of his talk with the hotel manager and his visit to Little Haiti.

"But I don't understand why you haven't been to the police!"

With an open road before them, Ken could afford to relax a little. "Sandy, the man and woman who brought your daughter here from Haiti are the two Labrousse told me about. Margal, and the woman who looks after him."

She made a quick, involuntary movement that he felt with his arm because she was sitting close to him. "The sorcerer?"

"The bocor, yes. That's why I haven't gone to the police."

"But—"

"I considered it. Then I thought, if I told them what kind of man Margal is, would they take me seriously? Suppose they only phoned the police in Gifford to go to that house and see if Merry was there. If you'd talked to Labrousse in Port-au-Prince about Margal and his powers the way I did—" He took his gaze off the road long enough to look at her. "But if you think I'm wrong, and feel we ought to go to the police anyway—"

She was tense and silent while they passed a noisy concrete truck. Then, "Ken, I don't know." There was a sob in her voice now as she, too, began to appreciate the complexities of the problem. "If the police can't do anything, what can we do?"

"Go there. Make sure first that Merry is at Jumel's. Then talk to the police up there ourselves, face-to-face, tell them what's going on and what kind of man Margal is, so when they go to the house to get her, they'll be prepared." When she was silent, he looked at her again. "Well?"

"I—suppose so." Then, after a pause, she added, "Oh, God, Ken, I hope we're not making a mistake!"

"Going to the police too soon might be a bigger mistake, Sandy."

For a while they continued to talk in starts and stops, with intervals of silence. The crowded interstate was behind them now, and after a stop at a toll booth they were headed north on the Turnpike. Suddenly, out of the blue, Sandy said, "Who is she, Ken?"

"She?" Did Sandy think he had a girlfriend?

"The woman Brian has been living with."

"Oh." He felt an explosion of relief—small, perhaps, but real. They had been getting to know each other again, and nothing must get in the way of that. "Her name is Carmen Alvaranga."

"I had a feeling. He slept with her before I married him."

"You can't fault him for that, Sandy. She's attractive, Latin, very sexy-looking."

"I fault him for leaving her."

"What?"

"It's because she's Latin and sexy that he walked out on her. Don't you see? Daddy, in Washington, would never have approved."

"But did approve of you?"

"Well, he came to the wedding. Long enough to say he'd been there, anyway." She made a face. "It's a little weird, isn't it? Daddy wouldn't have endorsed Carmen, who I understand comes from a really fine South American family, but I was okay."

"You were safe. Your father was an insurance executive. Your mother is now married to an attorney. Everybody's nice and respectable."

"And no threat to dear Daddy's career."

"Right. Never likely to embarrass him."

Again they were silent. Traffic on the turnpike was light, and Ken pushed the rental to seventy. Strange, he thought. At this hour there should be more traffic.

There was something a little queer about the road itself, too. He had been over it enough times to know it well—the curves, the stretches of pine trees, the golf courses and condo complexes crowding up to it here and there. But things seemed to be coming up in a different pattern now.

He was probably a little tired, both mentally and physically. A lot had happened since his arrival in Miami: the talk with the hotel manager, his visit to Alvaranga's apartment and her account of how Brian Dawson had walked out without an explanation, his conversation in Little Haiti. . . .

Something about the Little Haiti session troubled him. That fellow with the piercing eyes—what was his name? Odiol?—hadn't said much, had he? Hadn't spoken at all, in fact, except to ask for a cigarette at the end, and then money to buy some.

There had been something not quite right—even sinister—about brother Odiol.

Oh, hell, drop it, he thought. Think of something pleasant, like being a student at Miami U. again, when this lovely thing beside you was yours and the two of you were in love. Or thought you were.

He looked at his watch. Five minutes past eight. If he remembered the map right, they should be nearing Fort Pierce, where he must leave the turnpike and travel I-95 again for the few miles that remained to the Vero Beach exit. It should be getting dark soon, too. What time did daylight end in Florida in August? Odd how you could forget such simple things.

At his side Sandy slumped in a posture of sleep, her eyes shut. Tired, obviously. A long, hard day. This morning she had been in Port-au-Prince, talking to him on the phone.

The road remained the same: a four-lane divided

highway, all but deserted here, with clumps of pines and palmettos dotting flat green fields on both sides. But something was wrong. It was more like a dream road than a real one. Although the afternoon had been hot and dry, for the past half hour the car had been boring its way through patches of mist.

There shouldn't be a mist in weather like this. What was going on here?

Reluctantly he put a hand on Sandy's knee. "Hey. Wake up."

She opened her eyes, sat up, looked out the window. "Where are we? Are we there?"

"Not yet. It's only a little past eight. We should be close to Fort Pierce."

"I don't know this part of the state." Frowning, she rubbed the sleep from her face. "Where is this fog coming from?"

"I don't know."

"I've been asleep. I'm sorry, Ken. I didn't mean—"

The car suddenly entered a wall of mist that almost hid the road, and Sandy took in a sharp breath. "Ken, what is this weird fog? Has it been raining?"

"No. No rain."

"Then what—"

"I don't know," he repeated. "And you're right. It is weird."

Afraid of running off the pavement, he slowed to forty. A horn blared behind them and a Cadillac sped past with its lights on. Oddly, the mist did not distort their beams. Ken turned his own lights on, muttering, "Damned fool wants to kill himself."

Sandy glanced at him, obviously disturbed, perhaps even frightened. Leaning forward, she peered steadily through the windshield, then after a while, in a low voice, said, "Ken, are you sure this is the right road?"

There hadn't been a sign of any kind for at least half an hour, Ken realized. Strange. There had been plenty of them before: Such-and-such an exit so far ahead. Exit speed so many miles an hour. Next exit such-and-such. Nothing like that lately.

The car emerged from a tunnel of mist, and he concentrated on seeing a sign.

None appeared.

"Are you sure?" Sandy repeated, turning on the seat to stare at him. "Ken, I'm scared! I think something's happening to us!"

He pulled off the road and stopped. Looked at the map, then at his watch. "Hon, we can't have taken a wrong turn." The *hon* was a word out of their past; he had almost always called her that. "We can't get lost, either," he insisted. "Every exit is marked, with a warning before you reach it. Just keep your eyes open for the Fort Pierce sign."

But the one before Fort Pierce would have been Port St. Lucie, wouldn't it? And before that, Stuart? He didn't recall having seen those.

Shaken, he drove on at forty, searching the side of the road for something to tell them where they were. And kept looking at his watch, as well. And finally, when his watch read 9:10 and the road was totally dark, and they should have reached the sought-for exit long ago . . . finally there was a sign of sorts.

He stopped the car and stared, unbelieving, at a

small, shabby, amateur sign in red letters on a dirty white background. No such advertising would ever be permitted on Florida's proud turnpike.

DELLA'S MOTEL 1 MI.

Clutching his arm, Sandy said with a sob, "Oh my God, Ken! We *are* lost!"

"I must have turned off somewhere. But where? How?"

"I told you. Something is happening to us!"

Margal, he thought, remembering what Captain Labrousse had said about the bocor's powers. And, yes, something was happening, at least to him. He who almost never had headaches was having one now that was making him want to bang his head against the wheel. Was making him sick to his stomach. Dizzy. Unable to think straight.

"Look." His voice seemed slurred to him, as though he were drunk. "We can ask at this motel where we are, and get back on the right road. I'm sorry, hon."

"It wasn't your fault."

Margal, he thought again. *He knows we're trying to reach him and is trying to stop us. No, it wasn't my fault. But if I'm stupid again, it will be.*

If only his head would stop pounding. Was Margal responsible for that, too?

He drove on, more slowly now because he was unsure of his ability to handle the car. The road had changed completely. There was no longer a mist. But there was no four-lane divided highway either. This was a narrow strip of blacktop bounded by darkness.

The headlights picked out a few stunted trees struggling to exist in tangles of knee-high brush. Then a rusty mailbox and an old, unpainted house. Beside the house stood five small cabins in a row, with a lighted sign—DELLA'S MOTEL—on the roof of the middle one.

A smaller sign by the driveway, with an arrow, supplied the information that the house itself was the motel office. He stopped the car in front of the door. "I'll try not to be long, hon. You'll be all right?"

She nodded. But she was trembling, and her hands were clenched.

He tried the door and found it locked. He knocked, waited, then knocked again more determinedly. When it opened at last, he found himself facing a stocky woman with pink plastic curlers in her hair, wearing a shabby green dress and worn-out sandals.

Suspiciously she looked him over. "Yes?"

"I'm sorry to bother you, but I'm lost. Could you tell me where I am, please?"

"Lost?" With the same frown of suspicion, she peered at the car. "You're just off of Eighty, on the road to Ortona."

"I'm afraid I don't know were Ortona is."

" 'Taint surprisin', considerin' the size of it. Where'd you come from?"

"Miami."

"Well, let's see. You must've come up 27 to the lake and along 80."

"Please. What lake?"

"What lake? Okeechobee, o' course. What other

would I be talkin' about?" This time, as she peered at him, her scowl fairly dripped suspicion. "You drunk, mister?"

"No, no. I haven't been drinking."

"Sick, then?"

"I—don't know. I was trying to get to Gifford, near Vero Beach."

"Vero Beach!" she growled. "My Lord, you *are* lost!"

"If I'm near Lake Okeechobee, I must be."

"You're west of the lake, mister. A good long way west of it. What you better do, you want Vero Beach, you better go back to Twenty-seven, see, and head north to Seventy. Then turn right on Seventy and you'll pick up Ninety-five outside of Fort Pierce."

His head throbbing, his vision blurred by the pain of it, Ken leaned against the doorframe. "Just how do I get back to Twenty-seven, please?" Again he realized his voice was slurred, as though he were drunk.

She told him and he nodded, praying he would remember. Feeling she had been generous to talk to him at all, and was perhaps in need, he fumbled a ten-dollar bill from his billfold.

"Uh-uh." She stopped him with her hand before he could offer it. "Nobody pays Della Driscoll for a simple courtesy. Just hope I've helped. But I doubt it, mister. You don't look well enough to do any more drivin' tonight."

He didn't feel well enough, either, he thought as he thanked her and returned to the car. All he wanted at this point was to get off his feet and onto a bed somewhere, and shut his eyes until the pounding in his head went away. On reaching the car he stumbled and would have fallen had it not been there for him to lean against.

Peering in at Sandy, he felt himself go rigid. She, too, was apparently in no condition to go on tonight. She was slumped against her door with one arm under her head and the other dangling.

When he jerked his door open and the inside light went on, he saw she was asleep—or unconscious—with her mouth open in what seemed to be a silent scream of terror.

Chapter Nineteen

"Do you understand now who is the master here?"

Seated on his bed, the man with the fire-scarred face gazed implacably down at his unwilling pupil.

Still on his knees, still naked, Merry Dawson's father bowed his head. "Yes, yes. You are."

"You have no wish to feel the pain again?"

"Dear God, no!"

Margal was in no hurry. Their host, Elie Jumel, had been sent from the room hours ago, just after Dawson's humiliation. The fat woman, Clarisse, had been summoned soon afterward to bring food—only for the Haitian, not the American—and then ordered to retire to her living room mattress with the child.

A prisoner of the bocor's will, Dawson had not once in all that time striven either to rise to his feet or lie on the floor, though his knees were full of agony and he had not slept since his arrival at the house.

The hour was close to midnight.

"You must be aware, of course," Margal said matter-of-factly, "that I could have controlled your actions when I sent you into the kitchen. You were able to command Jumel to kill me only because I was testing you."

"Yes, master." Slowly lifting his head, Dawson looked into the sorcerer's glowing eyes and shuddered. "Now I know."

"So long as that is clear to you, you may get up now and use a chair. I wish to talk to you. Then I will let you sleep so that you may leave here at daybreak on a mission for me."

Struggling to rise, Dawson was so stiff that he fell forward on his elbows. A second effort brought him upright. Walking woodenly to a chair, he carefully lowered himself onto it.

"Not there," Margal corrected. "I said I wish to talk to you. Bring the chair here."

Dawson fearfully dragged the chair to the bed.

"I will begin by telling you that I am sending you to your father," the bocor said. "I would go myself, but the journey would present problems. So you will go for me."

"To my father? In Washington?"

"Confronting him, you will use the power I have given you—the power you demonstrated when you sent Jumel in here to destroy me. You will persuade your esteemed father to do certain things for me which I will tell you about before you leave."

"I need only command him? With my mind? God in heaven, how will I explain this to him?"

"Do I explain when I give you a command?"

"No, but—"

"But you are not my equal yet, eh?" Margal actually smiled. "Nor will you ever be, m'sieu. Nevertheless, your father will obey you."

"You don't know him," Dawson moaned.

"I know you, and you have the power now. But"—the smile became a scowl—"never think you can escape my mind, even though your mission will take you far from here. I will be with you every moment!"

The man on the chair bowed his head in surrender.

"You may sleep a little now." Margal tossed a pillow to the floor. "I will wake you when I wish to instruct you further. Before beginning your journey you will be allowed to shave and bathe, and be given food. Now sleep."

With a moan of relief Dawson sagged from his chair. Crawling across the floor, he collapsed in a sleep of total exhaustion even before reaching the pillow.

Chapter Twenty

"Sandy!"

As he reached for the woman in the car, Ken Forrest fought a savage torment in his head. "Sandy! What's wrong?"

A stupid question, for she was obviously unconscious. And he, too, was teetering on the brink of a black abyss. After trying repeatedly to lift her to a sitting position and finding he hadn't the strength, he backed out of the machine and returned on unsteady legs to the house.

The door was locked again. Della Driscoll must have resecured it after his departure. In response to his desperate but feeble pounding, it was finally inched open.

The woman with curlers in her hair scowled at him through the aperture. "You back? I thought I—"

"Please, Mrs. Driscoll. I need help."

"Again?"

"It's—my wife." If he used any other word, this kind of woman might not give them a cabin together, and Sandy could not be left alone. "Something's happened to her. We can't drive any farther tonight."

"Let me have a look at her, mister." She pushed past him and strode to the car. When he caught up to her, stumbling because of blurred vision and the savage drum sound in his head, she had the car door open and was peering in.

"She does look sick." Sudden anger twisted her face. "Are you two into drugs?"

"No, no. Believe me, I don't know what's happened."

"You been eatin' in crummy restaurants?"

"No. It can't be that."

She scowled at him. "Well—all right. Dunno why I should believe you, but we better get your wife inside."

"Thank you." Ken swayed forward, hoping he would be able to lift Sandy out of the car. He didn't have to try. With a gruff, "Out of my way, mister; you look as sick as her!" the Driscoll woman pushed him aside. For her, Sandy was no burden at all. All he had to do was stumble along beside her as she strode to the house.

Inside, she carried Sandy through the "office" into a small, drab living room and laid her gently on a sofa. "You stay with her while I make some of my herb tea," she ordered. "My tea'll fix most anything."

Rather like an army tank, she went lumbering into another part of the house.

Leaning over Sandy, Ken studied her face. Now that her mouth was no longer open in the silent scream of terror that had terrified him, there seemed to be nothing much wrong.

"Sandy."

Her eyes opened. "What—where are we?"

"You passed out in the car. We're at the motel."

"Motel? Where? Gifford?"

He touched her face. "We're not in Gifford yet, hon. We got lost, and now we're somewhere in the middle of the state, at a place called Della's." When she still looked confused, he added with a frown, "How much do you remember?"

"The road . . . didn't seem right. There was a lot of fog or mist, and then we weren't on the turnpike anymore."

"Does your head ache?" His own still did. Even when attending voodoo services on the plantation in Haiti, with the three drums pounding and that fiendish iron bar called the *ogan* clanking away for hours on end, his head had not hurt the way it did now.

The assailant then had been only sound. Now there was something evil in what was being done to him.

Who was doing it? Margal, the bocor?

"Sandy, listen." He put his lips close to her ear, so his voice would not reach the woman in the kitchen. "We can't go on tonight. If we try to, I'm likely to pass out at the wheel. What we need is a few hours' rest here, and I want us to be together. So I've told her that we're married."

"Her?"

"The owner."

Sandy tried feebly to grasp his hand. "Oh my God, Ken, I have to find my daughter! Please!"

"Just a little while, hon. Maybe only an hour or so. As soon as we feel better—I feel better—we can go on. I promise."

Softly, almost silently, she began to sob.

Could they go on without losing time here? If he drove very slowly, say? He could understand her feelings: the child missing for so long and now known to be in the hands of a fiend like Margal. But was he able to drive at all? She certainly wasn't.

He was still struggling to reach a decision when Della Driscoll came with a tray. Placing it on a table beside the sofa, she looked at Sandy. "You're awake, hey? That's good."

Sandy only stared at her.

"This here is my own herb tea, and it'll do you good." Kneeling, Driscoll took a mug from the tray and offered it with a gentleness that seemed out of character. "You drink some now, you hear?"

Sandy lifted the mug to her lips.

"Tastes good, don't it?"

"Yes . . . thank you."

"You finish it. Then your husband here can see about gettin' you to bed." She frowned at Ken. "You're lucky, mister. I only keep one cabin open for transients now. The rest I rent by the month to folks who work on farms around here. And the one I have ain't occupied tonight. You can use it."

"My wife thinks we ought to go on," Ken said.

"Go on! You out of your mind?"

"It's urgent we get to Gifford."

Driscoll's eyes narrowed to slits as she looked from him to Sandy. "Mister, the condition you're in, you wouldn't get five miles down the road before you fell asleep at the wheel and run off into a ditch." Taking the empty mug from Sandy, she struggled to her feet. "I'll show you the cabin. Just let me get the key."

She left the room, and Ken realized Sandy was staring at him, silently pleading with him. He reached for her hand.

"Hon, I can't drive right now. I just physically can't. The worst headache I've ever had in my life is making me weak and dizzy, sick to my stomach. And you can't handle the car; you've already passed out once. Just give me an hour to get over the worst of it."

"Ken, why are we like this?" she whispered.

Because, he thought, Haiti's special devil doesn't want us interfering with his plans for Merry, whatever they are. But he mustn't say that, of course. "Hon, I don't know. But we'll get over it. All we need—"

"You comin', mister?" Della Driscoll had reappeared, clutching a ring of keys.

He squeezed Sandy's hand in a plea for her to trust him, then followed the woman out. The cabin she led him to was the one nearest her house, he noted. Perhaps she liked to keep an eye on people she rented it to?

Opening the cabin door, she switched on a light. "Sorry it's only got the one bed. I expect you'd rather sleep separate tonight, feelin' the way you both do."

"It will be all right, Mrs. Driscoll. We won't be using it long."

"What you mean by that?"

"We must get to Gifford." Without even entering the cabin, he peered past her to see what it was like.

It was just large enough to hold the bed, an old chest of drawers painted pale blue with most of the paint chipped off, a couple of wooden chairs that had never been painted at all, and a dark, overstuffed chair about to pop its springs. Beyond the bed was a bathroom.

"I appreciate this, Mrs. Driscoll. How much do I owe you?"

"Twenty for the two of you. In the morning."

"No, now. We'll be gone before you're up."

"You're out of your mind. The minute the two of you hit that bed, you'll be out for hours."

"Please." He took a twenty from his billfold and held it out to her.

"Well, all right. Whatever you say." The bill went into a pocket of her dress. "You want help gettin' your wife over here?"

"Well—" Normally he could have picked Sandy up and carried her with ease. But could he now?

"All right, I'll get her," Driscoll said. "You wait here."

Standing in the doorway, he watched her go to the

house and come out with Sandy in her arms. So, he thought, I'm going to be in bed again with the woman I've never stopped loving. A woman who's married this time.

Despite the eeriness of the occasion and the problems they faced, he felt a surge of excitement. It lingered even after the motel owner strode into the cabin and deposited Sandy on the bed, and he saw that Sandy was again asleep or unconscious.

"Thank you, Mrs. Driscoll."

On her way out, Mrs. Driscoll turned at the door. "You need anything, just holler. Livin' alone like I do, I don't sleep too sound anyway."

The door closed behind her.

Gazing down at Sandy, he wondered what to do. Should he try to take off some of her clothes, to make her more comfortable? No. That mightn't seem right to her when she awoke. Besides, they would be leaving soon.

He took her shoes off. Removing his own, he lay beside her, on his back, and stared at the ceiling.

They had slept together in the old days, though not more than a few times. Only just enough to make him think it might be a permanent arrangement and to feel hurt and angry when she announced she was marrying Brian Dawson. The hurt was still in him, but not the anger. Losing her had been his own fault. You couldn't blame a woman for thinking of her future.

Turning toward her, he found her eyes wide open, gazing at him.

"Hello, Ken," she whispered.

"Hi. How you feeling?"

"Far-out. Kind of floating. Where are we? In one of the cabins?"

"Uh-huh." He reached out to touch her face. "I told her we wouldn't be staying long, though. Just until we felt well enough to try for Gifford again." He could manage only a small, sad smile. "It's been quite a while since we were together like this."

"Yes. I'm sorry."

He took her gently into his arms and touched his lips to hers. She pressed herself against him and they lay that way awhile before, with a shudder, she suddenly relaxed. Peering into her face, he saw she was again having trouble keeping her eyes open.

"Rest a little, hon. Sleep."

"Just for—" The struggle to concentrate made her frown. "Half an hour? Will you wake me?"

"I'll wake you."

With a sigh of surrender, she shut her eyes.

Chapter Twenty-one

Lying there beside her, he, too, must have dozed off. When he awoke, he was conscious of the pain in his head again, and that the cabin was full of the sound of drumming.

Rain. And not a welcome shower that would chase the heat, but a savage downpour that seemed likely to demolish the cabin.

He sat up. The bare bulb overhead still glowed; he had left it on, thinking Sandy might suddenly need him. Puzzled by the intensity of the deluge, now accompanied by a howling wind, he shook his head to sort out his feelings. But that only intensified the hammering inside his skull and made the contents of his stomach rise to his throat.

The cabin had two windows. When lightning flashed and a crash of thunder suddenly tore the night apart, both windows rattled so wildly, they seemed in danger of bursting. Then a second fiery flash of lightning turned them into monstrous eyes, alive and full of evil, glaring at him.

Without even a glance at the woman sleeping by his side, he flung himself from the bed and raced in panic to the door.

The wind all but tore the door off its rusty hinges as he flung it open. Outside, the rain slammed down in sheets, lightning streaked the sky, and a shrieking wind tore through the tops of tall pines.

In Haiti's Massif du Nord, violent mountain storms had been common. But not even there had he ever seen a storm such as this!

Why, then, was he rushing out into it?

The question found its way into his mind when he was halfway to the road. Lurching to a halt, he looked wildly back at the cabin. Its door was closed now; the wind must have slammed it shut. The light was still on inside, making the windows glow in the dark except when flashes of lightning set the whole night ablaze and blanked them out.

He looked toward the house. No lights there. No other lights anywhere that he could see. Only the drenching rain, the booming claps of thunder, the darkness that was slashed every few seconds by spears of lightning.

He could not stay here! Could not go back to the cabin! He had to escape!

Stumbling on, he crossed the road and found himself in a forest he had not known was there. It must have been there, of course; he just hadn't noticed it when they stopped at the motel. Strange, though. He should have noticed anything that unusual. It was a forest of huge cypresses, their trunks nearly as big as the cabin he had just fled from. And he was stumbling through dark, stinking water filled with cypress knees—those weirdly shaped growths sprouting up from the big trees' submerged roots.

Terrified, he stopped again, clinging for support to a knee as tall as his hips and shaped like—like what? A grotesque, oversized bishop on a chessboard strewn with other grotesques. A dwarf from Disney's *Snow White.* A human being with an ugly balloon face and no legs.

The last thought made him relinquish his grip and back away, as though the knee might possess some awful poison that would hideously destroy him, and he stumbled on through the swamp again. But other weird growths threatened him on all sides now. Shapes resembling panthers and wildcats. And some that were even more frightening because they were almost but not quite human.

Then the snakes. But the snakes were not cypress-knee phantoms. They were real.

Waist deep in stinking water, he first saw them gliding toward him when a gaudy flash of lightning lit up the whole eerie scene. The huge trees with their swollen trunks and sprawling roots. The awful congregation of upthrust knees, silently stalking him the way a pack of hungry jungle cats might stalk a terrified rabbit. Then the dark brown water moccasins, with darker bars and blotches on their thick bodies, slithering toward him for the kill. Dozens of them. Hundreds of them. Thousands of them! All huge, all with their broad, flat heads upraised and eyes gleaming and fangs bared. All deadly poisonous.

Now he knew he never should have fled from the cabin. Should have stayed there and bolted the door, and waited for an end to the nightmare. But it was too late. If he tried to go back now, the snakes would intercept him. In desperation he flung himself toward the roots of the nearest cypress, raking the dark water with his hands to help his feet in their struggle with the muddy bottom.

Out of breath, sobbing, he crawled up on the huge buttressed root beyond reach of the snakes and collapsed.

The storm raged on. Rain whipped the swamp water to a black froth. Lightning gilded the gliding snakes, many of them now hissing, as they endlessly circled his tiny isle of safety. High in the treetops the wind howled and shrieked with a voice too nearly human.

He clung to the root and prayed for the nightmare to end. For the hammering in his head to cease. For some degree of sanity to return to the insane world he was lost in.

Time passed, crawling, and at last the claps of thunder and flashes of lightning were less frequent, less terrifying. The cypress knees ceased to be a silent horde of grotesques hungrily awaiting his surrender and reverted to being only swamp growths again. The rain stopped.

Then, after an even longer interlude of waiting,

during which his arms and legs grew numb from the confinements of his perch, the worst of his tormentors, the snakes, began to glide back into the darkness that had spawned them.

He lowered himself slowly into the water and found the muddy bottom with his feet. Stretched his arms out for better balance. Took one step, two, three, away from his island of refuge, and dared to look back.

A flash of lightning showed him the snakes were not in pursuit.

With terror spurring him to one final, all-out effort, he broke into a desperate rush for the road.

The rush took him through water that was sometimes knee-deep, sometimes ankle-deep, and at times only an oily black film hiding what he was sure must be quicksand that would suck him down. Losing his balance every few strides, he crashed through the swamp like a terrified animal pursued by hunters, creating a din that must have been audible even to the people in the cabins he was struggling to reach.

Half drowned and layered with slime, he reached the road and stumbled across it.

But his strength was gone. With the road at his back, his legs turned liquid and let him down. Sprawled in the motel driveway, he tried to continue by crawling but collapsed and lost consciousness.

When he opened his eyes it was daylight. Not real daylight—the sun was not yet up—but he could make out the dim shape of Della Driscoll's house and the misty outlines of the five cabins, in one of which he had left Sandy. And on struggling to rise, he became aware that Driscoll herself was standing within three feet of him with her hands on her hips and her jaw pugnaciously jutting.

"Do you mind tellin' me what you think you're doin'?" the woman demanded.

Unable to rise, he turned over on his back and stared up at her. "I . . . don't know. The storm . . ."

"Storm?" she snapped. "What storm?"

"The rain. The wind. The thunder and lightning. I felt I had to get out of the cabin before something terrible happened." Succeeding at last in getting to his feet, he stood there swaying from side to side while looking around him in the gray dawn. The storm was over, thank God. "I guess I panicked," he heard himself saying. "I was ill when we got here. Something wrong with me. Something I don't—don't understand."

The woman's glare was uncompromising. "Mister, there wasn't no storm last night."

"But there was! It scared the hell out of me and I ran across the road into the swamp."

"Into what?"

"The swamp. Over there." He turned to point, and slowly lowered his arm as he realized he must have gone much farther than the other side of the road. From here, all he could see over there was a flat expanse of dry-land grass and scrub growth, with an occasional slash pine standing dark against the sky.

"A swamp," he heard himself repeating. "Somewhere. I got lost in it."

Della Driscoll's elbows were jug handles now.

"Mister, there ain't no swamp anywheres around here."

"But there is! A big one! I was trapped in it for hours by snakes!"

"A swamp with snakes, hey? When I opened my door just now, I seen you comin' from that field acrost the road, staggerin' like you was drunk. If you was in a bog somewhere—which I don't know where it'd be—why ain't your feet wet? And if it was stormin' like you say, why ain't you wet all over?"

Ken looked at himself. Yes, why wasn't he wet? And why didn't he reek of the stinking black water he'd been forced to wade through?

"Well?" Driscoll demanded.

"I don't know. I don't understand."

"You don't, hey? Well, I do. I've had your kind stop here before, mister. And I'm tellin' you, you come to the wrong place. Any swamp and snakes you seen around here was all in your mind, put there by drugs. Now you take your missus, if she is your missus, and clear out of here before I call the sheriff. I don't stand for nobody usin' drugs on my place. I'm respectable."

"Mrs. Driscoll, I haven't been using drugs. Believe me, I—"

"Out!" She took a menacing step toward him. "Right now! Take your missus and git!"

There was no use trying to convince her, Ken decided. Were he in her shoes, he might be equally angry. Turning away, he walked slowly toward the cabin where Sandy must still be asleep.

Dear God, what if she, too, had been a victim of hallucinations?

But she was peacefully sleeping, and when he waked her by gently shaking her shoulder, her only remark was a perfectly normal one. "Oh." She blinked up at him. "What time is it?"

"Daylight."

"Ken! You promised me—"

"I'll explain later, hon." He helped her to her feet. "We have to get out of here."

While putting on her shoes she raised her head to give him a puzzled look, but then went to the bathroom without saying anything. When she reappeared, he took her arm and led her to the door. Having expected to stay no more than an hour or so, they had brought nothing in from the car last night.

In the gray beginning of a new day, Della Driscoll was waiting there with a bulldog look on her face.

Ken halted. "Mrs. Driscoll, I'm sorry about this. I don't know what happened, but it wasn't what you think."

"So you say," she growled.

"Tell me again how to get to Gifford. Please."

"Mister, I'm tellin' you nothin'! You just clear out o' here right now!"

In the house on Petrea Road in Gifford, Clarisse knocked on the door of Margal's room and was told to enter. Bearing a tray, she went to the bed to serve the bocor his breakfast. But before she could put the tray down, she had to move a magazine he had been looking at.

"Are you finished with this?"

"Yes. Take it away."

The magazine was open to an article on the Florida Everglades, and as she walked to the door with it Clarisse looked with interest at some of the photographs. One showed some decidedly ugly snakes—cottonmouth moccasins, the caption said they were—gliding through dark, weedy water. Another, that took up an entire page and made her feel she was right in the midst of it, was a picture of huge trees in a swamp, with strange-looking growths rising from their submerged roots.

Florida was not a nice place, Clarisse decided as she tossed the magazine onto a table. Not nice at all.

Chapter Twenty-two

"Through your eyes, Dawson, I see an exit ahead, and a restaurant. You may stop there if you are hungry. Are you hungry?"

"Yes."

"Only 'yes'?"

"Yes, Margal."

"I prefer 'Yes, master.' "

"Yes, master."

"You are moving your lips. Do not move your lips when you communicate with me. It is not necessary."

"As you say, master."

The eating place had been advertised on roadside signs for the past fifty miles, at least, and its enormous parking area was crowded with cars from almost every state on the eastern seaboard. Definitely not the sort of establishment the son of Rutherford Dawson, presidential confidant, normally would have chosen to patronize, even when driving alone. But the hour was now 6:15 P.M. and, being hungry and tired after driving all day, Brian Dawson more than welcomed the permission to stop.

Here in South Carolina he was more than half way to his destination, and his last meal had been a meager breakfast prepared by Margal's Clarisse. He would not easily forgive the bocor for what had happened immediately afterward.

His daughter, Merry, had been asleep on an old mattress in the living room. To reach the car he had to walk past her and, of course, had halted. If he could but kneel and touch her before leaving the house . . .

But Margal's voice inside his head had thundered, "No! Not until you complete your mission and return!" And so he had been forced to depart from that terrible place without even saying good-bye.

The master should not have done that. No. There was no excuse for such pointless cruelty.

Finding a parking space in the crowded lot, he drove into it and shut off the engine, closing his eyes for a moment as he leaned back to ease the ache in his shoulders. How much sleep had he had last night on the floor of Margal's room? Not more than four or five hours, surely. And none at all the night before that, while playing the role of pupil to a relentless teacher. Now, after twelve hours of driving, nonstop except for gas, he was close to the end of his endurance.

Getting out of the car, he lost his balance and had to grasp the door to steady himself. Then, on lurching away from the machine, he stumbled to one knee.

"Hold it right there, sir."

Afraid to rise, he only turned his head to look behind him. A state police car was there. A young man in uniform strode toward him.

Oh, God, he thinks I'm drunk.

The trooper took his arm and helped him to his feet. Stood there holding him. "You been drinking, sir?"

"No, no. I'm just a bit stiff from driving."

The other's gaze shifted to Dawson's silver Jaguar. "Where you headed for?"

"Washington. That is, Virginia. Alexandria."

"From where?"

"Florida."

"And for what?"

"To visit my father."

"Your driver's license, please."

Brian fumbled out his billfold and offered it open, with the license visible. After examining it, the trooper flipped through other cards and peered even longer at one of those.

"You're Brian Dawson, and with the State Department?"

"Yes."

"The father you're going to—would that be the Rutherford Dawson I saw on 'Meet the Press' Sunday? The one that's an adviser or how they call it to the President?"

With a sigh of relief, Dawson said, "I didn't know he was on television Sunday. I was in Haiti. But yes, Rutherford Dawson is my father." He paused. "Look, Officer, I've been pushing a little, but I'm not drunk, not sick, and I'm in a real hurry."

"Why not a plane, then—sir? You could have made the trip by plane in—"

"I dislike flying. The flight from Haiti to Miami was all I could handle."

"Oh." A pause, then a shrug as the trooper handed the billfold back. "Well, okay, sir. Sorry to butt in. But when I saw you almost fall down—"

"I understand. But I . . . Wait."

He's impressed that I'm with State, Brian thought. *He's awed that I'm the son of a man close to the President. This could be my chance! If I tell him about Merry, he can phone the police in Gifford or Vero Beach, and they can go to that house and get her out of there!*

"No!" screamed a voice in his head, so savagely it caused him to take a backward step and clap his hands to his ears. "Do that and you die! And so will the child!"

"Sir?" The trooper stared. "Are you sure you're okay?"

"I—I will be. It will pass."

"You're white as a sheet, sir."

"Tell him you need food!" the voice in his head shrilled. "Go into the restaurant!"

"I'm just hungry, I guess." Brian struggled for composure. "I'm—well, to be honest, I'm a diabetic and have to eat on time, and today I didn't." He had certainly behaved enough like a diabetic to be believed. "I'll be all right when I've had some food, Officer."

"Well—okay, sir. I hope so." The trooper turned away.

"Now," the voice ordered, "satisfy your hunger as instructed. And never again even dare to think of disobeying me. Do you understand?"

"Yes. I mean—yes, master."

"I am not a patient man. Remember that! Or a forgiving one, either!"

"I will remember."

"I do not tolerate disobedience!"

"I—hear you."

"Go, then."

He had a terrible headache as he turned and trudged toward the restaurant. It began to fade, though, soon after he was seated and had ordered something to eat. Then, as he sat there waiting to be served, he began to think—vaguely—of a thing the young trooper had said.

If this visit to his father was so urgent, why hadn't Margal sent him by plane instead of letting him drive? Even if there were no scheduled flights to Washington from some city close to Gifford, with his State Department connections he could easily have arranged for a private flight.

Was the monster fallible, after all?

Chapter Twenty-three

The hammering in Ken's head was back, worse than before. It had begun when he strove to recall the Driscoll woman's directions for reaching the town of Gifford. The directions she had angrily refused to repeat.

Now, with the car stopped at the side of the road, he studied the map until his eyes burned.

Sensing his anguish, Sandy Dawson reached out to touch him. "Are you all right?"

"I guess so. Yes—I'm okay."

What had happened to him last night, anyway? Why had a seemingly nonexistent storm caused him to flee from Sandy into an unreal swamp, to be terrified there by a nightmare horde of poisonous snakes while an audience of grotesques looked on in fiendish glee?

Was Margal actually responsible? Could a sorcerer distort a man's mind that way without being close enough to hypnotize him? And if Margal had caused it to happen, why had Sandy remained unaffected?

But she hadn't been totally unaffected, had she? Like him, she had seen a nonexistent mist on the highway and been duped into thinking they were on the right road when they were not. Then she had passed out in the car, seemingly terrified, when they stopped at the motel. So Margal must have gotten to her, too, at least for a time.

No good would come of speculation. The important thing now was to get to Gifford in a hurry, to make up for lost time. They were west of big Lake Okeechobee, Driscoll had said. They must return along 80 to 27 and go north to—he peered at the map again—to cross-state 70. Then east on that to pick up 1–95 outside Fort Pierce.

Could he drive that far? Last night's ordeal had left him exhausted.

He glanced at Sandy. She, too, looked worn out.

There is so much I don't know.

He had never mentioned Sandy when talking to the men in Little Haiti, he was certain. So if one of them had chosen to tell Margal of his visit, the sorcerer still would not know Sandy was with him now. Was she just absorbing an overflow of whatever unholy force the bocor was directing at him?

He changed his mind about asking her to drive. "Tell me something, hon. When we got to that motel and you passed out in the car, you looked frightened. Do you remember why?"

"Yes, I do. I had a feeling something awful was going to happen to you there."

"That's all?"

"Isn't that enough?"

The overflow, he decided. Margal had been working on him. He, Ken Forrest, had been thinking mostly about her. She had picked up the bocor's vibes. That would explain her seeing the fog, as well.

Then why had she slept through his ordeal in the swamp? Had Della Driscoll's "tea" been a soporific?

"All right." He thrust the map at her. "I know the way. Talk to me, Sandy."

"What?"

"Talk to me. God knows what we're up against, but if we're talking, maybe I won't be such an easy victim."

Thank God Merry's kidnapper couldn't control the car. It picked up speed, and the woman at his side turned toward him, tucking one leg under her. "What shall we talk about?"

"For starters, why not tell me more about you and Brian? I thought you had a good marriage."

"It wasn't ever good, Ken."

"Wasn't in what way?" If he could get her talking about Dawson, maybe that old jealousy would build up inside him again, leaving fewer openings for Margal's mind control.

"Really, I don't want—"

"Pretend you do. Unless you want us to wind up in some other forsaken part of Florida. Come on, now."

But she had something else on her mind. "Ken, why can't we go to the police?"

"Oh, God."

"Why do you say 'Oh, God'? It's the logical thing to do, isn't it, after what happened last night? We need help!"

"Sandy, look at us, for God's sake. Are we in any shape to confront a bunch of hardheaded cops? To talk to them about a kidnapping in Haiti by a sorcerer with no legs? And about a storm that didn't happen? And my going nuts and plunging into a swamp that wasn't there?" With his gaze fixed on the road because he feared being vulnerable again, he shook his head violently. "Even the Driscoll woman accused me of being stoned, Sandy. The police would be sure of it."

"I don't see how it could hurt to try," she persisted.

"Do you want to risk another delay? If they think there's something wrong with us, they'll hold us. Please. Forget about the police, at least for now. Tell me about you and Brian."

She was silent for so long that at last he stole a glance at her, just in time to see her bite her lip. Then, in an unsteady voice, she said, "Well, all right."

"Good."

"To begin with, I suppose it was as much my fault as his. Because I didn't really love him, I mean."

"Why did you marry him, then?"

"Because of you."

"Me? I didn't walk out on you, Sandy."

"I know. But you weren't serious about us, either. You weren't serious about anything."

"And he was?"

"Oh, he was! As the only son of Rutherford Franklin Dawson, he had his future all mapped out. First there would be a State Department job—"

"Which is why Alvaranga wouldn't do. Here's Route Twenty-seven, hon. We go north through Moore Haven." He turned left onto a four-lane highway. "Did he know you and I had slept together?"

"No. At least, I never told him. After all, we weren't living together."

"Worse luck. If we had been, I'd have realized what was bugging you about me and done something to fix it."

Her hand touched his knee. "Would you, Ken?"

"Yes, damn it. Maybe I wouldn't have mapped out a future the way he did, but I'd have thought more about it. That was the trouble, wasn't it? You were afraid you'd end up supporting me."

"Something like that."

"Well, go on about Brian. Is he a good father to Merry?"

"Yes, I have to give him that."

"Really loves her?"

"Worships her."

"That's something. Is he hard to live with? Outside of having other women, I mean. Or at least one other woman."

Sandy shrugged. "He's very self-centered. Everything has to be just so and on time, as though I were a paid servant. In Haiti that could have been my own fault, because I wouldn't hire all the help he thought we ought to have."

She voiced a brief laugh. "I remember one day our cook, Edita, was out sick and I was sick—we both had what they call the fever—and I was in the bathroom for the umpteenth time, throwing up. And he walked in and looked at me in disgust and said, 'When are you going to get my dinner?' "

"Brother."

"I'm not a wife to him. Not loved. I'm simply someone he thought might be right for his career."

"You do sleep with him, I suppose."

"It isn't the same."

"Same as what?"

"The way you and I were. Shall I elaborate? Is that what you want?"

It was, he realized. And not just to keep Margal from taking possession of his mind again. He wanted to hear more about the intimate side of her life with Brian because, damn it, he was jealous. And even more important, because he was beginning to feel there might be a chance to get her back.

After all, he had never stopped loving this woman. No one else had been able to take her place.

"All right." Again Sandy shrugged. "In bed he was the kind of man who doesn't make love to a woman but rapes her. I say *was* because I haven't been in bed with him in over a year. We sleep in the same room but in separate beds, and the space between is a Grand Canyon." Her fingers squeezed his leg. "You wouldn't know what I mean by 'the kind of man who rapes a woman.' "

"You mean I didn't come on that strong?"

"Oh, you came on strong enough. You knew what you wanted. But you were tender and considerate. Even the few times when I didn't really want to go to bed with you, I ended up being glad I was there."

"Thanks, hon." He paused. "Why don't you leave him?"

"He won't let me. This is a critical point in his career, he says. A divorce would hurt his prospects."

"But he can't stop you from walking out on him."

"Yes, Ken, he can."

"How, for God's sake?"

"By refusing to let me have Merry. He said if I leave him, I'll never see her again." She paused and frowned. "What are we stopping for?"

They had been rolling north on Route 27 with the big lake on their right, and had talked all the way through the lakeside town of Moore Haven. Now a two-lane blacktop branching off to the right bore the number 78. Ken said, "Look at the map, will you? I think this is a short cut to 70 through a Seminole reservation."

Her frown told him she had her doubts. Or was she thinking that after yesterday's brush with horror it would be safer for them to stay on a main highway? He himself was no longer afraid of being savaged by Margal again. All she had to do was keep on talking to him.

"Well?" he urged.

"Well—all right, I guess."

The shortcut was all but deserted at this hour of the morning. A breeze blew across it from the water, despite a flood-control dike that hid the lake itself. A white heron stood statue still in a ditch, waiting for its breakfast to swim within reach. An armadillo crossed the blacktop like a miniature tank and disappeared into scrub growth. Houses were far apart. Sandy talked again of when they had been lovers.

After a while Ken was no longer at the wheel of a car on a mission filled with mystery and peril, but naked on a bed with her. On a table beside the bed glowed a lamp, and he found himself remembering the time they had bought it together at a flea market, laughing at themselves for being idiots because it was a hideous plaster imitation of Rodin's "The Kiss." Now by its dim light he looked down at Sandy's small, perfect breasts and flat belly and began gently to caress her ever-so-lovely body with the tips of his fingers, to make her want him. And presently she stopped lying there so quietly and began to caress him the same way, then tugged him over on top of her and pulled his head down to bring their mouths together. And oh, it was good, so good, to know that this girl loved him and wanted him the way he loved and wanted her. It made the future so wonderfully certain.

Their lovemaking finished, he rolled over on his back and smiled up at the bedroom ceiling and began humming a song. And the girl in the car on the road through the Seminole reservation heard him and stopped talking about their old relationship and said, "That's pretty. What's the name of it?"

He sang the words. *"Ti maman, fé ti ba pou mwen, pa kité, m'allé . . ."*

"It's Haitian, of course. I think I've heard it."

"An old Haitian love song. 'Sweetheart, give me a little kiss, don't let me go.' "

"Sing it all? Please?"

He put a hand on her knee, and while he sang the whole song for her the hand slowly burrowed down between her legs until it encountered a soft warmth that reacted to his touch by becoming moist. Then he stopped singing and began talking to her in Creole.

She frowned. "I didn't know you spoke Creole that well. How did you learn it so quickly? Most people find it hard."

Again he used the tongue of the Haitian peasant, this time so rapidly she seemed frightened by it and looked at him in alarm.

"I've never heard anyone but a Haitian speak it like that!" she breathed. "Ken—what's happening? What are you doing?" Then suddenly, in a shrill voice: "Ken! What are we turning in here for?"

With only one hand on the wheel he had unexpectedly brought the car to a near stop and swung it off the blacktop onto a pair of sandy ruts. Now he freed his other hand from between her legs and steered the lurching vehicle between walls of brush and tall grass. Fifty yards in from the road he braked it to a halt.

"Ken!" Sandy moaned. "What are you—"

His right arm went around her neck, brutally pulling her closer to him. His left hand went where his right had been before, but not gently this time, just jabbing and clutching.

A cry of pain all but turned her protest into a scream. "Ken, for God's sake, what—"

"Oh, stop it!" he snarled. "You know damned well what I want! Don't play hard to get with me!"

"Ken, I'm not playing hard to get! But not now. Please! Not here!"

"Oh, for Christ's sake!" Angrily he let her go, but only to fling the car door open and lurch out. Striding around the machine, he had his shirt off and discarded even before he reached her door. There he kicked off his loafers, rid himself of slacks and shorts, and was naked except for his socks when he reached in and grasped her by an arm.

"Get out here, damn it! I want you and I want you now!"

She grabbed at the wheel and tried to hang on to it while he tugged at her: But his rage made him too strong. Much too strong. In a moment she was out of the car, sobbing at him to stop it while he fumbled at her clothes.

"Please, Ken. Oh my God, I'll make love to you, but not like this and not now! We have to find my daughter! Ken! Stop it!"

He silenced her by fiercely pulling her into his embrace and crushing his mouth against hers, pawing at her with both hands while she struggled. It was the pawing that cost him his triumph. When she felt his grip slacken, she flung her arms up and pushed with all her strength.

He stumbled backward. Lost his balance. Fell naked into something with wickedly sharp thorns that pierced his skin and wrung a yell of pain from his throat.

With a swiftness born of terror Sandy Dawson leaped back into the car and squeezed herself behind the wheel. Turned the key. Sent the machine roaring down the ruts in reverse and somehow miraculously managed to reach the highway while still in control of it.

The sound of the fleeing car died away in Ken's ears as he extricated his naked, bleeding body from the thorns and struggled to his feet. Then he stood there with his mouth agape and eyes tight shut, flailing the air with both arms, as though once again battling the fetid waters of a snake-filled swamp.

Chapter Twenty-four

Like many others who earn their bread in the capital, Rutherford Franklin Dawson lived across the river in Virginia. His apartment fit the lifestyle of a man who worked in the White House as a close friend and colleague of that establishment's number-one resident.

This Sunday morning he chose to prepare his own simple breakfast of prune juice, toast, and coffee. Then he elected to relax in bathrobe and slippers with a new book. Being the work of a columnist who was one of the President's most cynical detractors, the book would undoubtedly raise his already high blood pressure, but he felt it his duty to sample the thing, at least. By the time he had read a chapter or two he would probably throw it across the room in a fit of temper.

Rutherford Dawson's favorite chair was a recliner well suited to his six-foot-three frame. Settling into it, he glared for a few seconds at the author's photo on the book's dust jacket, then began reading.

His phone rang. With a soft "Damn!" he got to his feet and strode across the room to the telephone table.

"Your son is here, Mr. Dawson." It was the security guard in the lobby.

"What?"

"From Haiti, sir."

"What in God's name—All right, Eddie, send him up."

" 'Your son is here,' " Dawson echoed in a growl on his way to the door. "Don't bother to phone first. Don't let anyone know you're coming. Damn it, suppose I'd had somebody here?"

Someone of the opposite sex, he meant. It was a situation he enjoyed often, but not one he wanted known at the White House. A man of his influence was expected to be more discreet.

He heard the elevator doors open in the hall, and then footsteps. His doorbell buzzed. Opening the door, he made no attempt to hide his displeasure. But his frown was quickly displaced by an expression of concern.

"My God, Brian! What's wrong with you?"

They shook hands. It was as close as they ever came to embracing. "I'm just a bit beat, Dad," the son said.

Leaving the South Carolina restaurant last evening, Brian had returned to his car and closed his eyes, intending only a brief nap before resuming his journey. When he awoke it was after midnight, and through the rest of the night he had pushed on like a zombie. Did he now have the strength to carry out Margal's orders?

His father led him to a chair. "When did you leave Haiti?"

"Well, I—oh, several days ago."

"Why? You in trouble?"

"No, no. I had to talk to people in Miami about the immigration problem."

"People in Miami? Then why are you here, damn it?"

This was not the way it was supposed to go, Brian told himself. He was forgetting what the man in Gifford had so painfully taught him.

"Dad." Leaning forward, he fixed his gaze on his father's face. "Look at me, please."

"Damn it, I've *been* looking at you! And all I see is a man who must have been on a bender for . . ." The voice of Dawson Senior began to fade. "What—are you doing? What's happened to your eyes?"

"Next to your mind, your eyes are your most effective weapon. Use them!" Margal the sorcerer had said over and over again. No doubt they were tinged with red now. Not the flaming red he had seen in the Haitian's eyes, perhaps, but enough to alarm his father.

The two sat staring at each other, the father obviously uneasy, the son now using his eyes and mind in concert.

After a moment of total silence Brian said in a low

voice, "Do you begin to understand me a little?"

Dawson Senior fumbled in his robe and produced a pack of cigarettes, a lighter. Having filled his lungs with smoke, he placed the cigarette on an ashtray while the smoke drifted from his half-open mouth as though he had no control over it. "What—are you doing to me, for God's sake?"

There had to be a test, Brian remembered, before he could safely continue. Margal had warned him. Or was the bocor warning him now, this minute? It was sometimes difficult to know.

"What am I commanding you to do?" The words did not actually leave his lips. His lips did not move. But he was fiercely concentrating now and knew his eyes were hypnotic.

Aloud, his father replied feebly, "You are telling me to—to take up my cigarette—and—and—"

"Why are you not doing it, then?"

With palsied fingers the older man fumbled the burning tube of tobacco from the tray and put it into his mouth. Slowly he chewed and swallowed it.

On the son's mouth a smile of triumph took shape. Aloud now, to save himself the exhaustion of too much concentration, he said, "If you go to your office today, will you be likely to see the President?"

Rutherford Dawson responded like a man talking in his sleep. "On Sunday?"

"I am asking you."

"Well, he is there today. He was to go to Camp David this weekend but changed his mind and stayed to do some work."

"And you could help with that?"

"I believe so. Yes."

"He would welcome your help?"

"I think he would."

"You will go there, then, and make every effort to see him. Time is of the essence. Now listen carefully to what you must do."

"May I—may I smoke? Please?"

"You may smoke."

Dawson Senior fired up aother cigarette and inhaled deeply, as though to restore some vital life force that had been sucked out of him. Recognizing the act for the desperate thing it was, Brian smiled again and began talking. After ten minutes he leaned back and said in conclusion, "You may go and get dressed now."

"Yes." It was a word his father had used repeatedly while being instructed.

"Perhaps you'd better take a shower, too."

"I took one before breakfast, when I shaved."

"You've been sweating. Take another."

"Yes."

"Yes, what?"

"Yes, my son."

"I prefer 'Yes, master.' "

"Yes—master."

"Now go. And don't be long."

It took the man who worked at the White House only a few minutes to shower and dress. When he reappeared, he looked a little more normal. He was, after all, the man from whom Brian Dawson had acquired his good looks, and the father was still more handsome than the son. But a close examination of his eyes, of something lurking behind his not quite steady gaze, would have betrayed a haunting or possession. Recognizing this, Brian escorted him to the door and said with a frown, "Are you able to drive?"

"Yes, I can drive."

"Be very careful. Time is of the essence, as I told you, but it will not help for you to have an accident."

"I will use care."

"Come back here as soon as you have carried out my instructions."

"Yes."

"Ring the bell when you return. I'll be resting and don't want you to walk in here, using your key, and find me asleep. Is that clear?"

"I must ring the bell."

"Now go."

Dawson Senior walked down the hall to the elevator. When the car rose to his summons and he disappeared into it, Brian shut the apartment door.

He was very tired again. All that had sustained him through the interview was the knowledge that he must not incur the wrath of his master by postponing it. Going into the bedroom, he took off his shoes and lay on the bed, gazing at the ceiling.

After a while the face of the Haitian bocor seemed to float there above him.

"Have I done well, master?" Brian asked without speaking aloud.

"Well enough for now. I was not pleased when you fell asleep in your car at the restaurant."

"Please . . . I didn't mean to do that. I was just so tired. Why didn't you wake me?"

"Because if you had driven right through without rest, you would have arrived too tired to be effective. And if aroused from sleep at such an early hour, your father might have been even more difficult to handle."

"I—see."

"Rest now. If he brings what you told him to, you will start back here at once, no matter what the hour."

"Yes, master."

The face faded. With a deep sigh, Brian closed his eyes and sank into what—just before it became sleep—seemed to be a slough of quicksand from which he struggled in vain to escape.

Chapter Twenty-five

Except for his socks, he was naked. Why was he naked?

Standing in scrub at the edge of a dirt road that was little more than a pair of ruts, Ken Forrest looked at his body and saw blood on it. Blood still oozed from punctures apparently made by thorns.

Had he fallen? He must have. Merely walking through the underbrush here would not have drawn blood from his upper arms and shoulders.

So he had fallen. But why had he been walking in such a place? Where was the car? Where was Sandy? And why was he naked?

Frightened, he looked around and saw his clothes in the road, close to fresh tire tracks in the dirt. The kind of tracks a car would make if clawing for quick acceleration in a drag race. A car had been here, then, and left in a hurry.

His car? Had he driven it here?

He had stopped at the junction of a shortcut along the western shore of Lake Okeechobee, he remembered. Sandy had questioned the wisdom of leaving the safety of the main highway when neither of them knew what the man in Gifford might do next. But he had overruled her objections.

Then what? His mind was a blank. He remembered nothing.

He stepped into his shorts, pulled his slacks on, knelt in the dirt to put on his shoes. As he struggled into his shirt, he saw a flash of yellow speeding along some kind of road nearby. A pickup truck, perhaps. The road could be the lakeshore highway he should be on with Sandy.

Why had he turned off it, along these ruts?

He began walking, though scarcely able to put one foot in front of the other. His head was made of lead but filled with stabs of pain. Lifting his left wrist, he peered at his watch and saw with dismay that the hands stood at twenty past ten.

They had left the motel at daybreak and couldn't have come more than thirty miles. Where had the time gone?

Where was Sandy?

Just a few yards ahead of him now, another vehicle sped along the road. A car this time, old, with a young black couple in it. Too late he called out and struggled to wave. They had not seen him.

The effort sapped the last of his strength and he pitched forward on his face in soft sand.

This time when he came to he was not on his feet, naked, but still sprawled in the road. And looking through the spokes of a bicycle wheel at a pair of tanned bare legs that disappeared into cutoff blue jeans. Lifting his gaze higher, he saw a freckle-faced boy about twelve years old clutching the bike's handlebars and peering down at him.

"Hello," Ken mumbled.

Jerking the bike with him, the youngster abruptly stepped back, as though intending to leap onto the saddle and ride away.

"Wait, please! I need help!"

Jerking the bike again, the boy did leap onto the saddle.

"Please! Wait! Help me!"

But the bike and its panic-stricken young rider had reached the blacktop. In a moment they were out of sight.

Ken struggled to his feet again. Again he began walking. On reaching the end of the ruts he turned to his right. How far was it to the nearest town? Miles. Too many miles for him to walk in this condition.

Please, God, let some good Samaritan come along.

He lost track of the time then, and his watch was no good to him. Something must have happened to it when he fell the second time. It had stopped and would not start again. The road went on and on, and though he halted on hearing cars coming and begged with outstretched hands for help, no car even slowed.

The sun pulsed like boiling metal in a cloudless sky. Heat waves floated up from the blacktop. Drenched with sweat, he plodded on.

Then up from behind him rattled an ancient green pickup, and in desperation he staggered into the middle of the road so it had to stop or run him down.

With squealing brakes it stopped. The two men peering at him were past middle age. Their prominent cheekbones and high coloring reminded him that he was on a road that ran through an Indian reservation.

They dropped to the road and approached him. From ten feet away one said, "Whatsa matter wit' you, mister? You tryna git yourself kilt?"

Ken hardly had the strength left for a reply but managed one. "I need—help—please."

The two halted a couple of yards from him and stood with arms akimbo, heads thrust forward, scowling. The clothes they wore were as decrepit as the pickup. They made no move to come closer.

He stumbled toward them. "Please . . ."

They glanced at each other and abruptly spun themselves about. Running now, they clawed themselves back into the truck as though fleeing from a devil. The engine came to life with a roar and the vehicle lurched forward.

Passing Ken, the driver veered so wide to avoid hitting him that the vehicle was briefly in danger of ending up in a roadside ditch. Then, all at once, its engine stalled and it came to a bucking halt.

Calling on his last reserve of strength, Ken ran after it.

A door flew open. He found himself looking at the muzzles of a double-barreled shotgun.

"You come one more step and I shoot, mister!"

He stumbled to a halt. The truck's starter snarled and its engine sputtered to life. As it pulled away down the road, the man leaning out of it continued to point his weapon at Ken.

Then it was gone, leaving silence in its wake. Through the stillness Ken staggered to the side of the road and sank into tall grass beside the ditch.

Why? Why had the boy with the bike fled from him in panic? Why had these Seminoles been willing to shoot him rather than give him a lift?

Why had Sandy gone off with the car, leaving him in the middle of nowhere?

He put his fingers to his face, half convinced he would feel some awful change there. Some transfiguration that could have occurred while he was lost in the swamp with the snakes. But it seemed no different from the face he shaved every morning.

He looked at the ditch, ten feet wide and water-filled. Unwilling to rise, he reached it on hands and knees, parted the grass at its edge, and peered at his reflection.

"My God!" he heard himself whisper.

It was not the same face. Oh, it might have passed for the same in a black-and-white photo if the camera wasn't too probing. All its parts were in place. But there was something in the eyes that did not belong there. Something too intense, cruel, even evil.

He put his hands to his eyes and rubbed them. Looked again at his face in the water. A breath of breeze had stirred the surface, and the reflection now seemed about to disintegrate. But the eyes—good God! They were even more fiercely staring than before, and seemed flecked with color.

Not their normal brown. These eyes were red.

Turning, he crawled back up to the road's edge and struggled to his feet. He had to go on. Had to find help.

Then find Sandy.

And then, with her, get to Gifford and rescue her daughter from the man who was causing these horrors to happen.

Chapter Twenty-six

When his father returned at seven, Brian Dawson was waiting apprehensively in the older man's apartment, thinking about the house in Gifford.

About the people in that house. His daughter, Merry. The man with no legs. The fat woman. The mousy Jumel.

There was no way he could free Merry by force or subterfuge, he knew now. That could be accomplished only by obeying the bocor's instructions. Meanwhile he was rested, had showered and shaved, had cooked and eaten a steak from his father's refrigerator, and had helped himself to a discreet amount of Scotch from his father's liquor supply.

There still remained the question of whether he had been able to carry out the bocor's commands.

It was a relief, in a way, to hear a knock on the door.

He went to the door and opened it. Looked at the man in the hall and almost felt a twinge of pity. In a single day the handsome Rutherford Dawson had aged ten years.

Brian drew him inside and shut the door. "Are you all right?"

"My God, my God, what a day." Clutching his attaché case, the older man sank onto a chair and leaned back with his eyes closed.

"You can rest later." Brian stood there glaring. "Talk now. Did you get what I told you to?"

The eyes grudgingly opened. A trembling hand thrust the attaché case toward him. "Here."

Snapping the case open, Brian eagerly took from it the three articles it contained. A bloodstained handkerchief. A sheet of paper covered with handwriting. A typewritten letter on presidential stationery, with a signature.

"These will do, I think. How did you manage it?"

"I did it." The voice was a groan. "Isn't that enough?"

"Tell me. This, for instance." Brian waved the letter.

"I had it in my desk. I was to check it for accuracy before sending it out."

"And this?"—holding up the handwritten page.

"He was rough-drafting a speech. I suggested he let me type it to make the rewrite easier." Anger flickered for a second in the eyes of Dawson Senior. "Damn you, Brian! This is the first time I've ever deceived that man. I despise you for making me do it!"

"You'll live with it." Brian held up the bloodstained handkerchief. "And this? Why the blood?"

"You said to bring you something he had worn or used."

"I know what I said."

"Well, for Christ's sake, I couldn't ask him to take something off and hand it to me, could I? So I—well, look." Rutherford Dawson thrust his left hand into his son's face. The tip of the longest finger had been sliced by something sharp, and there was dried blood in the wound. "I had a penknife open in my pocket. When I went in to give him the typed speech, I put my hand in and deliberately cut myself. He thought it an accident."

"And tried to stop the bleeding with his handerchief?"

"That's the kind of man he is. I went off with it wrapped around my finger."

Disappointment curdled the son's face. "So this is only your blood? If it were his—"

"What are you talking about? Brian, I don't understand any of this, but I know I don't like it!" The older man sat up straighter, finding strength in anger. "If anything happens to him because of what you've made me do, I—I—"

"You'll what?" Brian sneered.

His father was silent.

"All right, I'm leaving now." Brian replaced the items in the attaché case. "I'll be taking this."

"No! It was a gift from him!"

"Even better."

"You don't understand! It belonged to him!"

"He used it, you mean? Handled it?"

"Yes!"

"Good."

"But you can't—"

"Be quiet, Dad."

"No! I tell you—"

"Be quiet." This time the command was unspoken, but the senior Dawson seemed struck by a bolt of lightning.

"Y-yes," he whimpered. "Yes, master."

With the case in his hand, Brian walked into his father's bedroom. Reappearing a moment later, he tossed a remark over his shoulder on his way out of the apartment. "Be seeing you, Dad. You'll be coming to Florida soon."

"I will not!"

"Yes, you will." *You will, Daddy dear, because a certain Haitian sorcerer wants you there. And because this attaché case now contains, along with those other items, an old pair of shorts that you've worn many times.*

The shorts might not be needed, of course, now that he also had a handkerchief stained with Daddy's blood. But Margal had instructed him to obtain them.

On his way to the elevator he looked back and saw his father watching from the doorway. "Florida, Dad," he called back. "And I doubt you'll be coming alone."

Chapter Twenty-seven

Even for August the day was hot. Trudging along the blacktop, Ken felt the road's heat through the soles of his shoes, as though he were walking barefoot through fire.

He had seen that done once at a voodoo service near Savane Zombie in Haiti. Holding a red-hot iron bar aloft in both hands, a barefoot woman possessed by Ogoun Fer, one of the fire loa, had stood ankle deep for what seemed three or four minutes in the charcoal fire from which she had snatched the bar. Then she had stepped out unharmed, singing the loa's praises.

He plodded on. The heat waves rising from the road blurred his vision and made him dizzy. His watch had stopped. He had no idea of the time. But he must make himself keep walking. He must pray

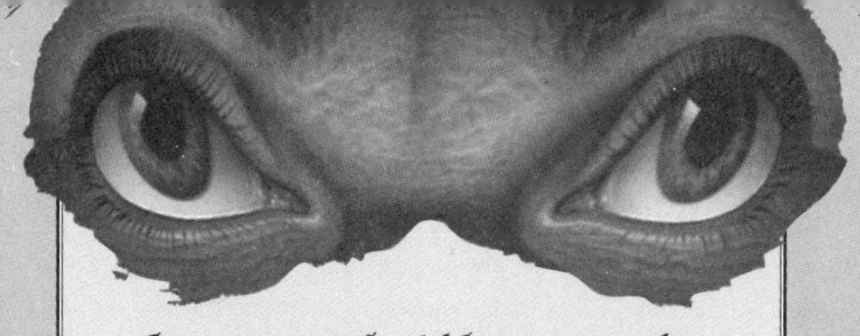

that someone would come along who would help him in spite of what the sorcerer in Gifford had done to his face.

He walked. He sat by the road to rest, then walked again. When he could no longer put one foot in front of the other, he sank onto the roadside grass again and slept.

For how long? When he struggled to his feet and trudged on again, the sun, on his left, was close to the horizon. He was still on the road through the reservation.

Through the heat haze he saw a car coming. It was going the wrong way, but in desperation he stumbled into its path anyway and weakly raised a hand.

It stopped. It was the car he had rented in Miami. Behind the wheel was Sandy Dawson.

Leaning from the wheel to open the door for him, she stared apprehensively as he approached. When he dragged himself onto the seat, she continued to stare. Not until he had pulled the door shut did she find her voice.

"Your eyes are still the same," she said. "But you don't know, do you?"

"I know. I saw my face in a ditch."

"Oh, God, Ken—what's happening?"

"It has to be Margal's work. I don't know how or why."

"Wait." She turned the car around, not the easiest thing to do there with grass growing in loose sand on both road shoulders. Shutting the engine off, she turned to study his face intently.

"At least, your eyes aren't as frightening as they

were when I left you," she said at last. "You must be getting over it."

"I don't know what they were like when you left me. I don't know why you left me." They were wasting time, Ken decided. "Look, we have to get to Gifford. We can talk while you drive."

With the car in motion again he leaned back in gratitude. God, how different this was from trudging along a fiery road under a blazing sun, with his head pounding!

Sandy said, "I came back to give you what you wanted."

Puzzled, he turned to look at her. "You what?"

"After getting away from you I drove nearly to Gifford. At least, I think I did. Then I realized I couldn't do anything by myself, not even go to the police. I don't know the name of the man whose house Merry is in. Or the address or phone number. Only you know those things. So I came back." She paused, then said again, "To give you what you wanted, in return for your help."

"What did I want?" He was almost afraid to ask.

"Don't you remember?"

He shook his head. "We took the shortcut, though I seem to remember you were afraid of it. What happened next I don't know. I came to with my clothes on the ground and blood on me from—I think—falling naked into a mess of thorns."

"You didn't fall. I pushed you."

"What?"

"You almost had my clothes off. You would have raped me."

"Oh, my God," he said.

"We'd been talking about the time we were in love, before I left you and married Brian. About how good it was, and how foolish I was to walk away from it. Then, without any hint of what was on your mind, you suddenly drove off the road and stopped in the middle of nowhere and dragged me out of the car and tried to tear my clothes off. Look." She twisted toward him to show him her blouse, which had buttons missing and was ripped across one breast, exposing her bra. "And your eyes were like something in a horror movie."

"My God."

"I panicked. I didn't know what was happening."

"That bastard Margal was happening," Ken said savagely. "Can you ever understand? Ever forgive me?"

"I'm here."

"I know you're here, but—"

"I came back for you." She reached out to touch him. "You'll never know how I prayed I'd be able to find you. All the way back, one prayer after another."

"Well—you needed me, you said."

"Yes, I needed you. But there was something else. Something more. Since we've been back together . . ."

She left it unsaid, and Ken responded by grasping and holding for a moment the hand that was still touching him. It was enough for now. He would be a long time forgiving himself for trying to take her by force, even if it had been Margal's idea.

"You must be tired," he said. "Want me to drive?"

"Should you, do you think? He has some power over you, Ken."

"Well, yes."

"Next time might be even worse. He might persuade you to drive into a ditch, or an oncoming truck. Something really final."

"All right. But if you get too tired . . ."

How, he wondered, had Margal known she was with him? Was it because they had been talking about the time before Brian, when they'd been in love and sleeping together? The Haitian was a reader of minds, and that conversation had created some vivid mental images.

Did he know what I was thinking about and order me to do it, to turn Sandy against me? To make her do just what she did, so we wouldn't be able to find him?

Sandy interrupted his thinking. "You know, if you had just told me you wanted me, the way we used to sometimes with each other, I'd have loved it. I know I wanted you. We were talking about it, remember?"

"Hey. We were trying to get to Gifford."

"Well, it was there. On our minds, I mean. We were planning it for later, sort of."

"Don't talk about it now," Ken warned. "Don't even think about it."

She shot an uneasy glance at him. "You mean you think—"

"He can read our minds. Mine, anyway. Talk about something he can't get a grip on."

"Well . . . suppose you talk. I'll just listen." She

frowned in thought. "Tell me about flying. What it means to you."

He hesitated. If he talked about flying, was there some way Margal could use his thoughts to destroy him? He didn't see how. Maybe if he were actually flying a plane, the bocor could give him a bad time, even cause a fatal crash, but what link could there be between thoughts of flying and this car, with Sandy driving the car?

All right, then. And, yes, it might be good for him to talk about what flying meant to him. Sandy had never really understood, had she?

Chapter Twenty-eight

In Gifford, Clarisse ate supper at the kitchen table with little Merry Dawson and the owner of the house, Elie Jumel. The three ate in silence, but suddenly Clarisse lifted her head as though listening. Then, abruptly, she stood up.

Sprawled near the back door, the two black dogs watched her every move. Both bared their fangs, as though to make sure she knew her place in this house.

Going to the door of the bedroom where Margal had eaten his supper alone, Clarisse tapped for permission to enter. Then she obeyed a second silent command and opened the door and said, "Yes?"

"Is there some way you can give me a bath, woman? I loathe the bathroom in this place."

"Well, I could bring a washtub from the kitchen."

"And hot water?"

"I can heat some."

"Good."

In the kitchen she filled the washtub at the sink and added hot water when the kettle spat out steam. Again the dogs watched her every move.

Returning to the bedroom, she placed the tub on a table beside the bocor's bed. Then, as she began to remove his red pajamas, which smelled of sweat on this too-hot August Sunday, she directed a look of annoyance at him and said testily, "How much longer are we to stay in this miserable place? If I may ask."

"Why?"

"Because I want to go home! And not to the heat and stink of Port-au-Prince, either. I want to go all the way home, to my mountains!"

"Be quiet," he commanded. "I have more important things to think about."

With his legless body naked, she began the daily ritual of bathing him. Actually, she enjoyed doing so. It was amusing to fondle his privates with soapy hands and watch his reactions. How did that old Haitian proverb go? *M'sieu fe sa li vlé; madame fé sa li kapab.* Or, as they would say it here: M'sieu does what he wants; madame does what she can.

A man didn't have to be a bocor for that to be true, either. It was true in most Haitian households. And maybe in many American ones, too.

Margal accepted her soapy caressing in silence, but the softness of his eyes and the ghost of a smile at the corners of his mouth told her that he was in a good mood. She could dare ask a few questions, then.

"Have you done anything about the man from Haiti who is trying to find us?"

"The pilot? Oh, yes."

"He is a pilot?"

"He flies for one of our sisal plantations, Marcel Odiol said."

"And what have you done about him, if I may ask?"

"Yesterday he lost his way and went miles in the wrong direction. They had to spend the night in an old motel."

"Is that all?" He could do better than that, she now knew. It might be difficult, though, having only a piece of paper money the fellow once held in his pocket.

Margal's retort was crisp. "I gave him a night to remember, if you must know. He fled from an imagined storm that terrified him. He wandered for hours in an unreal swamp full of snakes, in the presence of tree roots he thought were alive and waiting to devour him like a gathering of Erzulies."

"Erzulies? Devour him? What are you talking about?" The voodoo loa Erzulie was a goddess of love!

"Not the one you're thinking of, stupid," he said. "Not Fréda. I mean the one with the red eyes, Jerouge, who eats people."

Oh-oh, she thought. *Your personal loa. The one who puts that awful redness in your eyes.* It was a thought she wouldn't for a moment dream of expressing aloud. Certain facets of his sorcery were never to be discussed, he had warned her.

"What do you mean, they spent the night in a motel?" she asked. "Is someone with him?"

"A woman. And don't ask me who she is. In telling me of the white man who asked so many questions about us, Odiol did not mention a woman. I discovered her myself in the man's thoughts. And I used her this morning when he was thinking about having her naked in bed with him."

"You used her? How?"

"I persuaded him to rape her."

"How could that help us?" Clarisse demanded. "Or do you just enjoy manipulating people?"

"I expected her to become enraged and leave him."

"Did she?"

"Yes. In fact, she got away before he was able to rape her. But"—he shrugged—"she returned to him later."

Clarisse continued to bathe him, but something puzzled her now. If this pilot from Haiti was trying to find them, and if Margal had been able to delay him in the ways mentioned, why couldn't the sorcerer do something more drastic?

She put the question while gently washing his stumps. "Why can't he have an accident? Run into another car, for instance, or a tree, and be killed or badly hurt? You may be proud of yourself for what you've done, but is it enough?"

"Some men are more difficult than others," he

growled. "This one isn't made of putty like the child's father."

"What about the woman, then?"

"I told you I don't know who she—"

"Don't shout at me, please. I'm only trying to help." His bath finished, Clarisse took up a towel and began to pat him dry. "Could she be the child's mother, do you suppose?"

"The child's mother is in Port-au-Prince, trying to find her daughter."

"Are you sure? What if she somehow learned her daughter is here?"

"How could she do that?"

"The man did, didn't he? You take too much for granted, Margal. Why not exert yourself a little and find out who she is?"

"By reaching into the man's mind? I've tried that. No doubt he thinks of her name at times, but I haven't had the luck to be there when he does so. All I've heard is a pet name, *hon*, which I suppose is a contraction of 'honey.' "

"Well, is she the woman who used to walk with the child in Rue Printemps?"

He scowled into space. "Now that you mention it, she could be. But I never saw that woman up close, Clarisse. I can't be certain."

"Try the child," Clarisse suggested.

"What?"

"The child, Margal. You reached the father through her. If the woman is Madame Dawson, you should be able to reach her, too." She was patting his belly dry as she said this.

Its owner frowned at her until she finished, then slowly began to move his head up and down. "Fat one"—he reached up to touch her face in what was almost a caress—"I underestimate you sometimes, don't I? Of course I must try using the child! Bring me clean pajamas and get me ready!"

She brought the pajamas and put them on him. Lifting him in her arms, she placed him on the floor, far enough from the bed so that he could draw the usual circles when she handed him his chalk. While he drew them, she went to the chest of drawers for a candle.

While he lit the candle and carefully set it upright in the usual puddle of its own black wax, she watched him in silence, admiring the way he was able to move about using only his hands. She would never tire of serving this man, she thought.

Just think, not so long ago she had been only a fat country woman living in Margal's mountain village, aware of his presence but fearfully keeping her distance from him. A nobody. A nothing, with no future. Then he had lost his legs, and because he had needed someone big and strong, he had hired her to look after him. Now, praise the Ioa, she was the trusted companion and confidante of her country's most feared bocor! It was a miracle.

His face a grotesque mask of eagerness in the flickering light of the candle, Margal lifted his head to look at her.

"Ready?" she asked.

"You know I am! Bring the child!"

Chapter Twenty-nine

With Sandy at the wheel, Ken talked about flying. He had learned to fly, he reminded her, during his first two years at Miami U., when most of his classmates were spending their spare time at the beach.

He tried to explain what flying had meant to him as a student. How being able to rent a plane and soar above the grind had probably kept him from flunking out of school.

He tried to tell her how he had felt when flying over a city like Miami, looking down on wall-to-wall cubes of concrete that resembled so many tombstones in a cemetery. How he had shuddered at the lines of bumper-to-bumper vehicles crawling along the city's streets. How sometimes he had let out yells of pure ecstasy at being alone in a bright, clean world above all the ugliness.

"I was a country kid. Miami gave me the horrors at times. And I wasn't one of your brilliant students who could breeze through school without hitting the books. I had to hit them hard. So, when I could get away, I headed for an airport."

"I've never flown in a small plane," Sandy said. "Is it so different?"

He tried to tell her how it was different. While he talked, she handled the car with easy competence and they turned from the reservation road onto Route 70, leaving the town of Okeechobee behind them. He was still talking about flying when they neared Fort Pierce and swung north on I-95.

The afternoon was gone. Dusk lay like smoke now in the citrus groves.

"It must be a thrill to fly a small plane in Haiti, as you do," Sandy said. "I mean, there's so much of that country you can't see by road, even with four-wheel drive."

"When we get back, I'll fly you over the Citadelle. Have you ever been there?" He meant the famed mountain-top fortress of King Christophe, not far from the north-coast sisal plantation where he worked.

"Only the usual way, on horseback from Milot."

"From the air it's different. Incredible. You understand why it took years to build and cost so many lives. The whole Massif du Nord is incredible, for that matter. No roads. Only footpaths. Some of the villages in that wilderness are so remote, their people regard a trip to the coast as an expedition."

And the man we are now seeking once lived in

such a village, Ken thought. Or in his own private compound on the outskirts of one. With, if the tales are true, an enormous black woman looking after him, and zombies of his own creation doing the work around the place.

He talked about the times he had ridden into the Massif on muleback, to see for himself what the interior of that much-maligned country was really like. "Because, you know, Port-au-Prince isn't Haiti, hon. Not the real Haiti. Have you been to any of those voodoo ceremonies the tourists are taken to?"

"A couple."

"What did you think?"

"Well, they seemed real enough. Both were out of the city a few miles, in yards lit by lanterns. There were lots of people milling about. It was spooky."

"And good theater. You got what you paid for; no one cheated you. But it wasn't voodoo."

"What was it, then?"

"The trappings without the substance. The dancing, singing, drumming, all the things you'd been led to expect, but only for show."

"But—"

A sign on the right warned them that they were approaching the Vero Beach exit. Sandy made the turn and now, with their destination close, Ken felt some of the tension drain away. A few miles ahead lay Vero Beach itself, where they would swing north on Route 1 for the last short lap of this unreal journey. Dusk had become darkness. There was a hint of misty rain in the glow of the car's lights.

"Had you gone to those same *tonnelles* when they

were not expecting sightseers, you might have seen some actual voodoo," Ken said. "A planting service to Zaca, say, or a blessing of drums. Maybe even a *brulé zin*, with the initiates putting their hands into boiling oil. The people are genuine enough. It's only for tourists they put on a theatrical performance. Anything too close to the real thing might offend the loa."

Sandy reached out to touch his hand. "I'd like to attend a real service. With you."

"Good." He saw her take her other hand off the wheel as she turned to direct a strangely intent look at him—the kind of look he must have hoped for when he tried to undress her. "Hey!" he warned. "Watch your driving!"

It was too late. In trying to grab the wheel again she lost her balance and only made matters worse. Swerving to the right, the car lurched off the pavement into soft sand. With Sandy's foot still on the gas pedal, its right front wheel struck something solid and it careened over on its side.

Ken found himself on his back with Sandy on top of him, his arms loosely encircling her waist. His neck and one knee hurt. He had trouble breathing. But after a moment he was able to say, "Are you okay, hon?"

"I—think so."

"See if you can open your door." The driver's door was above her. The one on his side was under him, on the ground.

She reached up and tried the handle. To his relief, it worked. He let go of her waist and in slow motion, she climbed out of the machine. Then she reached in to help him do the same.

Together they stood there, some twenty feet from the road, gazing helplessly at the car. When he had recovered enough to realize there was no way they could get it back on four wheels without a wrecker, Ken turned to frown at his companion. In her eyes lurked a reddish tinge that made him feel as though something with many small, cold feet were crawling up his back.

He turned to look at the road. No one had witnessed the accident, apparently. Some distance away, bound east in the direction they had to go, a high pair of headlamps approached at no great speed.

He looked again into Sandy's eyes and grasped her hand. "Come on. Maybe we can hitch a ride to Vero."

There he could rent another car, he supposed—if there was a rental place open at this hour.

The headlights belonged to a van of some sort. Hoping for the best, Ken stepped into the road and raised both arms in a plea for assistance. The vehicle came to a stop beside him: a gray van with the words ZODT'S TV SERVICE and VERO BEACH in large blue letters on its side. And a phone number.

The driver leaned across the seat to open the door in Ken's face—a slender, swarthy fellow about thirty, with a touch of something unwholesome about him. That could have been the effect of his complexion—pockmarked, with a boillike lump under one eye—or the badly neglected teeth he displayed when opening his mouth to speak.

"What's the trouble, folks?"

"We've had an accident." Was it wise to ask help from such a man? Ken wasn't sure, but what if no one else stopped? Unless they took a chance here, they might have to walk to a service station he had seen at least a mile back, near the exit from 95.

"We'd be grateful for a lift into Vero." He had to say something.

The fellow eyed Sandy, who had taken a step forward and was closer to him now than Ken was. He stared at her face, which Ken could no longer see because her back was toward him. A crooked grin worked its way over his slack mouth. "Sure! Climb in!"

It happened without warning. Sandy took another step forward, a swift one, as though she could not reach the van fast enough. Using both hands, she pulled herself up beside the driver before Ken had even begun to move.

He was close enough, though, to hear what she said to the man at the wheel. Close enough to be shock-frozen into immobility even if he had been moving.

"Get rid of him!" was what she said. "Leave him here!"

The driver's grin spread to engulf his whole ugly face as he slammed the vehicle into gear and stepped the gas pedal to the floor. As the machine shot forward, Sandy pulled the door shut.

Wide-eyed and helpless, Ken stood there as

though turned to stone while the van sped down the road without him.

Margal, he thought as panic seized him. *He knows who she is now and has found a way to get into her mind. My God, what do I do now?*

Chapter Thirty

Heading south on Interstate 95, just past the city of Fredericksburg, Brian Dawson surprisingly found himself able to relax a little at the wheel of his Jaguar. It was as though a rope hauling him back to Florida had been allowed to go slack.

This puzzled him. (There was no way he could know that the man who owned his mind was presently more concerned with the mind of his wife.)

Was this his chance—at last—to get to the police?

Frightened by his daring to entertain such a thought, yet eager to carry it out, he watched for an exit sign.

Were there any good-size cities below Fredericksburg? He had forgotten. But never mind. Any exit would lead to a town with a police station.

A sign warned that he was approaching one, and

his eagerness increased. So did his fear. If Margal read his mind again, as the monster had done before in the restaurant parking lot . . .

Yet he must seize the chance. There might not be another!

What would he say to the police? He must be prepared, or they might not believe him. "Gentlemen, I am with the Department of State. My father is Rutherford Franklin Dawson. What I have to tell you may sound bizarre, but I entreat you to take me seriously."

Thank God he had shaved and was well groomed. Because he must win their confidence quickly, before the sorcerer became aware of his defection and took steps to make him appear drunk or drugged. If he suddenly became irrational, they must be informed enough to help him in spite of it.

The exit. Tense now, hands gripping the wheel so fiercely his knuckles were white, he forgot the wording on the sign the moment he was past it. No matter. Sooner or later there'd be a town, and he could ask for the station.

But hurry! For the love of God, hurry! It wasn't like Margal to be this careless. At any moment he might become aware of what was happening, and the punishment could be hideous.

Chapter Thirty-one

Ken was alone now—on an unfamiliar road, without a car, not knowing where Sandy had been taken or what might be happening to her.

If he had read the face of the van driver right, something terrible could be happening. Something ghastly, unless he could get to her in time to prevent it.

What could he do? He had so few options. A mile or so to the west was the service station he remembered. But how could they help him, other than by letting him use a phone? Vero Beach was east, but how far?

He didn't know this part of Florida. The Space Coast, they called it, because of the space flights from Cape Canaveral. In Vero he could go to the police, of course. But what then?

Would the police believe him? Or would they take one look at him and be suspicious? If his eyes still had that color, they'd have every right to be suspicious and might hold him for questioning. They might question him for hours.

Terrible things could happen to Sandy before he convinced them he was telling the truth. Terrible things could happen to her little girl, too, in the house in Gifford that seemed so hellishly hard to reach.

But what could he do alone? Even if a phone book supplied the address of the TV service, he would need a car to get there and someone with authority at his side when he confronted the man.

And what, dear God, if Sandy refused to be rescued? What if she thought she wanted to be where she was? Even the police would find their hands tied then, wouldn't they?

He began walking toward the city, forcing himself to a fast pace at first, then slowing to a shuffle as he tired. Cars passed, but none stopped until he walked at least a mile. Then it was the kind of vehicle a car-loving kid would drive, old but done over, with flashy wire wheel covers and a new red paint job.

Behind the wheel was a six-foot towhead who had to be a high-school fullback. His blue jeans were a second skin. His red T-shirt yelled in white I'D RATHER BE FISHIN'.

"Hey, you look tired, mister. Want a ride?"

Gratefully, Ken got in.

"Where you headin'?" the youth asked, putting the car in motion again.

"I don't know. The police, I suppose. I—we had an accident."

"We?"

"My girlfriend and I. The car went off the road back there. Turned over."

"Jeez." The youth made a face. "Where is she now?"

"That's just it. A van came along. The driver stopped to pick us up. But the minute she was in beside him he took off like a drag racer, leaving me there."

"You mean he kidnapped her?"

"It looks like it."

"Right here on this road? Jeez! It don't seem possible."

"That's why it worked, I guess. I just didn't expect it. If I had—"

"You any idea who the guy was? A van, you say? Commercial? A name on it?"

"Zodt's TV Service, Vero Beach. And a phone number I didn't really look at."

"Hell, I know where Zodt's is at. The driver a little skinny guy with pimples and bad teeth?"

"Yes, yes!" Perhaps this husky teenager would want to help.

"What's your name, mister?"

"Ken Forrest."

"Where you from?"

"I work for a sisal firm in the West Indies, flying. But I'm an old Florida hand. Went to Miami U."

"You're a flyer? A pilot?"

"Yes."

"Jeez!" A touch of awe sent the voice up half an octave. "Well, look, I bet we can find this guy, if you're game to try. You game?"

"How?"

"First we go to his shop. If he's not there, we look up his home address in the phone book and try that. Okay?"

It was less risky than going to the police. "Okay. And thanks. I don't know how—"

"Your name's Ken, huh?" The kid thrust out a hand that looked big and strong. "Mine's Wayne. Wayne Lawry. Glad to make your acquaintance."

"I'll bet you play football."

"I did last year, but I quit school. Got me a job in a fish house now, in Sebastian."

They were coming into the city, Ken saw, and Wayne Lawry was a competent driver, handling his rebuilt car with ease in the thickening traffic. You had to be a good driver here; the streets must have been laid out by blind men. As he coped with seemingly senseless traffic patterns, the youth kept up a running commentary.

"Lemme see now . . . Seems to me that shop was out there in back of where Rent-a-Wreck used to be. Yeah. One of those warehouse-type places on a dirt road off Route One . . ."

They were on Route 1 now, Ken saw by a highway sign. Traffic heavy. A shopping center on the right, mostly car dealers on the left. What would he and the kid do if the man with bad teeth was armed? He had looked like the kind who might be—and who would use a weapon without hesitation if he felt himself threatened.

Young Wayne voiced a triumphant "Ha! Sure!" and swung so sharply onto a narrow dirt road that the car traveled for yards on only two wheels. After settling back down with a thud, it abruptly slowed to a crawl, then proceeded like a stalking cat for another hundred yards before coming to a halt.

Just ahead was a long aluminum shed with four closed doors. Above one of them a weathered black-on-white sign read ZODT'S TV SERVICE. Under it gleamed a thread of light. In front of it stood the van.

"Your girlfriend's in there," Wayne Lawry said. "I figured he wouldn't take her home. He's married." He flashed Ken an anxious glance, as though afraid that in this off-beat area, in the dark, his newfound buddy might have become timid. "You okay, Ken?"

"I'm okay."

"Leave him to me, hey? I'm younger'n you and most likely in better shape." Sliding out, he took time to close the car door quietly.

Ken was only a stride behind him as they approached the shop door.

It was a metal door with no glass in it. No way to see what was going on inside. Wayne put a hand on the knob and tried it. It would not turn. "Locked," he whispered. "Stand back so he won't see you."

His knuckles beat a tattoo on the metal.

No answer.

He knocked again, more insistently. "Hey, Mr. Zodt!"

Inside, a sound of footsteps. Then a voice close to

the door said, "We're closed. What you want?"

"Got a package for you from Bill's TV." Was there such a place in Vero? Ken wondered. There probably was. This kid was sharp.

A scratchy, metallic sound as the lock turned. The door inched open and an eye peered out. The voice said, "All right, give it—"

Wayne Lawry responded by hurling himself at the barrier as though he were only a yard from an opponent's goal with a football in his grip.

The door clattered wide and he was inside with Ken at his heels.

It was a poor kind of shop. A couple of dozen TV sets, obviously secondhand, covered the concrete floor on both sides of an open lane to a grimy counter. A wall behind the counter went only partway to the ceiling and displayed a row of calendars featuring nude women. The wall contained an open door to a dimly lit room in the rear, in which Ken could see an old refrigerator, a threadbare couch, and a work bench littered with sets being repaired.

In front of the couch, in bra and panties, stood Sandy Dawson, both hands behind her back, seemingly stopped in the act of unfastening the bra. On her face was a look of annoyance or anger.

Anger at what? Being interrupted in the act of undressing for Zodt's pleasure?

Ken started toward her but stopped. The TV man had backed up a few steps and dropped into a crouch. With knees bent and arms spread wide, he rocked gently on his toes, facing young Wayne.

"You ain't from Bill's. What the hell you want?"

"You," Wayne said.

"Out! Get your ass out of here, God damn it!"

"Shall I take him, Ken?" Wayne asked over his shoulder.

"Be careful," Ken warned. The crouch looked too—what? Professional?

"Try it, junior," the TV man challenged.

Wayne charged.

What happened was some form of karate, Ken guessed. Only once before had he seen anything like it: a night in Port-au-Prince when he and a couple of friends had gone to a theater on the Champ-de-Mars to see a Chinese martial-arts film.

Zodt leaped from his crouch and met the boy's charge with his right foot high. The side of his shoe took Wayne under the chin with a sound like that of a baseball bat clouting a home run. Without even a grunt, the youth flew through the air and sat down in a sprawl.

The vacant expression on his face said he would not soon get up again.

Zodt glared at Ken. "You too, sucker?"

With arms poised, Ken advanced. In the movie there had been a way to counter Zodt's brand of attack. After seeing it, he and his friends had retired to a little self-service bar in a nearby pension, the Etoile, to practice it, sort of. If he could just remember it now . . .

Zodt shot out of his crouch again, the right foot stabbing upward so swiftly, it seemed only a blur. Ken dipped sideways and grabbed the ankle in both hands. Lunging in close, he wrapped both of his legs around the other's left one, then pushed up on the karate man's right with all his strength.

They crashed to the concrete together in that position.

Zodt swore. Then, with his legs being forced apart, he stopped swearing and moaned. When the treatment worsened, the moans became whimpers.

Not until even the whimpers ceased did Ken let go and stand up, leaving him out cold on the floor. A little distance away, young Wayne Lawry was on his hands and knees, groggily shaking his head as he tried to rise.

Ken helped him up. "You all right?"

"Jeez. I thought my head came off."

"Are you okay?" There wasn't time for this.

"I guess so. Yeah."

Striding toward the back room, Ken looked down at the TV man. Zodt lay on his back with his mouth open in a frozen cry of agony. It would have been satisfying to apply one of his own karate kicks to his face, if only to knock the rotten teeth out. Instead, Ken hurried on by.

"Sandy . . ."

She was still in front of the couch, reaching behind her to unfasten her bra. A statue. A stop-action, life-size photograph. A figure in a wax museum. Staring straight at him as he took hold of her shoulders, she seemed not even to see him, though the look of annoyance was still on her face.

"Sandy!" He shook her and nothing happened. Slapped her face and shook her again. Kept shaking her until the look changed into one of bewilderment and recognition flickered in her eyes. Her eyes were still red, he noticed.

"Where are we?" She was looking around now, confused and frightened. "What are we doing here?"

It could wait. Turning, he saw her shoes on the floor and her skirt and blouse on a bench where either she or Zodt had tossed them. "Come on, we have to get you dressed!"

The red in her eyes was fading, thank God. There was still some alien color in the whites, but not so much of it. He helped her put her clothes back on. Knelt to guide her feet into the shoes while she leaned on him to keep from falling. Then he led her to the front part of the shop.

The TV man was still out on the floor. Young Lawry had the front door open, waiting. "Now what?" the youth asked, rubbing his jaw but grinning as the three of them hurried to his car.

"I don't know. We have to get to Gifford. If I can rent a car—"

"Gifford isn't far. I can take you there."

"Thanks, but I need a car anyway." Helping Sandy into the boy's made-over hot rod, Ken got in beside her. "Didn't you say something about a Rent-a-Wreck place?"

"Yeah, but they moved. They're north of town now."

"On the way to Gifford?"

"That's right. Yeah."

"Then if we could stop there—that is, if the place is open—"

"We can sure check," Wayne said cheerfully.

There was a light on in the Rent-a-Wreck office, and a man at the desk. A credit card produced a small two-door sedan. Ken turned to Wayne Lawry and clasped his hand.

"You sure you're all right?"

"Well—" The youth rubbed his jaw again, as he had done several times since leaving the TV shop.

"You may have to see a doctor. Look, take this in case you have to." Ken fingered a hundred-dollar bill from his wallet.

The boy shook his head. "Jeez, no! That's way too much!"

"Take it. Here's my card, too. If you have problems, write me in Haiti. I want to know."

"Well, gee . . . you're the one got your lady away from that creep, not me."

"Without you she'd still be there. So long, and God bless." Ken turned away, certain the lad would suffer for being a good Samaritan but not knowing how else to help him. They couldn't stay with him or seek a doctor for him. They couldn't even go back to the wrecked car for their luggage. They were only a few miles now from the house in Gifford where Sandy's daughter was being held prisoner.

That maddeningly elusive house.

Was it real, or just a phantom?

Chapter Thirty-two

"Can you direct me to the police station?"

"Eh?"

"The police station!" Brian Dawson was now so nearly terrified by what he was daring to do, his voice sounded like steel on glass.

Fortunately the old man on the curb did not interpret fear as rudeness. Or didn't care enough to make an issue of it. With a shrug, he turned from peering at Brian's not-now-handsome face to point to an intersection just ahead.

"Police station y'want? Just make a right turn there, mister, and go three blocks. It'll be on your right. Y'can't miss it."

There was no time to thank him. Getting here from Interstate 95 had used up all but a small fragment of Dawson's initial resolve, and he shook now with an all-consuming fear. Unless he reached the police station in a few minutes, he would not have the courage to enter it.

His silver Jaguar made the turn on squealing tires, but then had to slow to a maddening crawl behind a truck that hogged the street. Recklessly passing the offender at the next intersection, he covered the second block in only a few precious heartbeats of time. Then, as he feverishly waited for a traffic light to change at the final crossing, the voice of the man in Gifford exploded like a thunderbolt in his brain.

"Go to the right here, M'sieu Dawson!"

The light turned green and he sat frozen behind the wheel, incapable of moving hands or feet. The truck growled up behind him, its driver leaning on the horn.

"No, master," Dawson whimpered. "No, no—please!"

"Do as I say! At once!"

He turned to the right, nearly sideswiping a car and earning from its driver an outburst of profanity. Completely disorganized now, he almost welcomed the next command that crackled in his head.

"Draw up to the curb and stop!"

The drivers of passing cars eyed him askance while giving him a wide berth. Had the Jaguar been moving less slowly, it would have climbed the sidewalk.

It lurched to a stop with both right-side tires squeezed out of round against the curb.

"Now sit and listen. For I am on the verge of losing patience with you!"

Dawson's hands slid from the wheel into his lap and struggled there like dying crabs. There was a nearly intolerable ache inside his head. Moaning from the pain of it, he squeezed his eyes shut.

"Before I allow you to resume your homeward journey, m'sieu, take time to consider what may happen if you dare to challenge me again." Though quieter now, the voice seemed even more relentless, in the way a hysterically furious man becomes even more dangerous with his rage under control. "Are you hearing me?"

"Yes . . ."

"And paying close attention?"

"Yes, yes . . . I swear it!"

"I could cause you to drive at high speed into an oncoming truck. You agree?"

Merry Dawson's father squeezed his eyes more tightly shut while moving his head up and down.

"Answer me!"

"Y-yes, you could. I know it."

"I could cause you to drive off the road into a tree. Or into a roadside canal deep enough to drown you. Is that not so, too?"

"It is so. Yes, master."

"I could even, if I wished, cause you to stop your car by the side of the road and take the cap off the gas tank and drop in a lighted match, could I not?"

"You—you could."

"There are so many ways I could destroy you, m'sieu. So many, many ways, depending on my whim at the moment. Some of them could be most interesting. Think of how the newspapers might report them. 'Last night the son of the President's right-hand man was found naked beside a highway in Virginia with his wrists slashed, apparently a suicide.' You do carry a penknife in your pocket, you know. Such a pretty one, too, with mother-of-pearl inlays in its silver handle."

Not called upon to reply, Dawson only voiced a moan of terror.

"Or suppose the papers were to report . . . well, never mind. If I alarm you too much, you may have a legitimate accident. We don't want that, do we? You must arrive here safe with the items I sent you for. No?"

"What—ever you say, master."

"Good. Now return to the road you should not have left and resume your journey. And this time keep in mind that you are not alone. Until I no longer have a use for you, you will never for one moment be alone again. Let the ache in your head warn you that Margal the bocor dwells there, reading your every thought."

Brian Dawson opened his eyes and they overflowed with tears that trickled down his cheeks. His whole body trembled. But he was able to put the car in motion again and, as ordered, continue his homeward journey.

In Gifford, Clarisse stood beside the bed on which her master had just finished his dialogue with Brian Dawson. "You are tired," she said, peering with compassion at his fire-scarred face.

"Only *le bon dieu* knows how tired," he agreed,

exhaling heavily. "This business takes too much out of a man. Think of how many I am required to control—M'sieu Dawson, his wife, his child, and the pilot fellow who, let me tell you, is not easy. And soon I shall have to include Dawson's father and the biggest conquest of all."

Reaching out, he patted her hand as she bent over to adjust his pillow. "We must find a way to lighten the burden, my pigeon. Think about it, eh? Perhaps we can make use of our mouse, Jumel."

Chapter Thirty-three

Something about the woman beside him was not right, Ken decided. She looked like the Sandy of old, except for a hint of red remaining in her eyes, but she wasn't.

It wasn't a difference he could put a finger on. But since rescuing her from the TV shop he had been uneasily aware of it.

Now as he drove north on U.S. 1, on what ought to be the final leg of their nightmare journey to Gifford, he glanced at her and said, "Think, hon. Did he give you anything?"

"Did he what?"

"Did you use any drugs?"

"Ken, I've told you." She was annoyed with him for his persistence, he sensed. "I don't remember what happened."

"Not any of it?"

"No, not any of it!"

She didn't even remember wrecking the car, she had told him. In fact, she only barely recalled having turned off I-95 at the Vero Beach exit. All the rest, including her driving off with Zodt and leaving him there by the road, was a blank.

She must have been given something by the TV man to make her welcome the creep's advances, Ken reasoned—if only because such a man could be expected to have drugs on hand. And whatever he had dosed her with must have been potent. Her speech was blurred now, and even the slightest movement seemed to require a special effort.

He ought to be taking her to a doctor. But there wasn't time.

Vero Beach was behind them. The Sunday night traffic was light. Coming up on the right was a country-style bar with an oversized sign that read JAKE'S PLACE.

Wayne Lawry had mentioned the bar. This was Gifford.

The address Ken had was 21 Petrea Road. Where in Gifford that might be he hadn't a clue. Maybe he could find out in the bar.

He swung into the almost empty parking area and got out. "Hon, I won't be long."

"Ken, I'm frightened!" Sandy said.

"I'll be as quick as I can. Or you could come in with me."

"No, no! Just—if he should start working on my mind again and I'm alone—"

Ken hesitated, then saw that he might not have to go into the bar after all. Near its door stood a young black woman in a white blouse and bright red slacks.

Reaching into the car, he touched Sandy on the shoulder. "Just sit tight."

"You lookin' for someone?" The girl in the red slacks had her hands on her hips and a knowing look on her face as he approached her.

"A friend who lives on Petrea Road. But I don't know how to get there."

"You have a friend on Petrea Road?"

"Why not?"

"You the wrong color, mister."

The best response to that had to be a laugh, he decided. To his surprise she laughed back at him. "All right, Brother Whitey." She stepped closer to peer into his face. "Just go up that road over there and take your first left and . . ."

Knowing she probably wouldn't repeat them, Ken listened carefully to her directions. It was well that he did, for had he been less than attentive, her next remark might have wiped them from his mind. Extending a long forefinger with a gilded nail, she tapped his belt buckle and said with a scarlet-lipped smile, "After you through callin' on your friend, brother, if you decide to ditch that lady in the car and come lookin' for me, you not goin' be sorry. Y' hear?"

"Suppose you're not here?"

She shrugged. "Looks like I will be. It's real quiet tonight. So you think about it, hey?"

"I'll do that."

Returning to the car, he slid in behind the wheel. "It's all right, Sandy. I found out how to get there." When she didn't answer, he turned to look at her and saw that her eyes were closed. "Hey!"

Her eyes grudgingly opened. In spite of her fear of being left alone in the car, she must have fallen asleep. Drugged, he thought again. But what had the bastard given her? What effect would it have on her if, when they neared the house they were seeking, Margal took over her mind again?

"Did you—?" Gazing at him, she shook her head, as though to clear it. "Did you find out how to get there?"

"Yes. Relax now, hon. Sleep if you want to. I'll wake you."

She came back a little more from where she had been. "Ken—what do you plan on doing when we get there?"

He had been thinking about that. "First we make sure Merry is there. Margal may have moved her, knowing we're closing in on him in spite of all he's done to stop us."

"But—"

"When we're sure we'll be sending the police to the right place, we'll go to them." Sensing she was about to argue, he shook his head at her. "Look at us, Sandy. You've been drugged. I could be a drifter. The police won't want to believe what we tell them, and if we aren't sure of ourselves . . ."

And suppose Merry had been moved from Jumel's house, he thought. By themselves they would not be able to find her and would have to go to the police anyway—even if their chance of being listened to was close to zero.

It could be the end of the line.

With Sandy now silent he drove on, following the black girl's directions. Each turn seemed to produce a darker, less traveled road than the one they had left. The night itself was black, with few stars visible. For some reason even the car's lights seemed less bright than they should have been.

They were bright enough, though, to pick out the road sign he was seeking. Then a mailbox loomed up on the left with the name JUMEL on it, in front of a shabby house with glowing windows.

He drove past without even slowing. "Mustn't let them think we're anything but a passing car," he said when Sandy protested. A bend in the road took them beyond sight of the house and he sought a place to pull off. "I'd better hide the car, hon." Sandy would be less nervous then on being left in it while he reconnoitered.

He found a grass-grown pair of ruts that angled off behind a screen of twisted melaleuca trees. Driving in, he switched off the lights. "Now you wait here for me, Sandy. I won't be—"

"No!" As he opened his door, her fingers fastened on his arm. "You're not leaving me here!"

"But—"

"Not after what that man has already done to me, Ken! I'm going with you!"

She was right, of course. Margal was working on her mind now, as well as his. To leave her here could be risky. He might return to find she had driven off again without him.

"Well, all right. But remember, all we want is to make sure Merry is there. No confrontation if we find out she is."

They were both out of the car now. Reaching for her hand, he began to walk her along the ruts. "I understand, Ken," she said almost inaudibly. "I won't do anything foolish."

Together, in silence, they returned to the road.

But something had happened to it. It was not the same road.

In fact, it was not a road at all.

Ken halted, releasing her hand and drawing her close to him with a protective arm around her shoulders. "What the hell . . . ?"

He frowned down at his feet. The ground on which he stood was not the blacktop they had driven over in the car. Was it the floor of a cave?

No, not a cave. It was of stone, but this stone was in rough-cut rectangular blocks. In the cracks between them grew weeds and moss.

He turned to look for the trees on either side. They had vanished. In their place were walls of the same material as the roadway, turning the road into a tunnel.

He looked up. The tunnel had a stone ceiling. And he had been here before.

"Sandy . . ."

"Where are we?" she whispered.

He thought he knew but was not prepared to say so until he was certain. "Come on." Taking her hand, he drew her along the tunnel. If he were right, there would be apertures—gun ports, actually—along one wall. Through them he would be able to see . . .

They came to one and he halted. Yes, it was like those he remembered. But he had been here only in daylight and couldn't see what lay out there now, at night. Yet somehow he was sure the walls of a nearly two-hundred-year-old fortress rose high above the corridor in which he stood, and its massive entrance door lay frighteningly far below. And beyond the small strip of flat land leading to that door, an almost vertical mountain slope fell steeply into one of the many deep valleys of Haiti's Massif du Nord.

"Oh, my God," Sandy said. "Ken, where are we?"

"What to do you see?" Surely not what he was seeing, unless the illusionist was now able to manipulate both of them at once.

"A corridor with stone walls, a stone floor, a stone ceiling. It's like—like—"

"The Citadelle, in Haiti?"

"Yes!"

The Citadelle Laferriére. That never-completed but still incredible mountaintop fortress near the north-coast city of Cap Haïtien, built so many years ago by King Christophe. Both of them had been there, he more than once. Was that why Margal was able to take them back?

Take them back for what?

To mind came some of the grisly stories connected with the place, most of them no doubt true. How some twenty to thirty thousand peasant workmen had perished while building it, either from exhaustion while dragging the monstrous blocks of stone four and a half miles up from the valley, or by falling to their deaths while slaving to erect the walls. How once, to show an aghast English diplomat how magnificently loyal his troops were to him, Christophe had drilled a company of them on the windswept highest level and given a command that sent them marching off its edge.

Christophe himself, dead by his own hand after a paralytic stroke, was entombed here in the central courtyard.

And now, thanks to the wizardry of a Haitian sorcerer born in these same northern mountains, Sandy Dawson and Ken Forrest were here again.

At night, this time. Alone. In a world of ghosts.

For what?

"Come on!" Ken grasped his companion's hand. "Let's get out of here!"

They stumbled on down the corridor, its inky blackness unbroken exept for patches of faint starlight shining through the gun ports. Black cannon shapes loomed in front of some ports, with pyramids of equally black cannonballs beside them. A right-angle turn led to another tunnel, and they were trapped in a nightmare.

A nightmare of walking. No, not really walking; it was impossible to do that in such darkness, over rough stone floors that kept causing them to stumble into unseen walls. All they could do was cling to each other and grope along with their free hands outstretched to warn of hidden dangers ahead. On and on from one corridor to another, with only the gritty whisper of their footsteps to keep them company. Unless, Ken thought, one ought to count the ghosts of the many Haitians who, while toiling here, had given their lives to create this fantastic monument to their mad monarch.

Suddenly the dark was behind them. Stumbling from its clammy embrace, they found themselves confronted by a rising flight of stone steps misty with starlight and began to climb.

A small but persistent voice whispered a warning in Ken's mind: Don't do this. Don't! But he could not respond. Instead, he said eagerly to the woman behind him, "Come on, hon! I know where we are now!"

Yes, he knew. These narrow steps, whose only handrail was space, led to the Citadelle's topmost level, a vast stone platform as windy as the flight deck of an aircraft carrier. Always uncomfortable in exposed high places, he had broken out in a cold sweat while walking that upper level.

Unable to help himself, he toiled on up, turning at the top to extend a hand to Sandy as she struggled up behind him. They stood on the flight deck together, with a mountain breeze drying their sweat and pressing their clothes against them.

"Why—have we come up here?" Sandy asked fearfully.

Yes, why? He turned to look around, as though the surrounding peaks of the massif might hold an answer even though they were scarcely visible. To be standing here in the dark was awesome. The sky must be full of clouds. He couldn't see them, but they had to be there because so few stars were aglow in a tropical sky that normally would be ablaze with them. Staring, he slowly walked away from his companion.

Forgot about her.

Felt he was alone.

Moments must have passed, for when the sudden clatter of a kicked stone caused him to turn, Sandy was not at the top of the steps where he had left her. She too was in motion.

Seemingly unaware of what she was doing, she was walking straight toward the edge of the lofty drill area where Christophe had marched his troops to destruction!

"Sandy!" Her name burst wildly from his lips as he raced after her. "Sandy! For God's sake, stop!"

Chapter Thirty-four

Dear God, she was too far away. He would not be able to reach her in time.

"Stop, Sandy! Don't do it!"

She wasn't hearing him. Not paying the slightest attention. She was just plodding on as though mesmerized, with the edge of space only a few yards in front of her.

Like Christophe's sacrificial soldiers, she would walk blindly off the highest point of the fortress, to be shattered on the rocky mountainside far below.

He was hurtling toward her like a sprinter now, with head thrust forward, feet pounding the stone, the mountain wind lashing his face. No breath left to cry out her name again. She hadn't heard him anyway.

To reach her in time he would have to throw out

his arms and leave his feet in a diving tackle. It might hurl her over the edge, she was so close to it. The momentum of his dive might carry him over with her.

He had no choice. It was the only way.

His hands curled in mid-dive as he reached for her ankles. That was the first thing he felt—her ankles in his grasp. Then his knees and chest hit the rough stone with a lightning-flash stab of pain, as though he had attempted a swan dive into a waterless pool.

There followed an instant of blackout in which he had no idea whether his hands still circled Sandy's ankles or had fatally lost their grip.

When the blackout passed, Sandy was in front of him with her head and shoulders over the brink, staring down wide-eyed in a silent paroxysm of terror. But his hands had not failed her. Drawing her to safety, he helped her to her feet and led her back to the top of the stone stairway.

They had climbed the stairs without incident, but he could take no chances now. "Let me start down first," he instructed. "Then you turn around and come down backward, as you would on a ladder. Can you do that?"

"I'll—try, Ken."

He went down backward himself, having to feel for each step with his feet before bracing himself to reach up and guide hers into place. The mountain wind strengthened and began to moan through rooms and corridors below. Something white materialized in the darkness and, after giving him a moment of near panic while floating toward them, turned out to be a huge white owl.

Haiti's mountain folk had a superstition about white owls. If one circled a house at night, someone inside would die before daybreak.

Nonsense, of course. But in this brooding land of witchcraft, Christophe's monstrous Citadelle seemed to whisper fierce warnings against complacency.

They reached the bottom and he found himself able to breathe normally again as he reached for Sandy's hand. "Come on now. It's time we got out of here."

Again the corridors were black as caves except for starlight shining through the gun ports. Again the ghostly cannon, never used to repel the expected assault by French troops seeking to recapture Napoleon's lost colony, were hazardous as unseen obstacles to be blundered into in the dark.

Leading the way, Ken paused every few yards to be sure Sandy was still close behind him. Some chambers were roofless now as they neared the central courtyard. Here the cannon were half hidden by weeds that had established roots between the stones. And as corridors changed levels for no apparent reason, unexpected flights of steps increased the hazards.

And always there were footsteps.

Those were of their own making, of course. Had to be! Even if the Armée d'Haiti still quartered a few prisoners here to police the ruins, they would not be awake at this hour. Certainly not prowling in the dark through a place they believed to be haunted.

Yet the never silent echoes sounded like pursuers' footfalls, at times safely behind but at other times so close, Ken could not resist lurching about to see who might be there.

It was a relief to emerge at last into the huge central courtyard with its pervading mist of starlight. A blessing to leave behind the walls and stirred-up dust, and feel the clean mountain breeze again. Then, as he sought a half-remembered route to the lowest level and its door to the world outside, a sudden shaft of moonlight pierced the clouds and, like a spotlight in a theater, illuminated something white in their path.

A white block of stone, coffin-shaped, in the center of walkways outlined with equally white rocks. Ken stopped. "Christophe."

To this spot in 1820 the corpse had been carried secretly up the mountain from the palace of San Souci, in the dead of night, and lowered into a pit of lime to save it from desecration by a mob of the king's disillusioned followers.

Sandy clung to Ken's arm. "What did you say?"

"The grave. His. Wonder how he likes being buried up here where so many died because of him."

Together they gazed at the tomb, Ken no longer fearful they would have to spend the night here. It was not the first time he had stood in this spot. "I know the way out now."

Out to where, though? A mountainside in Haiti or a country road in Florida? A terrifying world of illusion or back to a reality equally perilous? Anyway . . .

Taking Sandy's hand again, he said, "Come on, hon. We're okay now."

But it was not to be so simple. His "way out" led only to more tunnels, more stairs, more darkness and pursuing footfalls. Soon, despite the chill caused by the damp stone of their prison walls, he began to sweat as he realized his memory was failing him.

But, damn it, all they had to do was descend, wasn't it? The way out of this hellish pile was at the bottom . . . wasn't it?

Doggedly he trudged on, aware that he was nearing the end of his stamina. How long had they been wandering in this nightmare? Perhaps not always, as he was beginning to feel in his desperation, but certainly for most of a long, eerie night. And if he was running out of endurance, what about Sandy?

Halting, he leaned against a wall and waited for her to catch up to him. Heard her stumble not once but twice as she covered only a few yards of darkness. Could tell by the sound of her breathing that she was even more exhausted than he.

She stumbled once more, this time into his waiting arms. For a moment she seemed unable to get her breath at all. Then she moaned softly, "Oh, God, Ken, I'm so tired. Can't we rest?"

Easing her to the floor of the passageway, he sat beside her and took her in his arms again. Would they ever find a way out, or were they doomed to wander here forever?

She slept. After a while, so did he.

When he opened his eyes, there was a sky above

instead of a stone ceiling. Its grayness seemed to herald the start of a new day.

Or was that the color of a day just dying?

At any rate, he lay not on cold stone but on his back in deep grass.

Was he still in Haiti? He had gone to sleep there with Sandy in his arms, and she was still asleep beside him. Yet the feel of being in Haiti had fled, and this bed of tall grass was certainly not in the Citadelle.

Over him stood a man with a black face, silently peering down at them. The face appeared to be Haitian.

But many residents of Gifford, Florida, were black, too . . . weren't they?

Chapter Thirty-five

At Elie Jumel's house in Gifford, in the bedroom where he spent most of his time, the man without legs gazed at the woman who had just come in with his supper. The grimy windows were beginning to darken.

"Clarisse."

"Yes, Margal."

"You and the child will sleep on the front-room floor tonight, as you did before. Her father will be returning."

"If you say so. Move over a little."

"What?"

"Move over. It's more comfortable for you to have this on the bed"—she meant the tray she was holding—"than on the table, where you have to reach for it."

He obeyed without an argument. A sign, she guessed, that he was as tired as he claimed to be.

Having deposited on the bed his evening meal of Creole chicken and rice, she stepped back with folded arms and frowned at him. "Has the child's father given you any more trouble?"

"No, he hasn't."

"And the other two—her mother and the pilot—what about them?"

"They are not so easy. He has a will, that pilot fellow. But in the end they will do what I want them to. Never doubt it."

"Where are they?"

"At the moment, just waking up with confused minds and tired bodies after walking all night and sleeping all day in exhaustion."

"Walking where?" Clarisse asked.

"What?" He was critically inspecting his food.

"You said they spent the night walking. Walking where?"

"Does it matter?"

"I suppose not, but I'm curious. If you don't mind."

"Very well, they were walking the back roads around here but thought they were lost in the Citadelle."

"Our Citadelle? In Haiti?"

"Yes."

"But why, Margal?"

"God in heaven, don't ask so many questions! But all right, just this one more. My mind is tired, no? With the way I've been forced to use it these past few days, it has a right to be. So when projecting my thoughts, it was less of a strain to project a setting I knew well."

"You could have taken them to our house," Clarisse persisted. Her beloved red house in Haiti's northern mountains was the one she referred to. The house she longed to be in right now.

"That would have been harder for me. They have never been there."

"And they have been to the Citadelle?"

"It was my guess that he had, at least. He worked there in the north." Margal shrugged. "And so long as one of them could accept the illusion and they were concerned about each other . . ." He shrugged. "As it turned out, both had been there."

"I see." Not being anxious to return to the kitchen, where she had left Merry Dawson sitting like a small zombie at the table, Clarisse risked another question. "Have you a plan for those two now?"

"Of course."

"May I ask what it is?"

"Another time. I'm tired now."

"Well, just one more simple question, if you will."

He looked at her.

"You told me, if you remember, that she is easy for you. Easier than he is, at least. Why, then, can't you get rid of them both by commanding her to kill him and then destroy herself?" So you and I can return to Haiti and forget all these distractions, she added silently.

"Because she is a woman."

"What is that supposed to mean?"

"He is stronger. If she tried to kill him, he would defend himself."

"If he were asleep? And she crept up on him with some kind of weapon?"

"My, we're full of ideas this evening, aren't we?" With his mouth full of chicken, Margal could hardly grin but made the effort. "Well, then, let me philosophize for a moment. First, one should never dispose of a tool one may yet need to use. Second, it amuses me to play with people's minds. It sharpens my skills." He shrugged. "Besides, it might be hard for me to persuade her to kill him. You see, she loves him."

"What?"

"It's true. Every time I get into her mind, I find his image there."

"What about her husband?"

He shook his head. "She has no such thoughts about her husband. Only about this man and her daughter. Has the daughter stopped complaining, by the way?"

"No, and it's natural. She's just a baby and is now frightened." Clarisse folded her arms. "She isn't to be blamed, you know. It was exciting in the beginning, with the sea voyage and all, but she's been cooped up for days now like a baby chick in a box. She has walked the house until she knows every crack in the floors. Now she just sits and shivers. And sometimes cries, brave as she is."

"Tell her that she will soon be with her parents again."

Clarisse brightened. "Do you mean that, Margal?"

"In my own way."

She gasped. "No! Are you saying that when you've finished using the three of them, you—"

"Didn't you just suggest I command the woman to destroy herself?"

"But I—" I love that child, Clarisse wanted to say, but was afraid to. Yet it was true. The two of them had been together now for half a lifetime, it seemed. Had played together, eaten together, slept together. By the hour they had talked, Clarisse discovering childhood memories of her own she had thought long buried.

Afraid to speak up now, she was even more afraid not to. "Master, I beg you—"

"Not now!" he said angrily.

"But—"

"Leave me! Let me have my supper in peace!"

When annoyed he could not be reasoned with. Later, perhaps—not now. Without further protest she departed, closing the door behind her.

In the kitchen little Merry Dawson sat motionless at the table, gazing moodily into space. Clarisse sank onto a chair across from her and reached over to touch the child's hand.

"Don't fret, little one. M'sieu Margal told me your daddy will be here again soon."

The sad brown eyes focused on her. "I want my mommy, too."

"Well, it's very likely she'll be coming as well."

"With Daddy?"

"Perhaps not with him. I don't know about that. But she—"

"They don't like each other," Merry said.

"Oh?"

"For a long time they haven't liked each other. They don't say so, but I know." She frowned. "Where did Jumel go?"

"I don't know, child. What do you care? He doesn't even talk to us."

"I just wondered. He looked sort of—scared, I guess. When he came out of Mr. Margal's room, I mean. He stood there in the doorway looking at me as if he wished I wasn't here. I mean as if he wished I'd never come here. Then he went out. You don't know where he went?"

"No, I don't."

"He took that big, long flashlight he has."

"Perhaps he had to do something in the citrus groves where he works. It would be dark when he got there. I don't suppose they have lights."

"I'm tired," Merry said. "Can we go to bed?"

"How can you be tired? We haven't done anything all day but sit around and talk."

"Well, I am."

No, you're not, Clarisse thought. *You're frightened. For a while Margal made an effort to keep you from being frightened, but now he doesn't care.* "Well, all right," she said. "But we have to sleep on the mattress again."

That was another thing. When the child's father was here, why did he have to spend his nights in Margal's room instead of with his daughter? Was he that essential to what was going on?

Couldn't Margal afford even one small grain of compassion?

She stood up to go into the front room and arrange the mattress. Merry slid off her chair. At that moment the two black dogs began snarling, and she heard a car stop outside.

"That must be your father now," she said on her way to the door.

It was. Looking close to exhaustion, Brian Dawson merely nodded as he stepped past her. Attaché case in hand, he went straight to Margal's room without even seeing the child who stood in the kitchen doorway with her arms outstretched, waiting to be spoken to.

Merry's look of eager expectation dissolved behind a trickle of tears. The dogs stopped snarling. Clarisse stood silent, biting her lower lip in displeasure.

Dawson opened the door of the bocor's room and walked in. Closed it behind him without being told to. Strode to the man sitting there and handed him the attaché case.

Without even greeting him, Margal fingered the case open and took out, first, the items brought by Dawson's father from the White House.

"A pen. A handkerchief. A page of his handwriting. His signature." He scowled. "This is all?"

"Everything you ordered me to get is there," Dawson meekly protested.

"Well, yes. And what are these?" He held up the

shorts Dawson had taken from the chest of drawers in his father's room.

"They belonged to my father. As you can see, he has worn them."

"What is the blood on the handkerchief?"

"That, too, is my father's." Dawson explained how it had got there. "The case itself belonged to the President."

"Ah!" the bocor exclaimed softly.

A look of desperation crept across Dawson's once handsome face. "Please, may I go to my daughter now?"

"You may not." Margal pointed to a chair. "Bring that here and sit. You have some talking to do."

"Talking! My God, I have just driven—"

"I must know what happens when your President takes a trip. Being the world's most powerful leader, he obviously does not simply drive to an airport and board a plane. I require knowledge of the details. How and when will he arrive here? Who will be with him? Tell me everything!"

"But there will be time enough for—"

"Not so much time as you may think. Perhaps not very much at all."

Chapter Thirty-six

When he could no longer stand the silence, Ken Forrest broke it by speaking to the black man peering down at him.

"Well—hi."

"Evenin', mister." The small eyes shifted their gaze to the woman at Ken's side. "And missus."

Sandy was awake. She had not spoken, but her hand had groped for and found Ken's and clung to it now with a pressure that told him that she was frightened.

"Are you all right, hon?" he whispered.

"I don't know. I think so."

He pressed her fingers. "Just let me get things sorted out."

"Me, too," she breathed. "I'm confused."

He struggled to sit up, aware that his head

throbbed and his sight kept slipping in and out of focus. "Where are we?" he asked the man gazing down at them.

"I believe that is your car over there."

Ken looked where the fellow was pointing. Yes, the car behind the screen of melaleucas was the one he had rented after Sandy wrecked the first one. In it Sandy and he had driven to Gifford, where a hooker had told him how to find the house they sought. After hiding the car behind the trees, they had been walking to the house when the road dissolved into a Haitian nightmare.

He looked at Sandy again and was reminded of his headlong dive to save her from walking off the edge of the Citadelle's loftiest level. Had it really happened? He had ripped his slacks on the stone, he recalled. Had bloodied his knees.

Examining the slacks, he found jagged rents in both knees, caked with blood. Easing the pant legs up, he looked at his knees. Both were raw. So raw that just touching them sent a wave of pain through him, nearly causing him to black out.

It had been no illusion, then. His desperate dive to save Sandy, the hours of frantic wandering through the old Haitian fortress, the pursuing footsteps, the white owl—all of it was real!

Or was it? How could he be sure he hadn't acquired his raw knees by falling from exhaustion after walking through an unremembered night here in Florida? How could he be sure of anything any more?

But something had pushed him to the brink of exhaustion. And Sandy with him. And what had the man just said? "Good evening?"

He frowned up at the fellow. "What time is it, friend?"

Their visitor looked at a watch on his wrist. "Half past eight, mister."

"In the evening?"

"Yes."

Sandy and he had left the car and begun their walk to Jumel's house later than that, so it could not be the same evening. What the hell was going on? Had they been lying here in the grass all night and all day? If so, why was he so dead tired?

"It will be dark soon," their visitor added, as though aware of his bewilderment.

Struggling to his feet, Ken drew Sandy to hers and put an arm around her while peering around them in disbelief. But the fellow was not lying. The light had faded even more in the past few minutes.

He scowled at the man confronting them. "May I ask who you are, friend?"

"My name is Jumel."

"What?"

"Elie Jumel. And I'm not here by accident. I came lookin' for you, to help you."

Too stunned to answer, Ken could at first only stare. Then he said lamely, "Let's go talk in the car."

"All right."

He settled Sandy on the rear seat and sat beside her while the little black man faced them from the front. Then, with the dome light on so he could better size up this man who claimed to be Jumel, Ken noticed a tinge of red lurking in Sandy's eyes.

Was she still in the bocor's power? She must have been when she tried to walk to her death at the Citadelle. Or was she still being influenced by drugs the TV man had persuaded her to take? Either way, he must be on his guard. Even on guard against her.

In a voice that now sounded unmistakably Haitian, Jumel said, "I know why you are here, friends, but you have come too late."

"Too late for what?" Ken demanded.

"To rescue madame's daughter from the man who stole her."

Oh, sure, Ken thought. *Now you're going to tell us she isn't in your house but has been moved to somewhere miles away. So we'll go looking there for her, and your bloody bocor can work us over some more.*

"Why?" he fenced.

"She is not at my house any longer. M'sieu Margal moved her."

"To where?"

"To a place you will never find without help. But I will help you."

"Why should you?"

Jumel's face sagged with a look of sadness. "Because I want no more of that man, m'sieu! Look what he did to me. I was living peacefully by myself in a fine house the people I work for let me use. Certainly a better house than I ever had in Haiti. I had a good job. I made good money. Then—" He wagged his head.

"Then what?"

"He came, with the lady and the child. I had to

put them up. I had to buy food for them because they had no American money. I became a servant in my own house!"

Sandy implored the man with her eyes. "Mr. Jumel, is my daughter all right?"

"She is well, madame."

"Is she frightened? Has she—has she cried a lot?"

"Only a little. The woman looks after her well. You'll see for yourself when I take you where she is."

Ken said, "You mean this woman is with her now?"

"Yes, m'sieu."

"And Margal?"

"No, not Margal. It was because he had other things to do that he ordered the woman and child from the house. But, like I said, I can take you to her."

"Why should you?" Ken demanded.

"M'sieu?"

"Why should you risk a bocor's displeasure to help us?"

"I told you: I'm afraid of that man. I want to put an end to all this before he ruins everything I have here."

"All right. Mrs. Dawson and I have to talk about it, so why don't you give us a few minutes alone together? Go for a walk."

"Of course." The little man opened his door and got out. Without even a backward glance he walked away into the deepening dusk.

Ken said dubiously, "Well, Sandy?"

"I—think I believe him."

"It could be a trick, you know. We're only a few minutes from his house. It could be a ruse to get us away from there."

"Ken—" The pink was still in her eyes as she stared at him. "Where were we last night?"

"Don't you know?"

"Were we in Haiti? At the Citadelle?"

"That's what he wanted us to think, at any rate."

"And we thought so, didn't we? I did, I know. And if he could do that, why would he need Jumel's help now? No, I don't think Jumel is lying. He wants to help us."

"But why, damn it? You must have noticed he didn't answer that when I asked him."

"But he did. And there's more to it than what he said, if you think about it. He wants us on his side when this is over. Otherwise he'll be considered an accomplice in the kidnapping."

"You want to go with him, then?" Ken said. "Instead of to the house or the police?"

She touched his hand. "I—think so. Yes."

"All right." She just might be making sense, he decided. At a time like this a mother's intuition might be a more reliable guide than cold reasoning.

He opened his door. "Jumel! You can come back now. We've decided."

Chapter Thirty-seven

In the Oval Office at the White House, Rutherford Franklin Dawson perspired so profusely that he had to keep patting his face with a folded handkerchief. But up to now the man behind the desk had not seemed to notice.

"Am I surprised, Mr. President?" Dawson said. "Not at all! As a matter of fact, I was going to suggest that very thing."

"We needn't be there long, you know."

"Of course. Just long enough to show the nation you are vitally interested in this particular shot. And it is of great importance, sir. I'm sure you'd be the first to say so."

"I already have."

"Forgive me."

"What time must we be there, Ruddy?"

"The shot is scheduled for three-fifteen P.M., Mr. President. We should leave here—"

"Just let me know in time to be ready."

"Of course."

The man behind the desk leaned forward, smiling. "You know, Ruddy, you never cease to astonish me. I swear we have some sort of ESP going for us."

The father of Brian Dawson felt he could smile now, too. Commanded by a voice in his head to make his President see the wisdom of this unplanned journey, he had entered the Oval Office full of trepidation. But now it seemed that his talent for persuasion would not even be put to the test.

He was enormously relieved. "ESP, sir? It would certainly seem so!"

"I swear, Ruddy, I had no thought of going to Florida until I awoke this morning. Then suddenly my mind was full of enthusiasm for it, and I wondered why I hadn't seen its importance before. After all, this is a key step in our new program. I should be there."

"As I remarked before, sir—I meant to suggest it, had you not brought up the subject first."

"Thursday, then."

"Thursday, Mr. President." Dawson rose to leave. "You know, I've never been to Cape Canaveral. Only seen these things on TV. I'm really looking forward to being there."

Chapter Thirty-eight

"Where are we, Jumel?"

"At the Sebastian River, m'sieu."

"It's damned dark."

"But there will soon be moonlight, and for that I will be grateful. I have only this." The Haitian tapped a long flashlight hanging from his belt. "As you see, there is no light on my poor boat."

They had left the car and were standing on a small, rude pier. Ken frowned at the boat tied to one of its pilings. All through the thirty-minute ride from Gifford he had felt uneasy.

For one thing, he had studied a road map of the area long enough to know that the shortest route from Gifford to Sebastian was along U.S. 1, a divided four-lane highway. Yet this mousy man who called himself Jumel, giving directions from the rear seat, had sent him along narrow back roads most of the way.

Why? To reduce the risk of meeting a police car they might flag down for added help?

Jumel wouldn't welcome that, would he? The fact that he was taking them to Merry—if indeed he was—wouldn't wipe the slate clean for him. He was involved in a kidnapping.

Maybe his awareness of that explained his offering only evasive answers to questions.

Most of the questions had been anxiously put to him by Sandy, of course, and concerned her daughter. But there was one still to be asked before they stepped into the fellow's boat.

"Jumel, tell me something: How do you know where the child is?"

Was there a hesitation? "Because I took her there, m'sieu."

"You?"

"This is my boat. But I was only doing what he told me to, you understand. At that time I was afraid not to."

"Merry and the Haitian woman—you took them both?"

"Yes."

"How long is this river?"

"The south branch, where they are, is about five miles long, I think."

"How far must we go?"

"Almost the whole way."

Again Ken had a mental picture of the map. This was a region of country roads, not a wilderness. "It doesn't go near any road up there? We can't go by car to save time?"

"No, m'sieu. I know this river. I take this boat upstream every Sunday to attend to my crab traps."

"Attend to what?"

"My traps, m'sieu—for blue crabs. People pay good money for crabs. You understand?"

"I guess so." What else was there to say?

Flashlight in hand, Jumel crouched in the stern of the boat and steadied it by holding on to the pier. He looked up at Sandy. "You are ready, madame?"

Standing there with Ken's arm around her, Sandy replied eagerly, "Yes, of course!"

She was too eager, Ken decided, remembering how she had left him standing by the road while she drove off with the TV man. "Easy now, hon." His arm tightened around her and he spoke in a whisper, with his lips touching her ear. "I know you think we can trust him, but we aren't sure."

Her murmured "I know" was only to humor him, he was certain. She felt she was now only a few moments away from finding her daughter. Reluctantly he let her go and watched her step down into the boat. Then he followed, knowing he was committed.

A few minutes later a moon appeared, as Jumel had predicted. It was not full, but when its light touched the river a kind of magic took place, and some of Ken's doubts were washed away. No matter what this Sebastian River might be in daylight, it became a fairyland stream at night.

They had embarked upon the stream just above a railroad bridge that now in the moonlight seemed etched against the sky in black ink. Leaving it behind, the boat moved slowly upstream, its engine purring more smoothly than Ken had expected. Then the river forked.

Crouching over the tiller like a gnome in an eerie world of his own, Jumel took the south fork.

Lights glowed in windows on the left shore at first. But the homes were not close together and the stretches of darkness between them became longer.

To Ken's surprise, small, wooded islands began to loom up in the moonglow. He would have blundered into some of the many false channels or cul-de-sacs if trying to pick his way among them, he was sure. Jumel made no such mistakes; in fact, he did not even reduce speed.

Was the tale of the crab traps true, then? No man could navigate this stream at night unless he had been here often.

The Haitian had been playing his flashlight's beam over the water, seemingly in search of something. Now it picked up a white, floating object the size and shape of a bowling ball.

"One of my traps."

Was that a note of pride in his voice?

The moving light produced something else: a rustling, scratchy noise in a band of blackness even closer to shore than the trap marker. Jumel ran the light beam along there and it showed them an ungainly brown water bird with a long, curved neck, squatting on a cypress root.

"Snakebird," he said. "Lots of them here. They come for the fish."

Half an hour passed. The river remained a tunnel of dark, still water between high walls of even darker trees. No longer were there lights on its shores. Even the moonlight filtering down through laced treetops failed to provide much illumination. The Haitian used his flashlight constantly. At one point its beam touched a pair of wide-apart eyes that appeared to be golden hued, then reddish.

" 'Gator," Jumel said. "A big one. I see them here in the upper river lots of times."

The River Styx, Ken thought. *And you could be the Boatman. What the hell do we know about you, really? Only that you're Haitian, and as such you're not very bloody likely to be trying to double-cross your country's most feared bocor. So what are you up to, bringing us to a place like this?*

If there were any houses here, they were in darkness and the powerful beam of Jumel's flashlight failed to disclose them. The light revealed only more trees, some with roots resembling tangles of serpents, and stretches of swampy shore choked with high grass. The stream had narrowed to twenty feet or so.

Suddenly, incongruously, the purr of the boat's small outboard seemed to produce an echo overhead. Startled, Ken looked up and saw the lights of a small plane low enough in the sky to indicate that it was climbing from an airfield.

"You have an airport around here?"

Jumel pointed to the left shore. "Over there two or three miles. Lots of small planes in the sky here."

"Even at night?"

"Well, I haven't been here at night before."

And wouldn't admit if it you had, Ken thought. But the Haitian was not likely to answer more questions just now. Leaning on the tiller, he had swung the boat's nose toward the right bank, where his flashlight's beam revealed a small, very old dock.

Whether he intended the beam to show them an equally old cabin in a clearing beyond, Ken could not be sure. For a few seconds it did. The cabin itself was dark.

"This is it, Jumel?"

"Yes, m'sieu." Jumel cut the engine, and the boat glided to the dock in silence. "Please to make the bow fast for me, if you will."

As Ken did so, a turtle the size of a dinner plate flopped off the bank into the black water.

With the craft secure, Jumel scrambled onto the pier and waited for them to join him. Ken helped Sandy up and followed her. Except for the creak of rotting planks under their feet, the stillness was eerie. If there was a moon, it was veiled here by trees.

"Now if you will excuse me . . ." Jumel began walking.

Sandy eagerly followed. As Ken brought up the rear, a sixth sense tingled to warn him of danger.

From the pier a narrow footpath snaked up the bank. Climbing it, the Haitian used his flashlight. With Sandy almost at his heels he crossed the clearing. At the cabin door he turned.

His left hand, holding the flashlight, swung the door open. In the process the light flicked inside like a snake's tongue to reveal a single room, empty except for a few sticks of furniture. At the same time his right hand darted into his shirtfront just above his belt and reappeared gripping a flat black automatic.

Sandy halted, gasping in dismay. Ken froze with a fury of self-condemnation exploding inside him.

"Be good enough to enter," Jumel said in a totally controlled voice. "You, m'sieu, light the lamp on the table."

Sandy stared at the weapon in his hand and began to sob. Ken looked at it with eyes narrowed in hate. Through his teeth he snarled, "You son of a bitch, I knew it!"

"The lamp," Jumel repeated calmly. "And don't force me to use this. Because I know how to, believe me, and I've been instructed to kill you if I must." He motioned with the gun. "Be warned, m'sieu, I am not alone here."

Startled for a second time, Ken peered into the surrounding darkness.

"You misunderstand," Jumel said. "I meant he is with me. In here." He tapped his forehead. "Now, if you please, the lamp."

Like a sleepwalker, Sandy went past him into the cabin. Ken followed, muttering profanities to mask his true intentions. Seeming to stare straight ahead, he used a corner-eye glance to measure the distance between himself and the Haitian. Then, when close enough to the cabin for Jumel to feel safe from attack but still a step short of having his movements restricted by the doorway, he whirled and left his feet.

Left them in a headlong dive like the one he had

used to save Sandy from walking off the edge at the Citadelle. And the dive should have taken him under the gun and the blazing eye of Jumel's flashlight, to let him slam the Haitian to the ground.

Should have—but didn't. For like a startled goat, Jumel leaped aside in time to avoid contact, then let out a yell that tore the forest stillness to shreds.

"Master!"

Ken hit the ground horizontally, plowing the soft earth with face and outflung hands. Stunned by the impact, he scrambled to hands and knees, then lurched off balance to his feet.

Rage possessed him now. Too much had happened that was unacceptable. This time the profanities he voiced were not muttered but snarled, and had nothing to do with hiding his intentions.

He was furious enough to hurl himself at the gun, no matter what the consequences.

But he could not.

Instead, while the Haitian stood there watching him, weapon ready if needed, Ken suddenly heard and felt cannons thundering in his skull, wiping out his awareness of where he was. For seconds the barrage filled his head with agony. Then it passed and left him feeling only sick and stupid.

Staring at the flashlight's eye, he struggled to bring Jumel's face into focus. "What—what—"

"Go inside, m'sieu. Light the lamp as I told you to."

"But—"

"M'sieu, my master is not a patient man! If you are able to reason, ask yourself why he should care at this moment whether you live or die!" Apparently unafraid now of being attacked, Jumel stepped forward, aiming the light beam at Ken's face. "Do as I say, foolish man, before he orders me to kill you!"

Ken looked down at the palms of his hands, which were covered with black dirt and decayed vegetation. He rubbed them on his slacks, then used them to wipe some of the dirt from his face. "All right." His voice sounded like that of someone drunk or drugged. A stranger. "All right," he mumbled again. Lurching about, he stumbled toward the cabin.

Jumel followed, lighting the way for him.

Inside, the Haitian shut the door and leaned against it. His flashlight yellowed two rickety chairs, a small plank table, a cot black with mildew. Next to a cardboard carton on the table stood an oil lamp with the words BLESS OUR HOME etched on its greasy globe.

"Light the lamp."

Fumbling a book of matches from the table, Ken succeeded after several tries. Then he became aware of Sandy.

She stood in a corner where Jumel's flash had not sought her out. Her staring eyes reflected the lamplight. She took two faltering steps toward him before the Haitian's voice stopped her.

"Go to the cot, madame."

She looked at Jumel with no expression on her face, not even fear. Was she in some kind of trance? Or just in shock?

Either way, she was not about to give the Haitian

any argument. Meekly, she walked to the cot and sat down.

"Stay there, please," the Haitian ordered. "And you may sit also, m'sieu. Use one of the chairs."

With only dullness in his head Ken had no desire to resist. It was almost a relief to let himself go limp at last, with his chin on his chest and his arms dangling.

Stepping to his side, Jumel laid the flashlight and gun on the table, making sure both were within swift reach. Sliding the carton toward him, he took from it a bottle of water that he opened and tipped to his lips. Then he took out a coil of rope and a fisherman's knife.

"Put your hands behind you, m'sieu, through the rungs of the chair back."

Ken obeyed without protest.

Kneeling on the grimy floor behind him, Jumel bound his wrists to the chair and to each other in such a way that he knew he could not get loose without help. The Haitian then cut two more lengths of rope, knelt in front of him, and tied his ankles to the chair legs. There was now no way he could walk, even if willing to drag the chair along with him. Or, for that matter, even stand up.

Rising, Jumel hung the flashlight on his belt, pocketed the automatic, and walked over to the cot where Sandy sat.

"Lie down, madame. On your back."

She obeyed as though hypnotized, and he bound her, too, fastening her wrists together and her ankles to each other, evidently considering it unnecessary to secure her to the cot itself. Finished at last, he moved the one empty chair to the cabin door and sat on it.

"Now we wait."

Ken's mind was beginning to clear, and the words had an ominous ring that chilled him. "Wait for what?"

"For the master to complete what he is doing, and tell me what I must do with you."

"How long will that be?"

A shrug. *"Qui moun connais?* Do you know what that means, man from Haiti?"

Ken knew. It meant "Who knows?"

Chapter Thirty-nine

JOHN KLOBEK'S WASHINGTON FILE

The President let it be known today that he will be among those present when Thursday's rocket flames into space at Cape Canaveral, in Florida.

This came as a surprise to most of us who follow the chief executive's day-by-day activities. First, we had not been advised that Thursday's launch was anything more than routine. An ever-reliable Delta rocket is to push yet another communications satellite into orbit; that's all. Why is this one so important that it requires the President's presence at a time when his calendar appears to be more than usually full? Is this "communications satellite" really something else?

No one seems eager to provide an answer. All we can be sure of is that Rutherford Franklin Dawson, the number-one man on the President's staff, left unexpectedly for Florida yesterday to prepare for his chief's visit. Taking with him, of course, the usual aides and security people.

However, we have learned from usually reliable White House sources that the President seems unusually keen on being there in Florida on Thursday, and may we hazard an informed guess as to why this may be so? Certain Florida politicians have also declared it their intention to be present at Canaveral when the countdown occurs. And perhaps they will be there not so much to watch the launch as to discuss their need for White House support in their efforts to be reelected in November.

Can anything less than that explain why the President would even think of leaving Washington at this time when so much of importance is happening or about to happen? The latest Middle East flare-up has reached a most critical stage, and the President was to host a dinner Thursday night for the ruler of one of the few states in that area who is still friendly to us.

Of course, the President won't be gone long. With the launch set for 3:15 P.M., he may well be back in Washington in time for the dinner. But why is he going to Florida at all? Is there something about this particular probe that we haven't been told?

REPORT FROM THE CAPITAL
by Vernon Vedder

To stand by with an eye on the Old North Church tower
Listen, my children, and you'll be told
A puzzling story about to unfold.
That man in the White House on Thursday will leave
On a trip that has all of us on the qui vive.
He's going, he says, to Canaveral's Cape
Where with hundreds of tourists he simply will gape
At the latest space rocket about which we've heard
So little to date that the trip seems absurd.

All over this city good people are asking
If those at Canaveral may not be masking
As merely routine and of no great import
A shot that with top-secret meaning is fraught.

For why at this time when the Arabs are here
For talks that would seem to demand Paul Revere
To stand by with an eye on the Old North Church tower
(Expecting a signal that this is the hour

To ride through the country and spread an alarm!)
Why, why should our chief without even a qualm
Depart from the White House to watch a mere rocket
Unless it's enormously high on his docket?

We haven't the answer, dear children, as yet,
But kindly be patient and we'll try to get
A little bit more than we already know
While the President's down there enjoying the show.

Chapter Forty

The cabin was a steam bath. When Ken awoke and looked around, sweat trickled into his eyes and blurred his sight.

It misted the outlines of the weathered pine walls, the single door, the two small windows. It veiled the rickety table on which stood the plastic bottle of drinking water and the carton of food. It did peculiar things to the chair near the door and the man who slouched on it, seemingly asleep.

Experimentally, Ken moved. Elie Jumel awoke with the quickness of a cat whose captive mouse had stirred. But at least that other captor, the one whom Jumel served, had not reacted. Nothing happened inside Ken's head.

Thank God for small mercies.

The night must have ended some time ago, for the

light filtering through the unwashed windows was not mere daylight. Sunlight colored one window deep yellow.

He turned for an anxious look at Sandy, asleep on the cot. Unlike Jumel, she did not open her eyes when his chair creaked. Let her sleep; she must be exhausted. For her to have come all this way with her hopes high, only to have them so cruelly shattered, must have been like a descent into hell. How long now since her daughter had disappeared? Long enough, surely, to seem the biggest part of a lifetime.

Would she wake if he talked to Jumel? If so, he wouldn't try it. But he didn't think she would.

He kept his voice low. "Jumel."

The Haitian only looked at him. The blurred Haitian. Damn this wicked heat and the sweat that kept trickling into his eyes, trying to blind him. If he could even rub his eyes . . . but with his hands tied he couldn't.

"Jumel, can't you open a window here? This place is murder."

Jumel shook his head.

"Why the hell not?"

"You would call for help. There might be someone on the river."

"I don't suppose it would do any good to ask you to give me a drink of that water and wipe my face. There's a handkerchief in my pocket."

"No problem." With a glance at the woman on the cot, the little man walked to the table. Lifting a paper cup from the carton, he half filled it with water from the bottle, then walked to the chair with it.

Ken tipped his head back, and the water flowing down his throat gave him new life, even a spark of hope.

He felt even better when Jumel fished the handkerchief from his pocket and wiped some of the sweat from his face.

"My eyes, too, please."

"Certainly." Jumel did that, then neatly folded the handkerchief and put it back.

Ken watched him return to the chair by the door. "You know, Jumel, you don't seem to be the kind of fellow who'd get mixed up in a thing like this. How did you?"

A shrug. "I am Haitian."

"What's that supposed to mean? Aren't you proud of being Haitian?"

"Proud enough. Also very much aware that a Haitian bocor like Margal is not to be disobeyed. You find that amusing, I suppose."

There was a bocor in a village near the plantation, Ken recalled. Many of the workers patronized him. For what? All sorts of things, apparently. To find something lost. To buy luck at the cockfights. To obtain a charm that would change a woman's mind, or a *ouanga* to do in an enemy, or a *garde* to keep the enemy from doing the same to them.

More than once he had seen workers wearing little goatskin pouches around their necks or dangling from their belts. Probably only the sorcerer knew what was in them. One he found on a plantation path had contained dried leaves, some dirt—grave dirt, probably—a dried-up toad, and small bones the company medic said were from a child's foot.

He'd been amused at the time. But two years of living and working in Haiti had taught him there were different levels of sorcery. And the learning was still going on.

"No, Jumel, I don't find it amusing." For a moment he gazed at the Haitian in silence, hoping his reply might loosen the fellow's tongue.

While waiting, he became aware of an intruding sound and looked up at the cabin roof. A small plane was passing—so low overhead it must be climbing from, or descending to, the local airport Jumel had mentioned. The mutter swelled, then receded. The Haitian had not spoken.

"Well?" Ken ventured.

"Well what?"

"Why don't you tell me what it's all about? Why are you holding us here? Why the change of tactics? Up to now, Margal has taken care of us himself by playing with our minds."

A shrug. "The master has more important things to do just now."

"Oh?"

"After all, he did not seize Madame Dawson's child and bring her here just to be difficult. He—"

Was it hearing the name "Dawson" that aroused Sandy from sleep, or had she been on the verge of waking anyway? She stirred on the cot and voiced a low moan. When Ken turned his head toward her, she said, "Oh, God, I need to go to the bathroom. Please!"

Jumel rose from his chair and went to her. Looked

down at her with what appeared to be genuine compassion. "Madame, there is no bathroom here. Only outside, and not really one there; it fell down. But if—"

"I have to go somewhere!" Sandy sobbed.

He knelt and untied her ankles, then took her by the elbows and helped her to stand.

"Please!" she begged. "Untie my hands!"

"Madame, I am sorry—"

"Untie her, damn you!" Ken said.

"I cannot."

Sandy looked at him in panic. "But I have to lift my skirt and drop my panties!"

"Madame, I will do those things for you."

"Oh, God," she moaned.

"Damn it, Jumel," Ken shouted, "untie her! What the hell kind of man are you?"

"Come, madame." The Haitian's shrug could have been one of indifference, but there was a look of concern on his face as he drew Sandy to the door.

In desperation Ken leaned as far forward on his chair as his bonds would let him. "Jumel, wait! For God's sake, man, there may be snakes out there!"

Just short of the door the little man halted. "Snakes?"

"In a place like this, yes! Of course! I was bitten by a cottonmouth moccasin here in Florida once and damn near died. You can't just—"

"I have never seen a snake here. And I visit this cabin almost every time I come crabbing."

"But it's just the kind of place moccasins hang out in!"

"Very well, m'sieu. While madame is relieving herself, I will stand guard over her with my gun." Patting the automatic in his belt, he added without expression, "It will be my pleasure."

"You bastard," Ken whispered.

"Come, madame," Jumel said, and walked Sandy outside.

They were gone a long time, it seemed to Ken. But there was no outcry from Sandy, and when they returned she flashed him a look of reassurance. Having led her to the cot, the Haitian waited patiently for her to lie down and make herself comfortable, then refastened her ankles.

He turned then to Ken. "And you, m'sieu? Why don't we take care of you, too, before I make breakfast?"

Ken hesitated. "I'm—not so sure I want to go out there."

"M'sieu, our chances of seeing a snake—"

"But, damn it, there must be cottonmouths here! They breed in places like this!"

"Very well, if you don't want to go. If you were bitten once, I suppose—"

"But I have to go," Ken groaned. "Just stay close to me with your gun, will you?"

"Of couse." Jumel knelt before him and released his ankles from the chair legs. Rising, he said, "Come."

"My hands. You're forgetting my hands."

"No, m'sieu."

"But the chair—"

"Will have to come with us, I fear. Come."

The protest had been only experimental. The reply was what Ken had expected. Struggling to his feet, he stumbled across the cabin with his wrists still secured to the chair and each other, and the chair legs bumping his own at every step. Outside, Jumel let him walk only a couple of yards from the door before stopping him.

"Do you want your slacks lowered or just your zipper opened?" The smile on the little man's face said he found the situation amusing.

"If I take a crap, are you going to wipe me?"

"No. There is only one man I would do that for."

"Your bocor friend, I suppose."

"Certainly not you."

"All right, I was only asking. That can wait, anyway. Just unzip me and—"

"I know what to do, m'sieu. I may be Haitian, but I relieve myself the same way you do."

Carefully standing a little to one side, with the automatic now in his right hand, Jumel extended his left hand to do what had to be done. As he did it, a sound in the sky signaled the return of the small plane Ken had heard earlier. At least it sounded like the same one.

It was a single-engine, high-wing monoplane, Ken noted. A Cessna 152. At an altitude of not more than five hundred feet, it was probably heading for the airport.

"Hey," he said sharply. "Is that one of your local fly boys up there?"

Jumel finished his task without even looking up, then straightened from his crouch and stepped back.

A smile touched his mouth. "You are clever, m'sieu."

"What?"

"If I had looked up from that position, I have no doubt you . . . What would you have done?"

"You're crazy. How can I do anything with this damned chair stuck to me?"

"I believe you would have tried."

"And got shot for my trouble? Forget it." Ken began to empty his bladder. "Watch out for snakes now! I don't want to be bitten again!"

He was disappointed when no snake of any kind showed itself. As part of his half-formed plan to get away from this place, he'd been hoping one would. Jumel crouched again to attend to his needs, then led him back into the cabin and refastened his ankles to the chair legs.

"Are you hungry?" The Haitian included Sandy in his glance.

"Yes," Sandy said.

Ken nodded.

Taking a can of corned beef from the carton on the table, Jumel proceeded to open it with its attached key but stopped when Ken began humming, then singing, an old and much-loved Haitian folk song.

Lè ou nan pé blanc, ou wé tout figue youn sel coulé—
Nan point mulatresse, bel marabou, bel griffon creole
Qui renmen bel robe, bon poude, et bon odeur
Ni belle jeune négresse qui connais bon ti parole.

Obviously surprised, Jumel swung about with his hands on his hips. "You know our Haiti Cherie in Creole, m'sieu?"

"Of course."

"You? A foreigner? May I ask—"

"I had a whole heap of Haitian friends on the plantation, Jumel. They often invited me to their homes."

"And they taught you—"

"Lots of things. They wouldn't like what's being done to me here, *compére.* Be sure of it."

Jumel continued to stare. Before he could quite decide to reject the seed so carefully planted in his mind, Ken resumed the treatment.

"Would you like to hear that particular verse in English?"

"What?"

"In English, Jumel. After learning the song in Creole, I worked out a translation. It's even more colorful in English."

"Yes. I would like to hear it."

Ken quietly sang it.

When you're in a white man's country, you see
all faces of the same color—
No mulatresses, no lovely marabous, or light-
skinned Creoles
Who like pretty dresses, powder, and scent,
And no beautiful Negresses who know how to
say sweet things.

The Haitian made sounds of delight and clapped his hands. "Beautiful!"

"But the man who wrote that lovely song is dead now, Jumel."

"Dead, m'sieu?"

"Just as Madame Dawson's innocent little girl may soon be dead if you don't let us out of here to rescue her."

Jumel's dreamy expression swiftly changed as his mind emptied itself of memories and returned to the present. Angrily he said, "As I remarked outside, you are a clever man, m'sieu!"

"Not at all. It's just that when you produced the can of corned beef, I remembered all the *beuf sal* I've eaten in Haiti. Then I remembered the song."

"And hoped to melt me with it, eh?"

"Okay, pal, if that's what you want to think."

Jumel finished opening the corned beef and produced a loaf of bread. He made sandwiches. With Sandy sitting up on the cot, he fed one to her, patiently waiting for her to chew and swallow each bite. Then he held a paper cup of water to her lips.

After repeating the performance with Ken, he returned to his chair by the door.

The day dragged on. With the door and windows shut, the cabin became an oven again. Even Jumel's passive face gleamed with sweat and had to be mopped more and more often with a soiled red handkerchief he pulled from his pocket. But when he seemed on the verge of heeding his prisoners' pleas for fresh air and actually went to open a window, the mutter of an outboard motor on the river changed his mind.

"No." He shook his head. "I can't risk it."

"After he's gone, then," Ken begged.

"No."

"But that's the first sound we've heard out there, except for planes from the airfield!"

"I'm sorry."

As the afternoon wore on he did, however, heed Sandy's plea to be taken outside again. This time the bathroom session seemed to take longer, and Ken was straining at his bonds when they returned. But again Sandy flashed him a glance of reassurance as Jumel led her back to the cot.

"You, too, m'sieu?"

"Thanks, but not yet."

"It will soon be dark. I can't risk taking you outside then."

"Well, all right." Damn, Ken thought. *Can the bastard read my mind?*

The performance was a repeat of the first one, Jumel too alert to be caught off guard. When I try it, Ken thought, it has to work. There wouldn't be a second chance. And he wasn't tired enough yet.

With the coming of darkness Jumel again lit the lamp. Again made corned beef sandwiches. Again fed Sandy, then Ken, and gave them water to drink. Then he returned to his chair with a sandwich of his own.

It could be a long night.

"Tell me something, Jumel."

"Yes, m'sieu?" Even the Haitian seemed eager to do something about the silence.

"When we were discussing Margal a while back, you said he did not seize madame's daughter just to be difficult."

"Yes."

"You also said he has more important things to do just now than play with our minds."

"That is so."

"Well, if he didn't kidnap the child for ransom and isn't interested in us just now, what the hell is going on?"

The time was right for the question, it seemed. Jumel was bored with being a jailer, perhaps even resented being turned into one. "The child was seized," he said, "because my master required the services of her father."

"Of Brian Dawson? Why, for God's sake? There's no way Dawson can help your man win control of the Haitian government, if that's what he's up to. Dawson isn't even top man at the U.S. Embassy there."

"He is the son of a top man in your government, however."

"What?"

"You underestimate M'sieu Margal. Control of Haiti is not his objective. At this very moment he is almost certainly preparing to take over control of *your* country."

Silence. Ken looked across the cabin at Sandy and saw she was sitting up with an expression of incredulity on her face. Incredulity and something else.

Perhaps shock. Or fear. He looked at Jumel and saw that the Haitian, having dropped his bomb, was eagerly awaiting more questions.

All right. If the basic premise could be accepted, there were certainly more questions!

"Just how does Margal propose to take over the United States, Jumel?"

"By possessing the mind of your president."

"And how will he do that?"

"The way he possessed your mind, and madame's."

Ken thought of his night in the unreal swamp near the motel. Of his attempt to rape Sandy. Of how he and she had spent a whole night trying to extricate themselves from the maze of tunnels in Haiti's Citadelle. Those had been merely the highlights of Margal's campaign to keep them from reaching Gifford.

"You interest me, Jumel. But just how can a bocor in Gifford—even one as powerful as your Margal—hope to reach the mind of a man in Washington?"

"By persuading the man in Washington to come here."

"But, damn it, how can he do that?"

"For an ordinary bocor it would not be possible. We both know that, I'm sure. But M'sieu Margal is not ordinary. Given something a person has worn or handled, he can reach into that person's mind. Not to take it over completely, perhaps, but to plant thoughts the person will think of as his own."

"You mean Margal has something that belonged to our president?"

"He has."

"How did he get it?"

"This woman's husband was sent to Washington for it. Or for them, I should say. There are several items."

"But how did he get them?"

Jumel smiled. "He was taught by M'sieu Margal to persuade his father to get them. As you may know, his father is close to the President."

Ken was leaning so far forward on his chair, there was danger of his tilting it off balance and braining himself on the floor. "And now?"

"Now, as I said, your president is coming here."

"To Gifford, you mean?"

"Not to Gifford. But it will amount to the same thing. He will come to Cape Canaveral for Thursday's launch. And my master will be there, too. The child's father will drive him there. And from that time on, in Washington or anywhere else, the mind of your president will belong to the great Margal. Once he takes possession he never lets go unless he wants to. Think of it!"

Jumel's voice suddenly shook the flimsy cabin walls, as though someone had turned up the volume on a shouted sermon. "Just think of it! Consider! The destiny of your great country will be in the hands of a sorcerer born as a peasant in one of the poorest countries of the world!"

And we, Ken thought—Sandy and her daughter and I—will be dead. Because even if this is only a fantasy in a bocor's mind, he will believie it and won't dare let us live to report it.

Chapter Forty-one

The house on Petrea Road had been a furnace all day. Now, at nine P.M., while she sat beside Margal's bed, bathing him because he refused to let her carry him to the crude shower in the bathroom, Clarisse probed for information. Incongruously, her hands were even gentler and more sensuous than usual while her tongue ignored Margal's efforts to silence it. "I want to know what you will do with their president when you possess his mind," she said.

"Be quiet."

"I will not be quiet. I swear I'll get an answer out of you if it takes all night!"

It might well take that long, Clarisse told herself angrily. Exhausted by boredom, little Merry Dawson slept fitfully on the mattress in the front room. Her father had been ordered to retire to the room usually occupied by Elie Jumel and to rest there for some duty soon to be required of him. Jumel himself, having disappeared the evening before on some mysterious mission, had not yet returned.

The two black dogs prowled the yard and seemed to know precisely what they were out there for. She herself had let them out at Margal's command. Even watching them through the window sent shivers of dread through her.

Never before had she heard them growl so much or seen them prowl that way, as if they actually expected a victim to come blundering within reach of their fangs. Heaven help anyone careless enough to do that!

"Well?" she said fearfully, placing a hand on Margal's privates in an effort to mellow his mood.

"Well what, woman?"

"I'd like to know."

"You'd like to know what?"

"What will you do when you're close enough to command him?" She used the hand in a way that always pleased him. "You can't prevent him from returning to Washington, you know. The whole country would at once be aware that something was wrong."

"Why should I want to?"

"What are you saying? That we must go to Washington?" Dear God, it was bad enough to be here in Florida! If she had to live in a monstrous place like this nation's capital, she would surely die!

Margal reached up to fondle her bosom, though

she was not naked as he was. "You'll like it there. I'm told it's a beautiful city."

"I want to go home to my mountains!" she wailed.

"Not just yet."

"But Washington! God in heaven! Jumel says there is so much traffic there, a person can't even cross the street safely. And the weather turns so cold at times, you have to wear an overcoat! Has someone drained all the good Haitian blood out of you?"

"I need to be close to him. You know how it weakens me to manipulate someone from far away." He fondled her thighs now, with his hand under her dress.

Clarisse reacted to his touch with a little sigh of surrender. She had not lived with this man before he lost his legs and with them his manhood—or, at least, his desire to demonstrate it. Every now and then she worked up enough courage to complain to *le bon Dieu* about that.

Now, as she went on with her probing, her voice was almost a caress in itself. "Margal, talk to me, please. What will you do when you own that man? Are we to be rich?"

He laughed. It was the laugh of a child just handed a fascinating new construction toy with which he could build anything he might imagine. "Clarisse, I have more ideas than there are grains on a stalk of *piti-mi.* More than there are dogs on the streets of Port-au-Prince at night. Or fleas on the dogs."

"Ideas such as what?"

"Well, we can be rich, as you suggest. And will

be; you can take that for granted. In a very short time we'll be far wealthier than we ever could have become in Haiti, even if I chose to return there and take control of that poor country. And, of course, I will control Haiti and make things most unpleasant for those who opposed me. Take that for granted, too."

Done with caressing her, he withdrew his hand. "But those steps will be only a beginning, believe me. Only the sip of rum before the grand feast. The possibilities are so enormous, they keep me awake nights trying to sort them out. To put it very simply, I may change the world. If only to amuse myself."

Reaching down, he moved her hand away from his body. "Go away now, eh? Let me rest."

"Just another little minute, please," Clarisse insisted. "Is it tomorrow we go to this place—this Cape Canaveral—where you will be close to him?"

"Yes, tomorrow."

"At what time?"

"Well, Jumel said it normally takes about two hours to get there from here, but I wish to be there early, to prepare myself." He paused in thought. "The event is scheduled for three-fifteen. We should be there about eleven, I think."

"And the child's father will be driving us?"

"In his handsome silver car, yes."

"Where is Jumel?"

"At a cabin a few miles from here, attending to the child's mother and her pilot friend. Because I have no energy to spare for them at this time."

"And what about the child herself? Is she to go with us?"

He shook his head. "She stays here."

"What if someone should come and find her here?"

"That is why the dogs are outside." His voice had acquired a note of impatience. "Jumel assured me that they are quite capable of preventing anyone from entering this house. Now run along, woman. I must prepare my mind for tomorrow."

He patted her on the bottom as she turned away. Then his voice trailed her to the door.

"After all, my pet . . . tomorrow will be the most unforgettable day of our lives. Be sure of it."

Chapter Forty-two

"What time is it, Jumel?"

Even if his watch had been running, Ken could not have looked at it with his hands bound behind him. All he knew was that the seemingly endless night was over at last, the east window of the cabin was again yellow with early sunlight, and the man slouched on the chair by the door had his eyes open.

Jumel lifted his left wrist and peered at it. "Ten minutes past eight."

Glancing across the room, Ken saw that Sandy was still asleep on the cot. Good. In an unsuccessful struggle to get comfortable, she had kept the flimsy bed creaking through most of the night. Now she must need all the rest she could get.

He looked at Jumel again. The Haitian's bleary eyes and drawn face seemed to indicate sleep had eluded him, too. To the best of Ken's knowledge, he had left his post only twice during the night to prowl like a demon spirit about the lamplit room. Now he must be almost as full of aches and weariness as though he, too, had spent the night bound to his chair.

Had the time come at last to put their lives on the line?

"Is there any more food, Jumel?"

"Some."

"I'm starved. But take me outside first, eh? Before I flood your little country home here."

The Haitian showed his displeasure with a Creole oath. "You need to go again?"

"God, man, it's been twelve hours or more. I'm not a stone statue!"

"All right, all right." Jumel shuffled across the floor and knelt to release Ken's ankles, then rose again, muttering. He did not enjoy being deprived of his sleep, it seemed, even when serving his admired master. "Come on, then," he grumbled.

With his wrists thrust through the chair back and its legs protruding behind him, Ken followed awkwardly. "Watch out for snakes now, Jumel. I've said it before and I'll say it again: This is exactly the kind of place they love!"

"M'sieu." The tone was one of strained patience. "I have not forgotten your foolish fear."

"I tell you, it isn't foolish! It—"

"Please. If you wish to relieve yourself—" Shaking his head, the Haitian stepped outside, halted by the nearest tree, and turned. Almost indifferently he drew the automatic from his belt.

In the cabin doorway Ken stiffened, feeling as though he had just been led blindfolded to a wall. *Did I wait too long? Is he going to kill me? He has to eventually, and it would save him a lot of trouble to do it now. . . .*

Half expecting a bullet to cut him down, he slowly shuffled toward the man. The gun remained silent. In a cold sweat he positioned himself, facing the sun. It was a low sun at this hour. Like a huge orange eye it glared at him through the lower branches of a live oak draped with yard-long beards of Spanish moss.

Filtered through the moss, the sun's bright light almost blinded him as he waited. Worse, it robbed the moment of reality, causing him to feel he was imprisoned in a dream. Would Jumel squat to unzip his fly and extract his penis from his pants, or blast a hole in his heart instead?

For God's sake—which?

For a moment the Haitian seemed unsure of what he ought to do. With the gun in his right hand only inches from its target, he almost seemed to be awaiting instructions. Perhaps he had mentally asked a question and was expecting an answer.

At last, with a shrug, he shifted the automatic to his left hand, dropped to one knee, and reached for Ken's fly. But apparently at that moment he sensed something amiss. His fingers froze and he jerked his head up.

"What are you doing?" His voice was sharp with suspicion.

"Looking, for Christ's sake!"

"At what?"

"Not *at*. *For*. I've told you a dozen times this is the kind of place—"

"Oh. Your snakes." As his fingers fumbled for the zipper again, Jumel's lips flattened in a sneer.

Suddenly Ken's whole body began to shake. His mouth trembled open. His lips struggled to babble out words.

"T-there's one by the t-tree, c-coming at you, Jumel! Kill it! K-kill it, for God's s-sake! Kill it!"

You primed the pump and the water came. Jumel might not have believed, but he jerked his head around.

When he did that, two things happened. First, the sudden twisting of his neck pulled him off balance, and he had to jab his gun hand at the ground to steady himself. Second, that blazing orange sun behind the veil of Spanish moss must have distorted his vision at least enough to make him think there could be a snake at the base of the tree.

Before he could recover from either, Ken's right knee took him like a battering ram just under his left ear and sent him crashing into the tree trunk.

The top of his head hit it first, with a noise like that of a watermelon dropped on concrete.

Ken shuffled forward. With the chair still riding him like Sinbad's old man of the sea, he stood there peering down at the crumpled body. It would be a long time before the Haitian moved again. It might be never.

There was a smaller tree some twelve feet away. Ken went to it, turned his back to it, and with a twist of his body slammed the legs of the chair against it. Two of them splintered off and fell to the ground. A second assault shattered the others and broke the chair's back. Though still bound to each other, his wrists were now free of the chair.

He returned to Jumel, not to look at the man again but to locate the weapon that had sailed from the Haitian's hand when he was kneed. It lay in the grass a yard from its owner. Easing himself to the ground, Ken fumbled for it with his bound hands—with care, because it might go off if picked up recklessly. With the weapon safely in his possession and out of the Haitian's reach if by some miracle Jumel should come to, he returned to the cabin.

It was a relief, being able to walk without a burden on his back.

Inside, Sandy sat half awake on her cot. "Hi," she said listlessly. "I need to go, too, I guess." Her eyes opened wide. "Hey, you're—" She sat up straighter. "Where is he?"

"Outside. Out cold." Ken started for the table but stopped to look at her. "Are you all right, hon?"

"Yes. But what—"

"Later." Completing his journey, he peered into the cardboard carton. "That knife he sliced the corned beef with—he didn't take it out of his pocket. It has to be in here."

Turning his back so that his bound hands made

contact, he tipped the box over. Its contents spilled out on the table. His fingers found the knife. After a number of failures he discovered how to grip it so the sharp edge of its blade could be brought to bear against his bonds.

In a couple of minutes he was free.

He cut the ropes from Sandy, then, and took her into his arms. Let her cry, he told himself when she began to do just that. Let her get rid of it. Even if it hadn't dawned on her that Jumel would have to kill them to protect himself and his bocor master, she must have been terribly frightened all this time. And even more fearful for her daughter.

But he could not let her cry for long. Time was even more important now than it had been. Stepping back, he said sharply, "We've got to get out of here, hon. Come on."

Outside, Elie Jumel still lay unconscious at the base of the moss-draped oak, like a gnome peacefully asleep in some fairy-tale forest. Except that his pillow was a pool of blood.

"Wait." Ken knelt to touch the man's neck. There was a pulse.

"Just a minute, Sandy." Hurrying back to the cabin, he returned with some of the rope Jumel had used on Sandy and himself. It took only a moment to make sure the gnome would not leave his magic forest if he awoke. "Soon as we can, we'll tell the police where to find him," he said as they went down the path to the pier. "He probably wasn't all bad. Just had to do what Margal told him to."

But on the pier he halted, swung around, scowled

back up the path. "Hon, wait. If that creep comes to and tells Margal we escaped, the way he called on Margal for help when I first tried to jump him . . . I'd better go back and make sure he can't."

Sandy pawed at him. "No, Ken! No!"

"But if we're to get Merry out of that house and stop Margal from—"

"Please! If you killed him, I couldn't live with it."

The eruption of fear in him subsided, and he expelled the ashes with a gust of breath. "All right. He may not come to for a while. Let's go." Untying the painter of Jumel's boat, he held the craft while she stepped into it, then dropped into the stern and shoved off.

The motor, thank God, started at the second pull. They were away. All they had to do now was get back to the car and—

And what? Go to the police with what any sane cop would reject as a tale dreamed up by someone who belonged in an asylum? Or dare once more to confront the devil's number-one disciple the hard way, without help?

Chapter Forty-three

He should have paid more attention to the river when Jumel brought them up it. Of course, he had been preoccupied then with his suspicions of the man. And Sandy had been oblivious of everything but the prospect of being reunited with her daughter.

Neither of them now could tell the main channel from the false ones and blind alleys. Not by the banks, which everywhere resembled those of a jungle stream. Not by the water's flow, either. There was so little current that fallen leaves, instead of drifting downstream, appeared to be decorations pasted on a mirror.

And as the sun climbed higher in a brassy sky, the heat became a torment.

With a hand on the tiller, Ken struggled with the

decisions he was forced to make. This wooded island coming up—should he try passing it to left or right? This thing on the left that seemed to be a widening of the main channel—should he try it or risk the narrower band of water that went straight ahead? If he took the widening and it turned out to be only a bay or a pond, the mistake would cost them precious time. Perhaps a lot of precious time.

The damned stream was unreal. How for God's sake could he ever have thought it beautiful?

Hearing the mutter of a small plane overhead, he welcomed it as a sound from a world of sanity and, glancing up, wished he were in that world instead of this one, with its heat and problems. And, yes, its peril. For the longer they took to get out of here, the greater the chance that Jumel would recover and call on Margal to stop them.

Think about flying that plane, Forrest. It worked before for a while. It could work again. You hear? This isn't a boat on a jungle stream. It's a Cessna in a clean blue sky. Go, man, go!

Faced with yet another choice of channels, he gambled on the wider one and sent the boat coughing on into a world of tall trees that all but hid the sky. A fantasy world of shadows and silence in which a lone white bird planed on ahead as though to guide them. But the bird was a false leader. Rounding a bend and finding himself confronted by a wall of Spanish moss, Ken knew he had erred.

In the bow Sandy turned her head. "Ken, I don't think—"

"I know. We have to go back." He swung the tiller.

Black as ink here with the sky blocked out, the water looked bottomless and sinister.

Sinister it was, bottomless no. Something scraped along the boat's bottom, caught hold of the prop, and whipped the tiller out of his grip as it brought the craft to a shuddering stop.

"Damn."

With a warning to Sandy to hang on, he stood up and tried to rock the craft free. The effort produced only more rubbing sounds, more vibrations from solid but unseen things tearing at what he stood on. Sandy gazed at him in silence with an expression of surrender on her tired face.

"Got to go over the side, hon. See if I can free it."

"Ken—" Her voice seemed loud in so much silence. "What about snakes?"

"What about them?"

"You said—"

It was a relief to have something to laugh at. "Hell, that was for his benefit." Sitting to take off his shoes, he remembered to take Jumel's pistol from his waist and place it in the boat. Then he wriggled over the side and felt for the bottom with his feet.

As he'd suspected, the obstruction was a submerged tree. One with a maze of twisted limbs. But when he worked his legs down through the maze, the stream bed was of soft mud that would not support his weight.

There was no way he could brace himself in the mud to tug or push the boat loose. Maybe if he could get a foothold on the tree itself—

But that particular tree must have dropped into the stream long ago. When he tried to stand on its slimy limbs and exert pressure on the boat, his feet slithered out from under him and he fell into the water. Again and again the same frustration. Close to exhaustion, he at last gave up.

Half in the boat again, he glanced from Sandy's frightened face to the bank he knew their car was on, somewhere downstream. "Hon, we'll have to swim ashore and walk it."

He knew she could swim. Back in that other life that now seemed only a dream, they had gone to the beach together often. But could she bring herself to try swimming in water as dark and sinister as this?

She did seem to hesitate, but only briefly. "All right."

"It might even save us some time. If we did get the boat out of here and kept taking wrong turns—"

"That's right."

He watched her slide over the side and ease herself down until her feet found some part of the tree. Then he reached for Jumel's gun and followed her.

How to keep the gun dry was going to be a problem. He would have to swim a one-hand sidestroke, keeping the other upthrust like a periscope. "Ready, Sandy?"

"Yes."

"Stay close to me. There's nothing here to hurt us." Except maybe one of the 'gators Jumel had talked about. Or a water moccasin—for even though he had raved about those only to lay the groundwork for an escape attempt, there should be some in a swampy stream such as this.

But, hell, the bank wasn't that far.

Remembering Jumel brought another thought, though, as he pushed off and began swimming. If the Haitian regained consciousness and got through to Margal, this could be the worst possible time for it.

It would be so very easy for Margal to say, "Stop swimming, you two. Stop struggling. You've earned a rest now. Just sink quietly into this cool, dark water and rest forever on the bottom."

So very easy!

After all, the man had led them over wrong roads and convinced them they were lost in the Citadelle. He was responsible for a nonexistent cypress swamp, an attempted rape, a wrecked car, a desertion.

A simple drowning, in this place made to order for his kind of black magic, should be duck soup for him.

You're not swimming in a river, Forrest. You're flying a plane. Remember that! Don't let go of it!

He swam on, wondering why the bank suddenly seemed so far away. Of course, with only one hand it wasn't possible to swim with any speed.

Flying, Forrest. You're flying. Concentrate on the instrument panel in front of you. You're at five hundred feet and climbing.

Behind him, he could hear Sandy swimming a slow crawl, and actually hers was the only sound in the stillness now. Using only one arm, and that never breaking the surface, he himself made no noise at all.

So concentrate on the purr of the plane's engine, man. You're in the sky, remember. It worked before. Maybe he's never been in the sky and can't project his commands up here. Could be he has to have a familiar mental image of where you are.

As he neared shore, the tall trees blocked out the light and there was no color in the water. The trees' roots slithered down the bank like fat snakes, to disappear into a sheet of tar. But suddenly the tar rippled. Suddenly it parted. Something like a bronze doorknob—gleaming like a bronze doorknob—thrust itself up into view.

A 'gator's eye? With a quiet "Hold it, Sandy," he stopped swimming. He could use the pistol if he had to. More than likely he would miss with it, but the sound might change the reptile's mind if it planned to attack.

Then the rest of the creature rose into view behind the eye, and the eye was not that but a head, and the 'gator became a turtle. A big one, true, but only a turtle. Its curiosity apparently satisfied, it abruptly disappeared.

"Okay, hon. It's all right."

"Whew!"

Yes, it's all right, Forrest. So don't let yourself be sidetracked now. You're still in a plane, still flying. Concentrate on that rev counter. That altimeter. Watch that turn and bank indicator!

But, hey, keep swimming. Except with your mind.

His forward progress carried him to an invisible

tree root as big around as himself, and he half swam up it, half climbed it, until he could get his feet under him. Rising, he turned to help Sandy. Together they ascended the tangle of roots on the bank and pushed through a jungle of trees to a patch of grass.

Ken shoved the pistol back into his belt. "Are you all right, hon?" She was wet all over, of course. So was he. There was even a long-dead leaf plastered like an elfin cap to the side of her head. But he wasn't concerned about her appearance. After all the earlier horrors, this ordeal with the river could have been the final straw for her.

"I think so," she said.

"We walk, then. Let's hope it isn't far."

For a while they followed the stream, and the going was rough. Where the ground wasn't swampy it was a snarl of creepers and close-packed saplings. Ordinary walking was out of the question; you bulled through like a tank. Yet from time to time Ken still remembered the danger they faced from Margal—a peril that might be increasing every moment—and tried to think himself back into a plane. It wasn't easy with so many real-life decisions to make.

Here, for instance, was a shack like the one they had fled from. Was it inhabited? It didn't appear to be, but who could tell? Should they keep going across its weed-grown yard or investigate on the chance of being helped?

What if it were occupied and its owner disliked strangers?

Flying at such a moment was difficult.

They left the cabin behind without approaching it. Came to a place where the untamed river's edge gave way to half an acre of lawn surrounding a house of some size. He remembered seeing the house on their way upstream with Jumel, soon after launching the boat. "Hey, we must be almost there!"

Across the lawn loped a black and tan German shepherd with bared fangs, growling. But no one from the house followed. No door or window opened. It seemed the dog stood guard alone.

There had been German shepherd guard dogs on the plantation in Haiti, and he had made friends with them. Had romped on the beach and hiked into the hills with them. Nevertheless, he drew Jumel's pistol.

"Don't stop," he warned Sandy. "Talk to him as if you know him. Talk to me, too."

Still growling, the animal stopped in a crouch with his forefeet apart and head outthrust. Saliva dripped from his mouth. But when they walked past, interrupting a meaningless conversation with each other to speak and nod to him, he neither attacked nor followed.

Ken returned the pistol to his waist. "Lucky," he said as they put the house behind them. "But we've earned some luck."

Ten minutes later they reached the pier from which their journey up the Sebastian River had begun.

The car was where they had left it.

Chapter Forty-four

"Are we going to the police now, Ken?" Sandy's voice was leaden with fatigue.

"Hon, there isn't time."

"But if we—"

"No, we can't. You heard what Jumel said. Margal is going to Canaveral this morning, with Brian driving the car. He may take Merry with him. My guess is he will, to keep Brian in line."

As the car sped toward Gifford, Sandy grudgingly nodded. "All right. But I don't see how we can get her away from that man by ourselves. You know what he can do."

Ken reached out to touch her hand. "He could do it to a cop, too, if we had one with us. And that's how many they'd probably send with us—one man to check out our story." He gave her hand a reassuring squeeze. "Hang in there, hon. We'll find a way."

From the river road he had driven out to U.S. 1, and now they were headed south on that four-lane highway with the town of Sebastian behind them. What time was it? His watch had stopped running when he fell on it. Sandy's was the kind that had to be wound, and she hadn't been able to wind it with her hands tied. The sun, however, was climbing toward noon.

What time would Margal be leaving Jumel's house for the Cape?

"One thing you're forgetting, hon. We have a gun now."

She glanced at Jumel's weapon. "Would you use it?"

"On Margal? You're damned right I would!"

"Will it work on him?"

"Of course it will! He may have a super mind, but physically he's no better than the rest of us."

He saw her mouth tremble.

The town of Wabasso disappeared behind them. At ten miles over the speed limit they sped past orange groves, and Ken tried again to think about flying. On the river it had been relatively easy to do that, with everything else there so close to fantasy. Here on a busy highway it was a struggle.

Anyway, why should it work? Maybe when he'd imagined himself in a plane before, it had worked only because the bocor was busy with other things.

That was why Jumel had held them at the cabin,

wasn't it? Because Margal needed all his energy for something bigger.

GIFFORD, a sign said. There was the bar where the hooker had given him directions.

He had to drive more slowly now. Gifford's roads had not been laid out for people in a hurry. With time to think, he asked himself the same question Sandy had asked, and knew he had better come up with an answer.

Just how were they to barge into that house and take Merry away from a man able to manipulate people's minds?

Maybe he *would* have to use the gun. And face being brought to trial for murder.

The turns fell behind. The road they were on now ran past Jumel's house to where they had hidden the car behind the melaleucas.

A car was coming.

He slowed and moved over, frowning as it sped toward them. A silver car. A silver Jaguar. Even without the leaping cat on the hood, its sleek lines would have branded it.

He had only a glimpse of its occupants as it purred by, but that was enough. Alone on the front seat, the driver was Brian Dawson. An older, less handsome Brian Dawson than the one he remembered, but still without question Sandy's husband.

The two on the rear seat he had never seen before. The woman, huge and black in a red dress, sat stiffly erect, peering straight ahead of them. The man at her side, also black, had gray hair and a badly scarred face.

Sandy had grabbed at Ken's arm. "Ken, that was Brian driving that car!"

"And the other two must have been Margal and the woman who looks after him. They're on their way to the Cape."

"Without Merry, Ken. Oh my God, what if they—"

"Don't even think it." He stopped peering into the rearview mirror. "We haven't far to go now, hon." The mailbox with Jumel's name on it should be just around the next bend.

It was. He pulled up beside it. Was the child dead, as Sandy feared? Probably not. Margal would keep her alive at least until he was certain he no longer needed her. But there were still some questions.

Had they left the child in the house here or in the care of some neighbor—some crony of Jumel's, say? He just might have done that, unless this house had a room with a door that could be locked, and no windows. Because a six-year-old could open a latched window, or even break the glass if she had to.

Then again, the bocor might have left her here in care of someone. Someone under orders not to let her be rescued.

"Careful," Ken warned as they got out. "Stick close to me, hon." Sandy was a woman whose emotions sometimes got the best of her discretion. He loved her for it, but right now she was likely to go racing toward the house without considering the risks.

In spite of the warning she did walk faster than

he. And was past the mailbox, halfway to the veranda steps, when a hair-raising snarl tore through the stillness.

Something huge and black charged from behind a shabby hibiscus bush and launched itself at her. A dog. As ugly a dog as Ken had ever seen, with jaws agape and drooling, fangs gleaming in the sunlight, its crimson, cavernous mouth resembling a fiery pit.

Sandy flung up her arms and tried to step back, but it was too late. One arm did protect her throat, but the black battering ram sent her stumbling and she went down. Down on her back, screaming, with no chance of escaping the full force of another assault.

At that moment a second snarling attacker launched itself over the rail from the shadows of the veranda and raced across the yard at Ken.

Ken snatched the gun from his waist. Took aim at the first monster. Squeezed the trigger just as the beast hurled itself at Sandy a second time. Missed and fired again. Saw the dog jerk in midair and fall to the ground only inches from Sandy's legs. Saw it leap straight into the air again, mouth wide in a silent scream, and then quiver in space like a shot bird before plummeting to the ground to stay there.

Sandy was safe. With the second black beast racing toward him, he wasn't. Bracing himself, with the gun thrust forward in both hands, he took aim between the killer's blazing eyes.

But when he squeezed the trigger this time, there was no explosion. Only a click. And again, click.

Click, click, click.

He had only seconds before it would be too late. Not time enough to run for the car, which he could not do in any case without leaving Sandy at the brute's mercy. Into his mind flashed remembrance of a game he had played with a guard dog on the plantation, at the instigation of its Haitian handler.

Voicing a savage growl of his own, he dropped the useless automatic and fell to his hands and knees.

He, too, became a dog. Mean. Dangerous. Poised for combat.

The black beast skidded to a halt. Froze in the same position Ken was in. Only six feet of bare brown earth separated them as they sought to stare each other down.

On the plantation the handler of the guard dogs had said calmly, in Creole, "Now you laugh, *compère.* That's right—laugh at him. We have a saying in Haiti: 'The wild pig knows which trees he can scratch himself on, and which have thorns.' "

Laugh? With those slavering jaws only a few feet from his face and the monster quivering like a plucked steel spring? Good God!

Laugh? With the other dog still alive and twitching, though probably dying? And Sandy on her feet again only ten feet away, terrified, waiting to see what would happen?

"Don't answer what I'm going to say to you, Sandy," Ken warned. "He may go for the sound of your voice."

Out of a corner of his eye he saw her slight nod.

"Don't try for the car, either. Let him concentrate on me."

Again he thought she nodded.

"I'm going to laugh at him. A thing I learned in Haiti. Don't think I've lost my mind."

The beast confronting him still quivered, still drooled, apparently still could not make up its mind what to do. Ken voiced a throaty growl, not too threatening, and was growled at in return. But not as though he had touched a naked nerve and induced a reflex action. There was a hesitation before the dog responded, and the growl was no more menacing than his own.

Then he laughed, and the black brute eyed him with apparent bewilderment, faintly growling in reply.

He laughed again and got no response at all. "Thank God for René Dubois," he said in a conversational voice. "He should be here to see this. You mind if I get up now, boy?" It took weeks of training to make a dog bad, René had insisted. But if the animal had the right stuff in him, it sometimes took only a few minutes to change him back.

Bless you, René.

Still in a crouch, the dog watched him slowly rise to a standing position. No longer growling, it stood with its head atilt, staring at him.

"All right, boy." Ken took a step forward.

The dog did not move.

"You going to let me touch you?"

The dog did.

"And go up to the house without any fuss? What

the hell, you can come with me. Let's go."

With Sandy watching them as though mesmerized, Ken strolled to the veranda steps and waited. The dog came to him. Ascending the steps, he crossed the veranda to the door and paused again. The dog followed. He tried the door and found it locked. Tried a window beside it. That was locked, too.

"I'm going to have to break a window to get in here, boy. Is that okay with you?" Turning, he addressed his next remark to Sandy. "You'd better wait in the car, hon. Walk to it real slow. I'll check out the house."

But she wasn't ready for that. With a stubborn shake of her head she rejected it.

After what the other dog had done to her, it must have taken real courage for Sandy to do what she did then. With her hands limp at her sides she slowly approached the veranda and climbed the steps and walked to Ken's side. The black dog sank into a crouch and bared his fangs in a silent snarl, then looked up at Ken.

"Easy," Ken crooned. "She's the woman I love, old boy."

The dog stopped snarling.

With an eye on the animal in case it mistook the move for a threat, Ken knelt and removed a shoe, then rose with it in his hand. To the dog he said quietly, "Don't lose your cool now, boy. We have to do this when people lock doors on us. Nothing personal in it, you understand."

When the shoe shattered the glass and sent most

of it raining onto the floor inside, the dog reacted by baring its fangs and crouching to spring again. Sandy added to their peril by involuntarily taking a quick step backward. But again Ken knelt—you were less threatening when not so tall, Dubois had insisted—and slowly put the shoe back on.

Junmel's brute was just curious enough to watch him instead of attacking.

"Good boy," Ken said. "If you can take a smashed window, I guess we're home safe." Rising, he put a hand through the broken pane and released the latch, then eased the window up and turned to Sandy. "You'd better go first, hon."

Sandy sat on the sill and swung her legs in. Once inside, she quickly stood up and looked around. Again Ken saw on her face a look of hope, of excitement, that surmounted the exhaustion and terror so long in command there. Without even waiting for him to join her, she made for the closed door of what was probably a bedroom.

With a last wary glance at the dog, Ken followed.

There was no lock on the bedroom door. Sandy pushed it open and voiced a cry of joy. Running toward a small, gagged figure on the floor beside the bed, she sank to her knees and took her daughter into her arms.

Or tried to. It wasn't that easy. The child's wrists were tied behind her to a leg of the bed.

Ken strode forward. Kneeling, he removed the gag—it was a dish towel—and, after a struggle, succeeded in untying Merry's bonds. Then he stepped back while mother and daughter clung to each other.

But only for a moment. "Hon," he warned, "we have to get out of here. Now. Right now." He laid a hand on Sandy's shoulder. "I have things to do, and every second we stay here makes it closer to being too late."

She looked up at him. "You mean Margal? The President?"

He nodded.

"But can't we phone the police and tell them? There's a phone on the table out there."

"I saw it, too. They've ripped the wire out." Anticipating her next question, he shook his head. "I'm not sure I could fix it, even if we had the time."

Merry said, "They did that so I couldn't use it if I got loose. They told me so. And they said the dogs would kill me if I tried to leave the house."

"Please, hon," Ken begged. "Let's go!"

Sandy could only nod.

The front door had the kind of lock that could be released from the inside by turning the knob. Ken looked along the veranda for the dog. It had gone back to the yard and now stood over its dead twin.

"Better hold Merry's hand, hon. Just walk to the car as if he weren't there."

Letting them go first, he followed far enough behind to protect them, or try to, if the brute decided to challenge their departure. It did look up, baring its fangs again and watching their every step until they reached the machine. It did slink forward to bar his way as he trailed them.

But when he stopped and spoke to it, the dog also stopped. It did not move again when he went on.

The slamming of the car door put an end to the uncertainty, and Ken let his breath out in relief. Then the feeling of urgency returned as he realized the enormity of the task he faced.

"Look." The car was already growling away from Jumel's mailbox. "I've got to follow your husband, hon, and I don't want you two with me. God knows what Margal will do if he learns I'm after him."

"Ken—must you?"

"Must I what?"

"Go after him?"

He looked up at his face in the rearview mirror. "What's the alternative? Go to the cops, looking like this?"

"But—"

"They'd laugh me out of town." With Jumel's road behind them, he stepped up the speed. "Try to see it through their eyes. A guy no one ever heard of walks into a small-town police station looking as if he hasn't shaved for a week and has just been dragged out of a river. He gives them a song and dance about a Haitian witch doctor being driven to Cape Canaveral by a son of the President's best friend, to take over the President's mind. Would you buy it?"

"I—suppose I wouldn't."

"I'm going to drop you off at a motel, hon. We passed some on U.S. One. The first decent-looking one we come to . . . You can wait there till I get back."

"But what will you do?"

"Try to overtake them. I should be able to if I don't

get stopped for speeding. They won't risk driving too fast."

They were approaching U.S. 1. The child between them, no doubt exhausted by her ordeal, appeared to have fallen asleep with Sandy's arm around her. Sandy suddenly turned her head to look Ken full in the face, and he saw something that would have filled him with joy at a less critical moment. She was terrified not for herself now, not even for her daughter, but for him.

"Ken—" She sobbed the word. "What will you do if you catch up with them? You can't handle that man alone!"

"I'll think of something," he said. "Don't count me out."

Chapter Forty-five

As he pulled away from the motel after letting Sandy and her daughter out of the car, Ken glanced at a road map to refresh his memory.

Which route would Brian Dawson take to the Cape—U.S. 1 or I-95? They were only a few miles apart, and parallel, but 95 was likely to be faster.

Just ahead now was a road that led to 95. What should he do? And—face it—what real chance did he have of catching that silver Jaguar in this rented hunk of junk he was driving?

The dogs at Jumel's house might not have done their job in the way Margal intended, but they had probably insured the bocor's safe arrival at Canaveral.

He turned left and found himself on a two-lane blacktop. Roseland Road, a sign said; speed limit 35.

Doing twenty more than that, he hit a pair of railroad tracks never designed to be crossed at such speed, and the car took off like a plane.

As he fought to regain control, a small plane did appear over the road ahead, like those he had heard at the cabin by the river. From the Sebastian airport, Jumel had said.

This was Sebastian.

The plane was descending. He watched it as the car recovered from its leap. To be descending at that low altitude, it had to be coming in for a landing. It disappeared below the tops of pine trees to his left.

The airport was that close?

Moments later a sign said it was. SEBASTIAN AIRPORT, WEST ENTRANCE, NO THRU TRAFFIC—with a dirt road running off to the left.

Instead of sensibly overrunning the road and backing up to it, he took the turn on whining tires. But once on it, he slowed and listened.

And heard the sound of a plane taxiing; the field was that close.

Knowing now what to do if the field was the kind to give him half a chance, he drove on at a crawl. The road was a nothing: only a hundred yards long through scrub oak and palmetto before it swung left at a wide iron gate.

The gate was closed. On the other side of it, the black runway of a sleepy, small-town airfield glistened in the sun. Just turning off the near end of the runway onto a taxi strip was a red-and-white Cessna 152.

This could be it, Forrest. Start praying.

Past the curve of the road, the scrub gave way on his left to a world of shadows created by slash pines. On his right were metal buildings fronting the taxi strip. He could see four small planes parked there. Others might be hidden by the buildings.

The Cessna came purring along the strip to take its place at the runway end of the row. As the pilot opened the door and dropped to the ground to head for one of the buildings, heat from the craft's engine created a phantom reverse waterfall in the air above it.

Okay, Forrest. Where to hide the car?

He had noted three or four possible openings in the slash-pine shadow world. Backing up, he chose an old pair of sandy ruts that faded away to nothing a hundred feet in. On getting there, he squeezed the car in a few extra yards, to be doubly sure it wouldn't be noticed from the road. As he flipped open the glove compartment, praying to find a piece of wire in it, the silence was cotton in his ears and he could feel his heart pounding against it like something struggling to escape.

There was no wire. But a plane like that could be hot-wired without a jumper, no? He had never actually flown a 152, but it must be similar to some he had flown. If he had to unscrew part of the instrument panel to get at the starter wires, he would find a way.

Go, Forrest! With its high wing and good visibility, this is just the plane you need. And it's already warmed up. You won't get another chance, for God's sake. And you'll never catch them in a car.

But was it necessary to commit a crime here? At an airport like this, it should be possible to rent a plane.

Not for him. Sure, his billfold contained proof of his qualifications and had come through its river bath intact. He knew that from having opened it at the motel to give Sandy some money. But even if he knew where to inquire about renting a plane, he didn't look like a man who could be trusted with one. Changing that impression would take time. Too much time. Too much talk.

Forget it, man. Let's go. Now!

With the car keys in his pocket, he hurried back out to the road. Crossed it. Eyed a pair of NO TRESPASSING signs on blacktop driveways leading to the buildings. There were no fences to put teeth in the signs, though. No evidence of life around the buildings, either.

With his hands in his pockets, he put the road behind him and strolled on through weeds and scrub, keeping as wide a gap as he could between himself and the nearest building.

Suddenly a voice hissed in his head, "White man from Haiti, stop!"

Without realizing what he was doing, he obeyed.

"So you have escaped from the cabin." The voice was acid eating at his brain now. "But you have not escaped from me, m'sieu, and you never will! You are a fool. You should have killed Jumel so he could not warn me!"

Oh my God, Ken thought. *But don't stop. Make for the plane. Think about flying! It worked before!*

He stumbled on, aware that the command to halt was more than a sound in his head now. It had become a sack of cement on his shoulders, bearing him down. It was a pair of leaden chains on his ankles, causing him to drag his feet. But he kept going. He was past the buildings and staggering across the taxi strip. Anyone watching would surely think him so drunk he was likely to fall on his face.

"I see you struggling to reach an airplane!" Suddenly the voice was thunder, adding to the agony in his head with every syllable. "But you will not reach it! Go back! Go back to your car and return to Jumel's house!"

How much do you know, Margal? Do you know Sandy and I have already been to Jumel's and taken Merry out of there? How much do you know, you son of Satan?

"Listen to me, m'sieu! You may not use that airplane! Touch it and you will die!"

"Screw you, Margal. Go back to hell where you belong, you creep. You can't stop me."

"You will perish, I tell you! You will die horribly! I am at the end of my patience with you! Turn back at once!"

"Make me, you lousy bastard. Make me!"

Again the agony exploded in his head, and again he stumbled. This time he would have pitched to his knees but for the plane itself. As he grabbed at the fuselage to hold himself up, the sunlight bounced off it to blind him. The metal was almost too hot to touch.

But you got here, man. You made it! Now defy him for another minute or two and you'll be flying!

But even as he fumbled to open the door, he knew he had lost. The wide red stripe under the handle had become a river of blood flowing past his eyes, threatening to suck him in and drown him. No way could he hold back the agony long enough to hot-wire the plane and get it into the air.

End of struggle. Period.

He was able to drag the door open, though. Was able to climb into the pilot's seat. There, straining one last time to break the bocor's hold on him, he gripped the wheel with both hands and squeezed his eyes shut.

"Go to Jumel's house!" The voice in his head was a hurricane wind accompanied by claps of thunder. "I have warned you, m'sieu. Get out of that plane or you die!"

"To hell with you, Margal. To hell—"

The explosion in his head threatened to burst his skull. His eyes flew open from the shock of it, and he saw the key there in front of him, waiting to be turned.

No need to hot-wire the plane. *Just fly it. Fly it!*

He put out his hand. The engine came to life with a growl. He opened the throttle and, in a daze, watched the rev counter jump in the blur of the instrument panel. Then, as the plane sped along the taxi strip and made the turn onto the runway, he vaguely saw two men running from one of the buildings, waving their arms.

Sorry, guys. There was just no other way.

Seconds later he was airborne and climbing, with the voice of Margal fading to a whisper in his skull.

In another moment the whisper died too, and the pain with it.

It was true, then. Here in the sky he was out of the bocor's reach. Here in his own element, where he had always functioned best, he was free to do what he had to.

Chapter Forty-six

He searched interstate 95 first, flying so low he could have been reported had anyone been in the mood to call the authorities and knew where to call.

The sky was perfect for the task he had set for himself. With the agony gone from his head he felt ready. It was good to be back in a cockpit.

The interstate was less congested than U.S. 1. Had they taken it from Sebastian, as he suspected, they should be well north of Melbourne by now. Perhaps even north of Cocoa.

And maybe almost to their destination, he thought with a sudden stab of panic. *Remember, Forrest, Brian Dawson is at the wheel of that Jag, and he isn't the type to worry about speed limits.*

* * *

In the car at that moment Brian Dawson was being asked a question by Margal's woman, Clarisse.

"Tell me something if you will, m'sieu. It seems to me most unlikely that we will be allowed to get close to your President when we arrive at this Cape Canaveral. It would certainly not be possible in Haiti. How are we to accomplish this?"

Traveling U.S. 1 in fairly heavy traffic, the driver did not see fit to take his gaze off the road as he answered. "Do you know what a VIP is?"

"A very important person?"

"Right. And as one of those, I have a pass that will take us where we must go. Leave that little problem to me."

"You are sure, m'sieu?"

"My father will be with the President, in his car. That is how sure I am."

"And can we be sure of your loyalty?" she demanded.

"Clarisse, your master has promised me certain rewards in return for my loyalty. I will earn them, never fear."

She turned her head to frown at the legless man beside her. "Rewards?" she said to Margal. "What rewards, Margal? If I may ask!"

Margal shrugged. "M'sieu Dawson has come to have great respect for the powers of a bocor. So I have promised to continue his education and make him my chief assistant in the weeks to come."

And if M'sieu Dawson is foolish enough to believe that, Clarisse thought, he will believe anything.

* * *

Following I-95—not the highway the Jaguar was on—Ken still felt reasonably safe in flying low above it. The road ran through open country and traffic was light.

At a hundred miles an hour, thinking he had spotted the car, he cut his speed and went down to seventy feet for a closer look. No. It was a sedan that shone like silver in the sun but not the one he sought. But coming up now on his right was something that told him he was running out of time.

Remembering the map he had studied, he climbed quickly for a better look.

Route 405, the divided four-lane road leading east to the main entrance of the Space Center. It had to be that. He could see it running a few miles across country before it took off over the glitter of the Indian River on a kind of dike.

If the car he sought reached the Space Center, he would have no chance. Not the flimsiest ghost of a chance, unless he opted to commit wholesale murder. He would have to give up.

There were cars on 405. *Please, God, let one of them be it!*

He flew low over the highway, wondering how long he would be allowed to get away with such forbidden tactics. There was sure to be air security so close to Canaveral. Probably extra special, with the President expected.

Sooner or later he was bound to be checked out by planes from, say, Patrick Air Force Base, nearby. It was inevitable. And probably sooner, not later.

But of the car he sought there was no sign. No sign at all.

Where, dear God, could it be?

His mind again shaped a picture of the map. They could have come up U.S. 1 to the Bee Line Expressway just south of here and crossed over the Indian River on that. Yes, of course! It might be an even shorter way to get there. To check it out, he need only fly south a few miles.

He tore through the shining sky at top speed and then slowed to ninety for a pass over the Bee Line. With the cars on it moving at forty-five to fifty-five, he could see them clearly as he flew low over the divided highway.

This would be a good road for what he had in mind, he thought. No wires. No trees. Just a flat strip of grass on either side between the highway and the river. To hell with worrying now about security planes. Where was the silver sedan that was carrying Margal to his appointment with destiny? If not here, it must still be on Route 1, on its way here.

He saw it. Or thought he did. A silver sedan that looked like the one he sought had just turned onto the Bee Line from Route 1 and was approaching the first of two close-together bridges there.

Dipping the Cessna's nose, Ken flew alongside the bridge for a closer look.

No question about it, the car was silver. It had a leaping Jaguar for a hood ornament. The driver was a white man alone on the front seat. Both passengers in the rear were black.

As he climbed into the sky's glare again, he remembered how Sandy and he had stared in disbelief as the same car passed them on the road near Jumel's house.

In the car, Clarisse had turned to her companion and was screaming at him in near hysteria. *"Mon Dieu,* Margal! What was that?" The plane, she would swear, had almost touched the machine with the tip of a wing as it roared past.

On the right side of the seat, Margal had been even closer to the plane than she. He sat rigid now, his handsome face turned to stone. "It was the American from Haiti."

"Here? After escaping from Jumel?"

"Here, obviously." For the first time since they had left the Caribbean, Clarisse detected a bitterness, an ugliness, in his voice.

Leaning toward him, she stroked his cheek. "You are still Margal, *mon cher*. Do something about him, no?"

He was silent.

"Don't you hear me?" she persisted. "Do something about him, Margal! Cause him to make a mistake in that thing and destroy himself!"

"I—cannot," the bocor muttered.

"What?" Never before—never—had she heard him use those words. "Mother of God, what are you saying?"

"He almost accomplished this before by using his mind." With a deep sigh, the bocor shut his eyes and let his head slump. "I am a creature of the earth, woman. I must have an earth connection."

The fat woman stared at him until she began to quiver. Then she shifted her gaze to the shoulders of the man in front of her. Reaching out, she began to pound Brian Dawson with her fist.

"Can you see the plane, M'sieu Dawson? Can you? Is it coming back?"

As the car continued to speed along the highway, Dawson leaned forward to peer up through the windshield. Apparently the calmest of the three persons present—at least for the moment—he said with a shrug, "Yes, I see him. He's over the river, turning."

"Can he stop us?"

"Of course not. He would have to kill himself."

"You are sure?"

"Positive. We've nothing to fear from him at all."

Ken was indeed turning to come back. The turn completed, he peered down at his target.

It was going to be rough, doing what he had to do from here on in. The Jaguar was on the second of the two bridges. From the sky it looked like a silver cat creeping up the side of a concrete hill. It was the only eastbound car on the bridge, thank God, and traffic in the other direction was light.

But this bridge was higher than the first one. Its slopes were longer. Once the silver car began its descent, it would almost certainly pick up speed.

So, then, it would be traveling maybe sixty miles an hour when it leveled out again, and he would have only a moment or two to make his move. There where the slope of the bridge ended and the road became flat again was the one suitable stretch.

The highway there ran along a kind of dike, with the Indian River lagoon on both sides. A parklike band of grass a hundred feet or so wide lay on either side of the concrete. Then water.

No trees. No fences. No anything.

Not here.

Only water.

But if he failed here, he would not be given a second chance, even if he were still alive to try again.

Would he still be alive? This had to be a maneuver that would make a Blue Angel proud. An eraser wiping a blackboard; that close.

If he misjudged and flew an inch too low, he might still complete the mission, of course. But Ken Forrest would be part of the funeral that followed.

The car was off the bridge. Ahead of it the road was level. With his lower lip caught in his teeth and his temples being pounded from inside by little sledgehammers, he dropped the plane's nose and took aim.

The road rushed up at him. The car came on without a waver, its driver defiant.

Chicken. It was a game of chicken, as when teenagers in hot rods raced toward a head-on collision.

Hang in there, Forrest. You're a better man than he is. Hang in for Sandy. For Merry. For the future.

The car loomed up in front of him. Nothing else on the road was in motion. There were vehicles in the westbound lanes, on the edge of his line of vision, but their drivers had stopped to watch the drama unfold. He dipped the plane's nose lower.

Aimed it straight at the approaching windshield.

Okay, Brian darling, it's up to you. Think about Daddy in Washington, and how you might take his place someday if you don't throw your future away here. Think about how you might even make President—if you live.

At the last second, or what seemed to be the last, he caught sight of the driver's face. Just a glimpse. A flicker of a glimpse. The face was frozen in contortions of terror. Its eyes were so enormous, they looked as though they could be staring into hell itself.

Then the car swerved, and Ken jerked the plane's nose up.

He felt a gentle upward nudge as some part of the Cessna brushed the car's roof. He felt a blaze of fear that was like the brief kiss of a blowtorch. Then he was past, clear, in the sky again, turning on a wing tip and looking down.

Just in time to see the car hurtle off the concrete highway onto the grass and go lurching toward the river.

Just in time to see it hit something soft at the river's edge and roll over, then miraculously right itself before plunging into the water.

There, after swirling near the surface for a few seconds like some prehistoric monster trying to master the art of swimming, it coughed up a froth of bubbles and sank from sight.

"We did it!" Ken heard himself shouting. "Sandy, we did it!"

Now, for God's sake, Forrest, get out of here!

Chapter Forty-seven

It would be stupid to fly the plane back to Sebastian. He would be jailed for stealing it, no matter what kind of tale he told to justify the theft.

Seeking a place to put it down, he flew high and spotted a golf course. Good enough. He flew low again and looked over the terrain. With a prayer that his luck would hold, he landed on what appeared to be a par five fairway close to a clubhouse. Adjoining the clubhouse was a parking lot.

Abandoning the plane, he made for a patch of rough that seemed a good place to hide. As he disappeared into it, a crowd poured from the clubhouse to find out why the golf course had been used for a landing strip.

With the building probably empty and all hands milling about the plane, he made his way through the rough to the parking lot. In a place like this, some careless driver just might have left a key in a car, no?

Someone had. The car was a pale blue Cadillac, almost new. If in the excitement anyone noticed his departure, he wasn't aware of it as he headed west to interstate 95 and then south to Sebastian. There was no pursuit.

At the Sebastian airport, which seemed as sleepy as before, he drove the Cadillac to the bend of the entrance road and left it there with the key in it. Unchallenged, he cut through the pines on foot to where he had hidden his rented car and drove out.

Now, at last, as he made for the motel where Sandy and her daughter should be waiting, he was able to think of what he had accomplished.

Were the three in the silver Jag now dead at the bottom of the Indian River lagoon near Canaveral? They ought to be, unless someone very good at miracles had been present to dive down and rescue them. He would know when he heard a news broadcast or read a newspaper.

As for the rest of it, the owner of the stolen Cessna would soon learn, of course, that his plane awaited him at the golf course. No problem there. And the car Sandy had wrecked on the road to Vero Beach . . .

Phone the rental agency from the motel, Forrest. Tell them you cracked up the car and must have walked away from it in a daze because you've only just remembered it. Tell them you're on your way to Miami and will come in to straighten things out.

Not a big problem. Not after the one he had just solved.

Then there was the car he was driving now. He had better phone that agency, too, to let them know he was headed for Miami and ask what to do with it when he got there.

There would be some details to work out, of course. Never mind. Sandy and he would work them out together.

And then, after Brian's funeral, Sandy would want to go back to Haiti, he supposed, to close up the house on Rue Printemps and arrange for her things to be returned to the States. No problem there. He would be present to help. So would the Embassy people. And then—well—what?

At the motel he voiced the last question aloud while lying on a bed with Sandy in his arms. Both were fully dressed; it was a little soon for anything else when he had only just finished telling her that she was free again. Besides, her daughter was on the bed, too—sitting like a golden-haired elf at the foot of it, happily smiling at them both.

"How about it, hon?" he said. "A month or so at the plantation down there would get you away from the media wolfpack and help you put all this behind you. My house is big enough for the three of us if you don't mind being a bit cozy. We could go for rides in the mountains, swim at the plantation beach, get to know what kind of people we are now."

He looked into her face and saw moisture in her eyes. "Unless, of course, you want nothing more to do with me after what's happened," he concluded anxiously.

"It wasn't your fault, what happened."

"I flew the plane."

"And did what had to be done." She wiped her eyes with her hand. "I'm not crying about that. Don't ever expect me to."

"You'll come, then? You and Merry?"

She raised herself on one elbow to look at her daughter. "Have you been listening, honey? Would you like to do what Ken suggests? Go and spend some time on the plantation with him, swimming and exploring and—well, you heard."

"I'd love to, Mommy!"

Sandy burrowed a little deeper into Ken's embrace. "You heard her. All I can add is 'Me, too.' "

Chapter Forty-eight

JOHN KLOBEK'S WASHINGTON FILE

Have you been reading the papers lately with your curiosity fine-tuned? If so, the reports of the recent death of the son of presidential aide Rutherford Franklin Dawson may have left some questions in your mind.

The younger Dawson, as you surely know by now, was at the wheel of a car that went out of control and into the Indian River while presumably en route to the launch of a communications satellite at Cape Canaveral in Florida. His father and the President arrived for the launch soon after his death.

(This writer would still like to know what

there was about a seemingly routine rocket launch that made it necessary for our chief executive to so suddenly decide it required his presence.)

In any case, the car in question, with Brian Dawson at the wheel and a black man and black woman on the rear seat, plunged into the river because it was dived upon by a small airplane. Who was at the controls of the plane is not yet known. We know only that, (1) the craft was stolen from a small airport in Sebastian, some fifty miles to the south, (2) after buzzing the car and causing it to go off the road, the unknown pilot landed at a nearby country club where he stole a car, and (3) the stolen car was later found abandoned near the aforementioned Sebastian airport.

Also still unknown is the identity of the black man and black woman reported to have been with Mr. Dawson in the doomed car. Were they Haitians? Mr. Dawson worked at the U.S. Embassy in Port-au-Prince and very probably had Haitian friends in Florida. But why would he have been taking two of them to Cape Canaveral?

Whatever the answer to that—and it could be most interesting, we suggest—we are not likely to uncover it soon, for when swimmers went down to the car soon after its fatal plunge, they encountered an enigma. While the driver was dead at the wheel, either from drowning or from a severe head injury suffered when the car rolled over, one of the rear doors had either sprung or been thrust open, and the two rear-seat passengers could not be found. Why, if they somehow managed to save themselves, have they not come forward?

There remain several other puzzling aspects of this most curious event. Mr. Dawson's six-year-old daughter, Marcia, we are now informed, was kidnapped in Haiti nearly two weeks before the tragedy, presumably by a legless Haitian called Margal, reputed to be an infamous bocor, or witch doctor. Mr. Dawson was in Florida at the time. His wife flew to Miami to join him on learning the stolen child had been carried to Florida.

When Mrs. Dawson learned from a television newscast of her husband's death, the child was safely back with her after having been held for days at the home of one Elie Jumel. Yet another Haitian, in the Indian River County town of Gifford. An anonymous telephone caller, she says, told her where Marcia was, and on going there she found the child alone in the house. Jumel, now in custody, claims not to know or even to have heard of the supposed kidnapper, Margal. The child was left in his care by her father, he insists. Her father?

It seems to be a strangely complex affair indeed, and we hope one day to unravel it for you. Meanwhile, the son of our President's closest associate is dead; two black persons who were in the car with him and may actually have kidnapped his daughter are missing; a third Haitian will not talk; and for the time being, at least, Mr. Dawson's widow has returned to Haiti with her child.

And no one—at least, no one who is talking—seems to know who flew the plane that day. Or why.

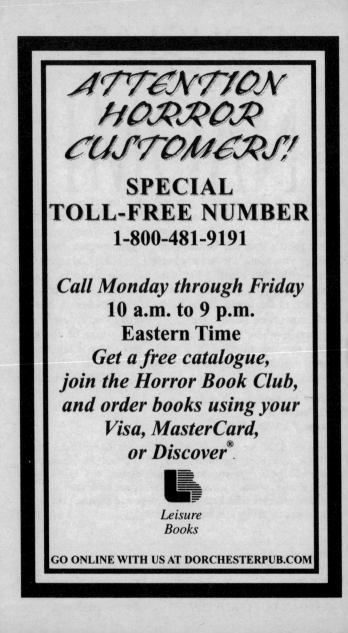